Wraith

A Novel

by
Raymond Bolton

Wraith
Published by arrangement with the author.
All rights reserved.

ISBN-13: 978-1-73581413-1

Horror
Paranormal Fantasy

For information about Raymond's other books, go to:
https://www.amazon.com/Raymond-
Bolton/e/B00HMY0B6U/
Or e-mail him at **author@raymondbolton.com**.

Bolton, Raymond (2020-01-01). Wraith. Regilius Publishing

ACKNOWLEDGMENTS

Aside from the author, three individuals have made this book possible:

Wraith's remarkable cover is the work of graphic artist Dean Samed, who hails from Ramsgate in east Kent, England and Natasha Brown of Littleton, Colorado.

If you choose to read this on your Kindle, Nook, or other electronic device, you can thank Clare Ayala, who resides in Southern California, for her excellent formatting skills.

1

"I'm a'right," Warren slurred as he lurched through the hotel's front door. Reaching out, he failed to grab it and stumbled onto the sidewalk.

"Sure you are," Jordan called after him as the doorman held the door open for the rest of their party. "You should have gone easier on the Irish cream."

Warren turned and grinned at the ones who were following him, his eyes flashing wickedly. "It was just desert," he said. Then, appraising his partner through the corner of an eye, he grinned and added, "You do believe in just deserts, don't you, Jordie?"

Jordan scowled and Warren decided he didn't much give a damn. While a small amount of alcohol relaxed him, a large enough quantity made Warren downright euphoric. It also loosened his tongue and made him undeniably obnoxious. He knew that in the morning he would hate himself for having acted like this, especially since he would have preferred a more subtle approach to addressing the matters that were recently brought to his attention. The thing was, for the moment it did not matter one single whit and that made his grin even broader.

" 'Sides," Warren chuckled, legs splayed, his body weaving when he halted. "A li'l Brandi will fix ev'ry thing, won't you, Sweetie?"

Warren's wife, Brandi, in the face of the example he was setting, was struggling to keep their two wriggling children under control. If she had heard his attempt at being clever, he could not tell, but she didn't react to him one way or another. In the course of snaring their ten-year-old son's wrist with her right hand and their eight-year-old daughter's with her left, lest they rush out into the night and beyond her control, her purse had slid from her shoulder to her elbow and now was dangling by its strap. Caught between the requisites of motherhood, while her children were complaining loudly, and maintaining a difficult decorum in the wake of her husband's inebriation, she was working hard to keep up. Bringing up the rear, Jordan's wife, Nancy, was frowning and her eyes flicked back and forth between Warren and her husband.

Ignoring Warren's harangue, Jordan looked up one side of the street and down the other. "Does anyone remember where we parked?"

They were on the west side of Powell Street, opposite Union Square, and Nancy reminded him, "We're in the underground parking garage."

"Oh, yeah," Jordan acknowledged, only a trifle less tipsy than his business partner. "What about you guys?"

"Warren refused to pay," answered Brandi, "so we're parked on the street a block or two above Market."

Warren chimed in, "Do you know how much those crooks wanted to charge us?"

"At this time of night," countered Jordan, "what's a few bucks in exchange for a little convenience? And besides, you're not exactly hurting for money, are you pal?"

"No thanks to you," Warren growled.

"What's *that* supposed to mean?"

"I'll need a clear head when I talk to you about it, so you'll just have to wait till I see you at the office." Warren was starting to head downhill when he halted. Turning back, he looked Jordan in the eye and said, "Give it some thought. I'm sure you can figure it out."

Glancing around at the almost deserted streets, Nancy asked in her gentrified Texas drawl, in an obvious attempt to diffuse the budding argument, "Walking this late at night would make me nervous. Why don't y'all let us give you a lift?"

She was referring to the fact it was edging into the hours when only questionable sorts were out and about. San Francisco was never a twenty four hour city like New York or Las Vegas, even on Friday. Already well past ten, late night diners were on their way home and avid partyers were now ensconced in fashionable lounges and cocktail bars.

"I need to sober up," grumbled Warren. "I have some business to attend to tomorrow morning and I'm gonna need the car. 'Sides, a little hike will do the kids good."

"Really?" asked Jordan. "Look, I honestly don't mind. I'm always up by five. I can drive you back bright and early."

"Nope."

"Please, Warren," Brandi begged. "I think Nancy's right."

"It's just a few blocks. We'll be there before you know it," Warren argued, beginning to grow more than a little angry at having to justify himself.

Jordan tried to intervene. "Hey, Bud… "

"I said *no!*" insisted Warren, pointing his finger at Jordan. Then, in a measured tone, he continued. "It'll be fine.

This is San Francisco."

"That's what I'm talking about."

"Don't *push*!" Warren snapped, extending his hands, palms facing outward. Then, in a less strident tone, he reiterated, "Anyway, you and I have something serious to discuss on Monday."

Jordan retreated a step, sighed, then relented. "All right. Just be careful."

As Jordan and Nancy headed for the crosswalk, Warren stuffed his hands into his pockets and stormed off in the opposite direction.

"G'night, bud," Jordan called after him. "We really enjoyed ourselves."

Warren heard Nancy add something more, but whether it was to him or her husband, he could not tell. The clanging of a bell and steel wheels rolling over the iron rails running up Powell, as one of San Francisco's iconic cable cars trundled past, trampled over her words.

"I think we should have followed them to the corner and turned left," suggested Brandi, trying to keep up while pulling the children along with her. When she caught up with him, she asked, "And what was all that about? That thing about Monday?"

Warren wheeled on her. "Did you honestly think I wouldn't find out?"

"About what?" Brandi asked.

"About the trip."

"Mommy? Are we going on a trip?" asked Robbie.

"Shh! Not now," Brandi hushed.

"Hah! Naturally, you couldn't tell the kids or Daddy'd

find out."

When Brandi presented an uncomprehending look, Warren rebuffed her attempt at innocence. "I've seen the reservations."

She fell silent and returned a minimal nod.

"Were you planning to leave a note on your pillow saying, 'Nice knowing you, Honey. Happy anniversary'? You do remember that our anniversary is coming up pretty soon, don't you?"

Brandi came erect and countered, "You're continually drunk and the children need someone to set a better example."

"And when you were going to tell them they had a new father?"

"You're still going to be our daddy, aren't you?" pleaded Robbie, gazing up at him.

Amazed at how someone so young could follow the conversation and perceive its nuances, Warren squatted down on his haunches, gripped Robbie by the shoulders and looked him square in the eyes.

"Of course I'm going to be your daddy. I'll always be your daddy and nothing's going to change it." He looked up at Brandi and glared. "Do you see what you're doing?"

He attempted to rise but instead stumbled backward, arresting his fall by placing one hand on the pavement.

"That's *exactly* what I'm talking about. Look at yourself! You should be ashamed. You can't even stand." Rebecca sneezed and Brandi glanced at her, then back at Warren. "We need to get them out of the cold."

Angry, but unable to argue against the obvious, Warren lowered his head, struggled to his feet and once again headed downhill on Powell. When he turned right at the next intersection, he ran into a wall of wind roaring up from the Pacific Ocean. Gripping his lapels, he drew his jacket around himself as the gust buffeted his pant legs, whipping them against his ankles and shins.

"Mommy, I'm cold!" cried Robbie.

"I want to go home," pleaded his sister.

"Hurry up, now," urged Brandi, grabbing Robbie by the hand. "We don't want to lose track of your father."

"You're hurting me!" the boy objected.

Warren, who, by this time, was rapidly moving downhill, slowed his pace to accommodate his children. *You're such an idiot,* he reprimanded himself. Despite what he had learned only this morning, he knew he should have taken Jordan up on his offer. San Francisco's streets running from west to east function like wind tunnels, funneling wind from the ocean to the bay. And while the gusts that were surging through Geary Boulevard weren't as strong as the ones driven up streets with higher elevations like California, he knew he needed to get them into some kind of shelter or they would all most likely come down with pneumonia.

He decided to turn left onto Mason, thereby putting its buildings between his family and the gale, before turning west again farther downhill where the wind was certain to be calmer. This stretch of their walk did seem somewhat better and, after traveling two more blocks, Warren turned west again with Brandi and the children close on his heels.

At one point, she looked around and observed, "I don't remember parking on Eddy."

"We're almost there," he insisted, uncertain at this point whether he had indeed parked on Eddy, rather than on Ellis which they had passed a block higher up.

He was not at all pleased with their current

surroundings. Like many American cities, San Francisco is a hodgepodge of diverse districts and neighborhoods. At night, as one proceeds westward of Powell and farther downhill from Geary, the buildings become less illuminated and the darkness increases. In a matter of half a dozen blocks, it is possible to transition from the well-heeled and tony to the dregs of despair. Instead of brightly lit restaurants, hotels and glamorous boutiques, the storefronts become shabby, more dilapidated than the ones that lie only a few blocks farther uphill or eastward. Hotels turn into low income extended residences and the spaces between are salted with dimly lit bars, tiny cafés, small, multicultural food marts and family-owned grocery stores. Along this portion of Eddy, the disparity between where they'd begun and the place where they had landed was obvious.

On their right, between two buildings situated like bookends, gaped a cavern a third building had occupied. A wall of plywood, thrown up by the demolition crew, was all that separated the pit from the sidewalk. As Warren and his family continued westward, they could not help but notice bodies in sleeping bags, looking like cloth-covered slugs along the buildings' foundations, or else tucked into iron gated entranceways. Windows were barred and outdoor lighting was minimal, providing the scantest assistance to pedestrians.

As Warren scanned their surroundings, he thought he detected movement ahead, only seconds before a large masculine form peeled away from the shadows and planted itself squarely in front of them.

"Warren," gasped Brandi and grabbed him by the elbow.

He halted as two other figures, both shorter than the first, stepped out to flank it.

"Hey," called Warren, raising a hand in feigned

nonchalance. "It's all right."

"Bet your ass it is," countered the man in the center.

"I mean, we don't want any trouble. If you'll just let us pass, we'll be out of your way before you know it."

Warren attempted what he hoped they would interpret as a good-natured laugh. Instead, it emerged like a cough. He tried clearing his throat, but like his mouth, his windpipe had gone paper dry. Met only with silence, he rasped, "What do you guys want?"

"What do you have?"

"N-nothing. We don't have anything."

"Don't give me that crap."

Brandi tightened her grip, digging her nails through Warren's sleeve and into his forearm.

"Do you want my wallet? I have some money," Warren offered as he reached back to retrieve it.

"I want everything."

"Every… ?"

Before Warren could finish, the stranger strode forward and, with both hands, grabbed his collar and lifted him up so that only his toes touched the pavement.

"Every. Fucking. Thing! I want your wallet. I want your watch, the lady's purse, her jewelry, anything inside the kids' pockets," he demanded, freeing a hand to point at Robbie and Rebecca.

"But… "

"Warren! Give the man what he wants."

"Do what the bitch says!" the man shouted, returning his hand and tightening his grip to the point Warren could hardly breathe.

Before Warren could answer, one of the others wrenched his arms behind him and the tendons in his shoulders started to tear. When that one had secured him well enough that all he could move was his head, the leader released his grip and circled around to a place Warren could only imagine. In a matter of seconds, Brandi screams were followed by the children's.

"My God!" he cried, straining to see. "I'll give you anything you want. Anything! But please leave my family out of this."

What had he been thinking? Too late, he realized that he hadn't been thinking at all. He had allowed the haze of alcohol to lead him blithely—blindly was more like it—from one street onto the next and into the very heart of the Tenderloin district, the city's soft underbelly of vice. Warren berated himself. *Why did I have to bring the kids?* All three were crying now, Brandi's gasps intermingling with sobs. He had brought the children to dinner, he now remembered, because of the price of a baby sitter. *A baby sitter? You cheap bastard!* Another round of cries brought him upright. Despite his recriminations and Brandi's infidelity, nothing justified whatever his family might now be enduring. When he endeavored to turn and get a better view, the man who was holding him yanked him back again. *Brandi, sweet Brandi,* he thought. *I've been such a jerk. You don't deserve any of this.* She cried out loud and the leader of the group laughed, before his voice hardened.

"I don't have time for this."

"Just do them," one of the men holding Warren urged. "Do them. Let's take what they have and get out of here."

"Mommeee!" shrieked Rebecca, agonizing Warren to the core.

"I'll get you!" Warren shouted. "If it's the last thing I ever do, I promise I will get you."

"Yeah, right," the first one snickered.

In the next instant, someone grabbed a fistful of Warren's hair and yanked back his head. Something sharp sliced through his throat and severed his windpipe. As the blood flowed away from his brain, his vision tunneled, the colors of the neon signs faded, and Brandi screamed.

2

Warren's final experiences before the world slipped away were the sounds of his wife screaming and Robbie crying. Rebecca's silence troubled him even more. *What are those bastards doing with her?* he worried during his final seconds.

Sounds and light faded, leaving only darkness. Time became meaningless, now that there was nothing to mark its passage—no heartbeat, no intake and outflow of breath. He could not say how long he remained in such a curious state, but after a while Warren thought he could make out the tiniest speck of light. Having nothing with which to compare it, he could not be certain if it lay at a distance or was close at hand. In fact, he initially wondered if it might be something his mind had created until, at one point, the speck of light began to expand. He did not actually witness it happening. It was nothing like that. But each time he tore his mind from his surreal predicament and returned to study his surroundings, the circle of light had grown perceptibly larger until, eventually, it grew large enough to fill all but his vision's perimeter. By then, he could not help but wonder if he was moving toward it. If that were the case, what would happen when he finally arrived?

He was lazing in his musings, lulled by how long the process was taking, when he remembered various accounts of people's near-death experiences in which they described something similar. Why he would now recall a scene from a movie he had seen in his childhood that cautioned, "Stay away from the light! Don't go into the light!" was puzzling, but the words suddenly commanded his attention. Without understanding the warning's basis, Warren responded to it. Realizing that the glow was threatening to surround him, he attempted to distance himself by backing away. Lacking a body, or anything with which to propel himself, his only tool seeming to be his volition. All his thoughts, all his desires focused on his wish to escape.

At first, nothing seemed to be happening and Warren feared he would fail. But as urgency turned into panic and his efforts increased in proportion to his fear, the luminescence's expansion halted, then slowly, very gradually, it appeared he might be moving away. In response to that success, he decided to strengthen his desire by focusing on it to the exclusion of everything else.

As Warren gained distance, familiar voices began beckoning him to return. He recognized Robbie's and Rebecca's. Along with those sounds, he started to see their faces, as well as those of long departed friends and relations. His mother, his father, and cherished family members began to appear inside the tunnel's glowing core. Almost more than anything—the operative word being "almost"—he wished he could join them. But rather than allow the soothing balm of their voices to dissuade him from leaving that place where all his problems could be set aside and forgotten, another compulsion arose that kept him moving: neglected matters from his past life were struggling to resurface.

Like an itch he could not reach, forgotten memories were trying to emerge, starting with hints, partial glimpses, vignettes from some fuller picture. *Why is it so hard to remember?* he wondered. His children's faces catalyzed the process by returning his thoughts to Eddy Street, to the trio of thugs and that pivotal moment that resulted in his murder. Matters that preceded his death and revolved around that particular event needed to be addressed. There were injustices that needed fixing, wrongs that wanted righting, and downright betrayals that demanded revenge. His instinct told him that stepping back into the world of the living was as important as keeping away from the light. The problem was remembering what those injustices were. There was something having to do with Brandi and something else about Jordan, but nothing he could remember with specificity. Who was it who informed him and what exactly had she said?

The question stopped him.

What had *she* said?

She? This person was a woman?

It was then Warren remembered that the individual who had made those disclosures had indeed been female. The effort to remember her identity brought back images of a breakfast at a bakery in downtown Tiburon, minutes from Jordan's residence and closer still to their field office. The only women who fit into this context, who would have had any knowledge of either his wife's or his partner's activities were either Nancy—whom he did not believe would share whatever dirt she might have about her husband or, for that matter, about Brandi—and Sabrina, who held down the fort in Tiburon and was intimately connected to both. The instant she sprang to mind, the image of Friday's breakfast solidified.

It had been a typical June morning, holding the promise of a warm summer day. The bay was still dark and glassy under a flawless blue sky, but the wind was already tracing cats' paws across the waters in Raccoon Strait, hinting that its strength was building. The breeze was not yet strong enough to deter the man and woman who were sculling in tandem toward Richardson Bay, but yacht racing crews would already be packing their foul weather gear to practice for the weekend's regatta. The streamer of fog that was snaking beneath the Golden Gate Bridge would dissipate and vanish as soon as the offshore marine layer lifted.

Sabrina had been waiting on the bay side of Main Street. Since the street still lay in shadow, she was wearing a lightweight sweater over a cotton summer dress. The man she was conversing with, Warren recognized, was a Tiburon merchant who owned one of those touristy shops that seemed to spring up from time to time, then dried up and vanished a few years later. Their talk was ending and he heard each of them say their goodbyes, just before Sabrina turned and saw him approaching. She was starting to smile when he greeted her.

"Good morning, Sabrina. You wanted to talk?"

Her smile flickered, then evaporated. "Let's get something to eat first."

She gestured toward the café where they were standing and Warren nodded. After picking out pastries from the glass display case to the left of the bake shop's entrance—almond bear claw with marzipan filling for him, cheese Danish for her—she led him to a table near the café's rear doorway that opened onto a postage stamp sized wooden deck. Once they were seated, a cheery teenage girl sporting strawberry blonde hair and looking as if she'd been sampling the goods on a regular basis, brought them two cups with saucers, a steaming pot of coffee, and two breakfast menus. Setting the latter aside, they enjoyed their sweets and discussed pleasantries while avoiding the obvious. Eventually, however, Warren could no longer contain himself. He blotted his lips and placed the linen napkin next to his plate.

"All right," he said, as he lifted his cup to his lips.

"What's this all about?"

Sabrina turned and studied the people who were sitting nearby. Warren mimicked her, since Tiburon is a small town where gossip travels fast. When it was obvious their neighbors were too absorbed in their own conversations to eavesdrop, Sabrina turned back and inhaled.

"I'm not looking forward to telling you this, but you're going to learn about it anyway. My guess is sometime next week. It's better you hear it from me now, than get blind-sided later."

Warren started to chuckle. "You're making it sound like… "

"Jordan's cooking the books."

Warren spat, spraying coffee over the table cloth.

"*What?*"

Incensed by the declaration's absurdity, he stared at her sideways, then set down the cup and started to push back his chair.

"That's ridiculous. I've heard enough."

Before he could rise, Sabrina pressed. "I had lunch with Michael from accounting when I came into the city on Wednesday and he explained what Jordan is up to."

"I spoke to Michael on Monday, right after the weekly meeting," countered Warren, only partially risen, still gripping the chair's armrests. "Why didn't he say something then?"

"He didn't learn about it until later. Please, Mr. Holmes, don't go. You should know me well enough by now to realize I'm not the kind of person who invents things— Michael either."

Warren frowned, recognizing the truth in her

statement, and settled into the chair. "Has anyone else said anything about it?"

Sabrina shook her head. "I'm pretty sure we're the first to find out. Michael stumbled onto it by accident Wednesday morning. We've been sharing confidences for some time now, so he knew he could trust me. We discussed the best way to handle it, and we decided we should bring it to your attention before we brought in the SEC." Before Warren could reply, she added, "According to what Michael has shown me, Jordan's been salting away money for almost three years into offshore accounts… "

"Offshore… " He broke off the sentence, his mouth hanging open.

" …in the Seychelles."

Warren stared. After a pause, he looked away and spent a moment considering. Finally, he looked back and said, "Jordan's rich. Why would he do something like that?"

"Apparently, not rich enough." Sabrina bit her lip and leaned across the table. "And that's not the worst part," she said, barely louder than a whisper.

"What could be worse than this?"

"When he leaves the country, I'm pretty sure he's planning on taking Brandi and the kids with him."

Warren slammed his fist on the table hard enough that several people turned to stare.

"That's it. I'm done."

Rising, he slid his chair back with so much force that he almost knocked down the server who was delivering dishes to the table behind him. His apology, amid gasps and comments from the other diners, stopped him long enough that Sabrina had time to reach into the bag she had placed next to her chair.

"You should take a look at these before we give them to SEC enforcement," she said, withdrawing a sheaf of documents. Looking up, she added, "This isn't hypothetical."

Warren regarded the papers she was holding and frowned. When he failed to accept them, Sabrina urged, "Please don't go, Mr. Holmes," and extended the papers toward him. "I promise, this is going to come as quite a revelation."

With his eyes on her offering, Warren again drew the chair underneath him. Easing himself into it, he studied her face and Sabrina returned his stare without blinking or showing any sign that she was being less than candid. Only then did he accept them and start reading. Ten minutes later, he was staring at the final page and finding it difficult to accept what he had read.

"Airline reservations?" he asked when he finally looked up.

Sabrina nodded. "Two adults and two children," she confirmed. "You will notice there is no return trip."

"But this doesn't necessarily indicate… "

"No, it doesn't. But can you think of anyone else matching that description he might care to take with him?"

Unable to respond, Warren shook his head and looked back at the page in his hand, trying to conceive of any possibility other than the one she had offered.

"Haven't you heard him complain from time to time that the passion's gone out of his marriage?"

"Things change. Relationships alter. You can't expect them to stay the same forever," he countered, setting the evidence on the tablecloth.

"Brandi's been at odds with you and your… " Sabrina paused, compressed her lips, then continued. " …excessive drinking for some time… "

"Who the hell are you to judge?" Warren snapped and Sabrina flinched. But when she failed to look away, he said in a quieter tone, "There has to be some other explanation."

"I'm listening, Mr. Holmes. After reading everything I've given you, what would you suggest as a reasonable alternative?"

Unable to respond, Warren exhaled. He picked up the records again, taken by how light they were, given the weight of what they contained. There must be *some* other interpretation to the evidence she had presented, his stubbornness insisted, if only he took the time to reexamine them.

"Do you mind if I keep them?"

"Not at all. We still have the originals."

He stopped and stared. "This isn't some form of blackmail, is it?"

"Have I asked you for anything?"

Warren shook his head.

"And I'm not going to," she continued, returning his stare with equal intensity.

He could see no sign of guile or deception, so he took the documents to the office and spent the better part of the day analyzing what she had given him. When each read returned him to the identical conclusion, he pondered what he should do about the two he had, until now, held above all others: his wife and his best friend. The more he thought about it, the angrier he became.

His present lifestyle would never have been possible

without his business partner. Without Jordan's insights he would still be working for somebody else, would still be toiling each day on the telephone in an effort to bring in new clients. He knew he owed Jordan for giving him the means to become his own boss, no longer beholden to others, but Jordan owed Warren too. Warren had taken the concepts Jordan had given him and transformed them into a powerful tool for turning the vast sea of corporate data into something quantifiable and readily marketable.

Was his contribution any smaller than Jordan's? Of course not. Without him and his software development skills, Jordan would also be struggling to maintain his own client base. He certainly would not be living at the tip of the Tiburon peninsula in a house overlooking San Francisco Bay. Consequently, regardless of how unsatisfying Jordan's marriage had become, it couldn't justify sabotaging Warren's.

And then there was Brandi—dear, sweet, loveable Brandi. He used to ask himself what he had done to deserve her. Aside from her family's wealth, her considerable intelligence and physical beauty—Warren could not think of another woman more striking—she had given him two wonderful children and was the best mother imaginable. She was certainly the best wife he could have wished for. Always caring and patient, amorous without hesitation, she had always put up with his numerous failings. Perhaps it was the salesman in him and his boyish charm, something he had deliberately cultivated when the two of them had met, that had drawn her to him. But after all these years, he had to ask himself, what wrongs had he done that she would contemplate deserting him? Try as he might to avoid the obvious, he knew it was his bouts with alcohol.

The more he ruminated over the pair's betrayal, the angrier he grew. Had she even *once* intimated that his behavior might be the thing that would sunder their relationship, he would have directed all of his efforts toward correcting this apparently fatal flaw. She had not. It was her silent enabling, her codependence that had led them to this situation, he decided. As for Jordan, that he would plunder their company's treasury for his solitary gain, to leave Warren and their employees unexpectedly lacking the means to carry on, was completely unforgiveable.

That was his emotional state on Friday. That was his emotional state now. Warren also cursed the trio of street thugs who had sent him here, to this limbo, this place where he had no means to redress these grievances. *Damn her! Damn them both! Damn all of them!* His fury rose and the more he dwelled on what they all had done to him, the more enraged he became. If only he were able to return, he would wreak vengeance and havoc, the like of which none of them could ever imagine.

The instant the thought surfaced, Warren started to wonder if, by sheer dint of will, he might be able to leave this place and return to the world of the living. After all, it was his intention to remove himself from the Tunnel of Light that had prevented it from capturing him. Could he then, by directing all of his efforts, all of his being, toward this solitary task, return himself to his previous reality? Suspended as he was between the Tunnel of Light and the world he once knew, he began to focus on that possibility.

He could not say how long he had been thus occupied. It could have been days or even weeks, considering however much or how little those measurements now meant, but after a while he felt a subtle shift in his perceptions. Where there had previously been only silence, little noises began to intrude. Whereas, aside from that luminous tunnel, there had been only darkness, faint glimmers of light began to appear in the opposite direction. Curious as to what they might signify and wishing he could examine them, he was delighted when he found himself moving in their direction. As wish became deed and the lights grew closer and the sounds became increasingly audible, Warren worked ever harder to reach them until he seemed to be moving at a remarkable velocity.

Abruptly, light was everywhere. Blinded by the brilliance, he closed his eyes until they finally stopped hurting. When he reopened them, the things he saw astounded him. The entire Bay Area with its bridges, buildings, and the great bay itself, replete with container ships and tug boats plying its waters, spread like a tapestry beneath him. From the cranes at Alameda's loading docks to Vallejo's Mare Island Naval Station and the yacht harbors of Sausalito and Berkeley, from towns and cities as far south as San Jose, then past San Francisco and Oakland to northern communities like Novato and Vacaville, Warren was intensely aware of the teeming life beneath him. It wasn't merely the activity. On a level he could not identify, Warren sensed the millions of hearts beating and the millions of breaths taken in and released. The life in which he would never again participate nagged at him, reminded him it was forever beyond his reach, raising his anger to a new level at the injustice of it all. What happened when his thoughts turned to his erstwhile partner amazed him all the more. In that instant, Jordan's thoughts came rushing in and Warren knew, beyond any doubt, good old Jordie's exact location. He grinned, knowing how easy it would be to find the cemetery.

3

"Hun, this just doesn't seem right," said Nancy.

Jordan was staring out of their living room's picture window at Raccoon Straits, flowing between their home and Angel Island. Half a dozen sailboats with their multicolored spinnakers set, were attempting to make headway through the channel against what Jordan knew to be the second fiercest ebb tide in San Francisco Bay, with only the one under the Golden Gate Bridge being any stronger. Off to his right, the Angel Island Ferry was transporting a load of picnickers, bicyclists and hikers from Tiburon's downtown jetty to the dock on Angel Island, where it would return later today to retrieve them. Farther westward rose Alcatraz Island, with San Francisco's skyline and the aforementioned bridge serving as backdrop. It was a million dollar view that didn't seem worth a penny, now that Brandi's children had been murdered and she was, even at this minute, barely alive.

The news of what had happened on Eddy Street almost leveled him. Jordan loved her, loved her with all his heart, loved her enough to accept her children as his own when she asked if he would consider bringing them along when they made their getaway. *Damn Warren to hell!* Somehow the son of a bitch had stumbled onto what he had been doing, or at least it sounded as if he had, especially that thing about "just deserts." Why couldn't those killers have just murdered

Warren and left the rest of them alone? For that matter, why couldn't Warren have left his children home with a baby sitter, or even his housekeeper watching? Everything would have been so much simpler. Instead, here was Jordan with travel plans that would amount to nothing if Brandi didn't pull through. Even if she did, he knew she would never be the same, now that her children were dead.

Of course, he couldn't discuss any of this with Nancy. They had been living what she perceived as an idyllic lifestyle for just over a year. It galled him that she didn't seem to care if her growing disinterest in all things sexual had devolved their relationship from heartfelt lovers into celibate roommates. And why should it? They had moved into their waterfront home just shy of five years after his and Warren's investment firm launched and, one year later, had taken off like a rocket. Back then, it had seemed as if he and Warren were invincible, unable to take any missteps. Every security they had selected graphed steadily uphill. They were doing so well that, at one point, the SEC decided to investigate whether they were using inside information. However, once he and Warren demonstrated the efficacy of their proprietary software by selecting nearly a dozen corporations they had not already purchased, and *those* stocks remained upward bound for the twelve months that followed, they were deemed a legitimate, if not one highly inexplicable phenomenon and were allowed to retain their license without penalty.

When he and Warren first met, they were a couple of cold call stock brokers. Each Friday after the market closed, they would meet at a bar in downtown San Rafael and discuss the preceding week over beers and Happy Hour edibles. Since Jordan had developed a reputation for not always adhering to the firm's daily stock recommendations, but had occasionally managed to pick an unexpected winner or two on his own, Warren eventually got around to asking what it was that had prompted him to select them. Jordan explained that, in addition to the usual indicators, he had noticed that before certain stocks took off, they had specific metrics in common that traditional analytics ignored. He also believed that, if he could find more time to study the vast array of publicly traded companies, he could probably identify many others with the same characteristics. His day job, however, ate up so much time that he felt lucky to spot the occasional candidate. Computers, he believed, would be the solution. They could do all the work, provided he had the right software. The problem was, Jordan complained, that he knew virtually nothing about those devices except how to use whatever programs were already available.

Warren had grinned, explaining how, before he had entered the world of finance, he had spent much of his youth coding software. If Jordan wouldn't mind describing his theory's particulars in detail, Warren told him he might be able to assemble the program Jordan needed.

The project had taken quite a while to complete, since Warren's specialty, it turned out, was in the world of gaming—not the gambling sort, which would have better lent itself to their purposes, but rather the Doom and Tetris variety. It was dogged persistence that finally got him to his goal, that and his admirable propensity for research. When the day finally arrived that Warren felt he had mastered the necessary algorithms, they tested his creation and quickly identified three emerging energy enterprises.

When those stocks shot upward, Jordan grew jubilant and the pair abruptly cut ties with their employer and launched their own endeavor. Since they did not dare bring their client lists with them—which certainly would have invoked the firm's ire and possibly drawn attention to their new analysis tool, while, at the same time, risking lengthy litigation over who held legal claim to it—the initial going was tedious. Tales of their repeated successes, however, eventually spread and clients began beating the proverbial path. A few more years found the two men millionaires.

Life—meaning Jordan and Nancy's marriage—would have been perfect if her passions hadn't cooled to the point she was treating him more like a brother than husband and lover. Granted, he had been working extended hours, even on weekends, but it was to get them to where they had landed. Yes, they were cordial, but cordiality is only part of a marriage. No, they had not argued, at least not as much as most married couples, and he prided himself on insuring that they had resolved their disagreements before going to bed.

Once the day came that Jordan felt comfortable enough with his business's momentum that he could throttle down and relax, he tried all the usual ploys—elaborate bouquets, well-thought-out dinner dates and nights on the town, romantic strolls through wooded glades, conversations sprung from the heart, even diamonds—and still he could not entice her to consider tussling between the sheets. Jordan had almost resigned himself to a monastic existence when Brandi approached him with complaints of her own.

"I don't know what to do, Jordan. I can't get him to stop drinking. It's bad enough he gets sloppy drunk around me, but he's slurring his words and knocking into furniture in front of the children."

"Has he ever hit you?"

She shook her head. "It hasn't come to that… yet. And I hope it never will. That's not the point. He should be someone our kids can look up to. But right now… " Her face sagged and she appeared to be on the verge of a breakdown.

That's when Jordan's radar went up. Although Warren never seemed to recall, he and Jordan had attended the same university. They had graduated three years apart. But during the year when their attendances overlapped, something happened that Jordan had done his best to ignore because, one, he genuinely liked Warren and, two, their mutual success as stockbrokers, and eventually business partners, demanded it.

The fact was, Warren had stolen Jordan's girlfriend. It wasn't something he had deliberately set out to do. Jordan and—he could not remember the girl's name for the life of him—had been having difficulties. She had left him for someone who was kind and gentle and, well, brilliant if the truth were told. And though it had happened all those years ago, the offense still nagged at him. Now, he was presented with an opportunity to repay Warren in kind.

Jordan and Brandi spent hours speculating about the reason behind Warren's drinking, some flaw, perhaps, that caused him to react in this manner to their good fortune. In the end, they decided it didn't really matter. Whatever the reason, his ongoing drunkenness was completely unacceptable. Whenever it became especially pronounced, Brandi phoned Jordan and they would find some discrete destination to hash out her grievances. Their talks became increasingly frequent until, what began as morning cups of coffee at a Terra Linda diner, turned into extended lunches with a growing need to turn them into something more. The first time Jordan took Brandi's hand into his as an act of consolation, he was pleasantly surprised that she didn't resist. Instead, she squeezed his in return, then gazed back with a smile that asked what neither was yet ready to put into words. That was when Jordan confessed about how Nancy's passion had died.

At first, they simply commiserated, sharing tales about their tragedies. Then, one rainy Tuesday two years ago, they drove to an unobtrusive motel on a frontage road where Highway 101 arches over Richardson Bay and broke their marriage vows. That midday tryst, brief as it was, put an end to Jordan's inertia. For the first time in years, he felt energized and set to work on a plan designed to pave the way for a new life and a new love.

"Did you hear what I said?" asked Nancy.

Startled, Jordan turned around to face her. "I'm sorry. No. I didn't."

"I said this doesn't seem right. We should be making plans for a weekend getaway, not getting ready for a drive down to Colma."

Colma, California was, in the words of the New York Times, "Where San Francisco's Dead Live." With a live population of around fifteen hundred, more than a million and a half of the Bay Area's deceased have been laid to rest in Colma's twenty six cemeteries.

Jordan nodded, then stepped forward to embrace her, torn between a social obligation to memorialize his partner's life and his distaste over what Warren had been doing to his marriage. Since he feared that explaining his ambivalence might somehow betray his feelings for Brandi, he elected to be politic. He began with, "I don't know if things will ever be the same again. How do we pick up now that… ?" then broke off as Nancy clung to him and started sobbing. When she finally tore herself free, wiping her tears and regaining her composure, he told her, "You're right. We have to go. It wouldn't look right if we missed the funeral."

"It wouldn't *be* right," she corrected.

… … … … …

The crowd that had gathered around the three excavations was larger than Jordan anticipated. As he and Nancy made their way through a virtual sea of white and gray granite headstones and the occasional pink marble slab, toward where several dozen mourners were already assembled, he began to recognize most of them. In addition to the firm's employees, he was surprised to see several former coworkers from their original brokerage house, not only stockbrokers like him and Warren, but some of the clerical staff and managerial team. Fellow members of both Chambers of Commerce to which they belonged— the San Francisco chapter, where their main office was based, and Tiburon's, where he and Warren maintained a nominal storefront—had turned out in force. Glancing around, Jordan quickly picked out the faces of Sabrina Babich, their Marin County salesperson, and Michael Sumner from the San Francisco accounting department. As if sensing he was looking, Sabrina's eyes flicked toward Jordan. When their eyes met, she appeared startled, her eyes widening for a moment. Her lips attempted to force a smile, but it evaporated as she leaned against the accountant and began talking to him with unusual animation. Michael's face came up. When his and Jordan's eyes met, without averting his gaze, he continued speaking to Sabrina, nodding as he did so.

Nancy tugged Jordan's elbow and he followed her toward the congregation's center, glancing back briefly and wondering about the conversation Sabrina and Michael were having. When his eyes finally focused on their new destination, he recognized several of his and Warren's clients. While he and Warren had only spoken to the majority of their customers by email or telephone, a few had made a point of dropping by their downtown office to offer their thanks for how well the pair had managed their investments. Their taking the time to pay their respects emphasized how much they valued his and Warren's services.

Quite naturally, friends and neighbors were here as well. When Jordan started toward them, Nancy wrapped her arm around his elbow and tugged him in a different direction.

"Hun," she said, as her eyes turned toward two couples standing with a traditionally garbed clergyman. "I think this is where you belong."

Of course, Nancy was right. Warren's mother, Sheila, attired in black skirt and matching beaded jacket, was standing graveside with her husband. Sporting the assembly's only hat—black with matching veil—along with a pair of black kidskin gloves, black handbag and single strand of black pearls, she was tastefully fashionable, even now in her moment of grief. It was she who had arranged for Warren's interment, here near the tombs of William Randolph Hearst and Phineas Gage. Although he had never met the couple who were with them, the woman's unbridled display of grief made it likely they were the bereaved grandparents.

Jordan nodded. "You're right as always," he conceded and patted Nancy's hand as she twined her arm around his. Departing the path that led from El Camino Real, they turned up the grassy slope.

Howard Holmes, Warren's father, noticed them first. He mouthed something into Sheila's ear and she broke off her conversation with the minister and turned to face Jordan and Nancy. Additional comments from Howard brought the other three around and Jordan steeled himself for what he expected would be a difficult encounter.

Even though the walk was not strenuous and a breeze was blowing down from Serramonte and the ocean beyond, sweat was beading across Jordan's forehead. The temperature was edging into the upper seventies and the suit and necktie Nancy had insisted on—lest someone else's attire make Jordan appear less respectful—was becoming stifling. He pulled the carefully folded handkerchief from his suit's breast pocket and dabbed at the perspiration, then tucked it into the pocket at his hip before extending his hand toward Howard.

"I'm so sorry for your loss," said Jordan as he and Howard clasped hands.

Howard managed a tight but seemingly sincere smile,

then nodded. "This hard for everyone."

God, I hate this, thought Jordan. What does one say, he wondered, on such an occasion that doesn't sound forced and hackneyed? Nonetheless, he turned to face Sheila and took her hands into his. She spoke before he could address her.

"Thank you both for coming," she said, glancing back and forth between him and Nancy.

"Of course, Dear," Nancy replied, relieving Jordan of the obligation. "How could we not?" Then, turning to the pair standing off to one side, she inquired, "I expect you're Brandi's kin."

As they nodded in acknowledgement, Sheila volunteered, "Yes, they are." Turning to the couple, she said, "Mark, Karen, I would like you to meet Jordan Weeks, Warren's partner, and Jordan's wife, Nancy." Turning back, she continued, "After Brandi authorized her to do so, Karen arranged for Warren and the children's remains to be released. She was kind enough to allow me to organize this ceremony."

Karen Burkhardt smiled at Sheila's comments. Up until this moment, she had seemed to Jordan to be out of touch with her surroundings, focused instead on the holes in which her grandchildren were about to be placed. Unwrapping her arm from Mark's bicep, she stepped forward and burrowed her eyes into Jordan's.

"Were you there when my baby was attacked and her poor little children were killed? Sheila said you were with them."

Jordan shook his head. "We had dinner together. But we didn't see the... " He paused a beat, reluctant to use the word 'murder.' " ...unfortunate incident."

"How did it happen?" Karen persisted. "I mean, how did they end up there? I've been told they were in a terrible part of town."

The look on her face told him she needed to hear anything that would make sense of such an incomprehensible loss. He did not believe that disparaging Warren for either his condition or the resulting lapse of judgment would have contributed anything beneficial. Consequently, he offered a partial explanation.

"It can be easy, in that part of the city, to take a wrong turn. They wouldn't have been the first to have done so."

In fact, occasional newspaper stories told about tourists who, a short distance west of Union Square, had elected to stroll to City Hall before finding themselves hiking through nearby tenements, then being beaten and robbed or suffering the same fate as Warren's family.

"What a horrible place!" Karen exclaimed, placing her hands over her mouth.

"Not at all, my dear," Nancy responded. "The kinds of things Jordie is talking about are exceptionally rare. If you stop and think about it, they happen in all major cities. It's so unfortunate this had to happen to your little darlin' and the kids." She stepped forward and grasped Karen's forearms. "If there's anything you need… "

Karen shook her head in several short nervous jerks and pulled herself free.

Nancy's gasp was almost imperceptible. Jordan noticed it, but knew her to be a social veteran who would not allow strangers to spot even the smallest chink in her emotional armor. "Just think of us as family," she said, returning her hands to her sides. Taking a deferential step backward, she emphasized, "Anything, anything at all."

As if to alleviate the situation, Sheila directed their attention to the minister, saying, "Jordan, Nancy, I'd like you to meet Reverend Castle. He has presided over our church for… " She paused a second to consider. " …Lord knows how long. Seems like forever, doesn't it, Reverend?" The minister smiled and Sheila continued. "Anyhow, even though Warren and his family were never part of our congregation, I thought something more dignified than a secular ceremony was in order."

"Thank you, Sheila," the minister replied. "And you're right. This is the best way I can think of to commend them into the Good Lord's hands." He glanced at his watch, then studied the gathering. "I don't see anyone else coming, so with your permission, I'd like to begin."

As the minister summoned the throng to gather around him, Jordan noticed the polished ebony box beside one of the graves. Its size told him it was Warren's. As he gazed into the pit, lost for a moment in vague recollections of their mutual history, he jerked upright when someone addressed him. Glancing around, he saw that all of the mourners were focused on the minister, so he turned his eyes to Reverend Castle as well.

Jordie, the person repeated. It sounded as if he were speaking directly into Jordan's ear, and it snapped his head around. No one but Warren, Nancy or Brandi ever addressed him that way, but it wasn't either of the women who had spoken. It was a man's voice and it sounded like Warren, but Jordan knew that was impossible. *It must be someone else*, he told himself. He surveyed the mourners who were listening to Castle, but there were no obvious candidates. The minister was beginning the eulogy and all eyes were focused on him.

"Dear?" asked Nancy. "Is something wrong?"

He saw she was staring and her eyebrows were furrowed.

"I… No. It was nothing. Just my imagination." He was

about to explain, "I thought I heard Warren," when a penetrating chill swept through him. He shivered and Nancy whispered, "You don't look well. We should leave as soon as this is over."

Jordan nodded and was about to reply when the voice spoke again.

It's all right, old friend. I just wanted you to know you haven't seen the last of me.

Jordan's eyes widened and his initial impulse was to ignore it. *This is crazy*, he told himself. *Things like this never happen except in movies or dreams.* But when something ice cold came in contact with his shoulder, Jordan jumped. This time, the people in his immediate vicinity did turn and stare. Regretting his reaction, he was offering an apologetic smile when the voice said, *Take care, good buddy. I'm back.*

"Back?" he responded reflexively.

Like I told you before, we have some unfinished business.

Jordan's heart was pounding. He took Nancy's wrist and leaned toward her. Although he knew it wouldn't look good, he grimaced and said, "I have to get out of here."

"Why on earth would you want to leave?"

"I have to go *now*," he hissed.

Jordan saw he was drawing attention. Sheila and Howard were frowning and Karen was showing something akin to hatred. It didn't matter.

"*Now!*" he repeated. "Will you come, or do I have to leave without you?"

Nancy glanced at Warren's parents, hesitated a moment, then said, "Yes. Of course. If you feel that bad… "

Jordan flashed what he hoped would be a smile, and mouthed the words, "I'm sorry," before turning to rush to his car. They had been standing at the center of it all, so he was forced to make a path between the mourners amid comments like, "Poor man. He looks so upset", "Can you imagine what he must be going through?" and "I've never seen anything so disrespectful."

When they had passed through the last of them, Nancy asked, "What's the matter? You look like you've seen a ghost."

"I wish you hadn't put it like that," he snapped. Then, a few paces farther, he turned to her. "I'm sorry. That was rude. But I distinctly heard Warren speak to me." When she responded with a disbelieving look, he added, "I heard him as clear as if he was standing next to me." He debated what he was about to say next, then decided to tell her the truth, as crazy as he knew it would sound. "He said he's coming back."

"That's ridiculous!"

Jordan could only nod in agreement as he began to question the state of his sanity. Nothing about this was rational, but he knew what he had heard. He also knew he had to leave. In the next instant, he realized how fast he was moving when Nancy caught her foot on something, stumbled and almost fell. He managed to catch her, then steadied her as she gathered herself.

"I'm sorry," he muttered, before resuming his trek and failing to keep to a walk. "When have you ever known me to invent things?" he asked when she caught up with him.

Nancy thought for a second, then shook her head. "Well, never, I guess."

"Then believe me when I tell you I heard him."

4

"That wasn't at all like you," said Nancy as she fastened her seatbelt.

Jordan shook his head in acknowledgement and floored the accelerator of his silver Mercedes Benz S-Class coupe. He swerved into traffic, but hardly felt the momentum as the car's automatic suspension tilted the vehicle's body to counter its inertia.

"Would you please slow down?" she demanded. "Now you've really got me worried."

"I'm sorry," he said and eased his foot from the accelerator.

"Now tell me again. What was that about hearing Warren?"

He remained silent a moment as he asked himself the same question. Were the situation reversed, he would have considered the declaration as verging onto insanity, or at least the ridiculous. He did not believe in the supernatural. And while he wasn't exactly an atheist, his mind never touched on esoteric matters. Ouija boards, séances and communicating with the departed were, to his mind, so beyond the acceptable as to land them solidly in the realm of kooks and weirdos.

Nonetheless, he had heard Warren speak. Of that

much, he was certain. All right, he acknowledged, he hadn't exactly *heard* him. The crazy part—There! Now he *was* admitting it—was that it wasn't at all like the monologue his mind conducted when he was debating with himself. The voice was clear and distinct to the point that it might as well have been spoken and he didn't know what to make of it.

"I don't know."

"So we left the funeral early and you can't tell me why?"

He inhaled deeply, then exhaled. "I know this sounds nuts, but I really did hear Warren talk to me."

"So you said." Nancy paused, then added, "And now I'm asking myself why I should believe you." Before he could answer, she continued. "I listened to you then because I know you're not one to go and invent things. I left when you wanted to, even though we're going to have to come up with something that sounds rational enough to satisfy Sheila… or Brandi's mother, from the look of it. But now, as we're sitting here and I've had time to think about what we just did, you have to give me a good explanation."

He turned his head long enough to see she was staring.

"Honestly," he said as he returned his attention to the road, "I wish I could explain it." He banged the steering wheel with the heel of his hand and felt it vibrate. "But I can't make the sound of his voice go away."

"Are you hearing him now?"

"No. But it's stuck in my mind."

"Do you remember what he said?"

Although she sounded genuinely curious, he wondered if the motive behind the question wasn't more about his level of sanity, rather than about what he had heard.

"He said he had some unfinished business he needed to attend to."

"I can understand why he'd feel that way. I do have to remind you, though, the dead stay dead while we go on with our daily affairs."

The last word stuck and he wondered for a moment if she weren't alluding to him and Brandi, before he dismissed the idea and accepted her comment at face value.

"Look. If I were in your place, I would probably feel the same way you do. But can we please drop this until I've had some time to work it out?"

"You don't want to talk about it?"

"Not right now… if you don't mind. We can discuss it once we're home and I've had time to settle down."

They rode home in silence. That troubled him almost as much as the problem he was facing. Aside from the vacuum that sexual abstinence had inserted into their relationship, he and Nancy were as close to being soulmates as he ever could have wanted. Shutting her out now seemed like a violation of the covenant they had made when they pledged their vows. All the way home, Jordan stewed over the encounter, visiting, then revisiting the event while hoping for some kind of breakthrough, something that would offer a rational explanation. Clarification never came and he pulled into his garage feeling troubled and confused.

Once inside, he poured himself a bourbon, then paced the living room while Nancy, supportive wife that she was, waited him out, knowing better than to intrude. By the time evening was approaching, however, she suggested they get something to eat at the restaurant at the bottom of the hill, rather than try to prepare dinner.

Peter, the restaurant's manager, greeted them. "Good

evening, Mr. and Mrs. Weeks. The usual table?"

"Is it available?" Nancy inquired, glancing at the half dozen couples who were standing in the vestibule.

"It is for you." In a confidential aside, he added, "You always have standing reservations."

And of course they did. They were two of the restaurant's most frequent patrons, not only because of the establishment's proximity, but also because of the quality of the fare and service that had made it Tiburon's oldest dining establishment. Jutting over the water on pilings, its singular view of the bay, of the Golden Gate Bridge, of Angel Island, as well as both Sausalito and San Francisco—even better than the one from their living room—was also part of its unexcelled ambiance.

"Would you care to let me in?" Nancy asked as Jordan nursed his glass of wine and stared out the corner table's window.

"I suppose I should. You're the only one who will listen." He took a sip and chuckled. "Not that you'll believe me."

"Your software idea was a bit of a stretch, and I believed you then." She reached out to take his hand. "And look where it got us. Although, I grant you, this time may be different."

Jordan set down his drink and turned to face her.

"How do you think I feel? This is way beyond the pale. But I have to tell you, Nan, I heard him. However it happened, I heard Warren speak to me."

She smiled and patted his hand. "I often hear my deceased father speak to me. Whenever I'm down I… "

"Please don't patronize me."

"I'm n… "

"It was *nothing* like that. I know what you're talking about: insistent memories welling up, past conversations. It was none of those things. *None* of them." Making a conscious effort to remove the edge from his voice, he continued. "I heard Warren's voice as clearly as I hear you now."

"I'm sorry, Hun," Nancy replied, looking at Jordan askance. "But I'm going to need something more substantial."

Warren's voice boomed inside each of their heads. *How's this for substantial?*

They both jumped. Nancy knocked over her glass, sending Chardonnay across the tablecloth. As they scoured the room for the source of the question, the contents of the serving tray their waiter was carrying exploded, spattering the server and diners with oysters on the half shell and beef tenderloin carpaccio. Amid screams from the dinner guests, Jordan and Nancy threw up their arms to protect themselves from the food and flying china. Stunned, the server allowed the tray to slip from his grip and bounce against the aquamarine carpet. He remained frozen in place for several seconds before he regained sufficient presence to start cleaning up. While the patrons straightened themselves, retrieving their wine glasses from the carpet and brushing morsels of appetizer from their jackets and blouses, Nancy and Jordan stared at each other.

"Are you all right?" Jordan gasped.

Nancy nodded. "What just happened?"

You asked for a demonstration and I gave you one.

Nancy gripped Jordan's wrist. "Did you hear that?"

They both looked around, but saw only dinner guests recovering and the waiter struggling to put the place in order.

Responding to the outbursts, the manager rushed in

from the kitchen. Surveying the aftermath, he demanded, "Eric, what happened?"

"I don't know, sir," the waiter replied, glancing up as he placed a broken saucer on the serving tray. "Everything just flew into the air."

The manager started reprimanding him for fabricating an excuse for his carelessness when Jordan interceded. "He's right, Peter. I've never seen anything like it. Did you feel a tremor?"

Peter halted and looked at him. "No, Mr. Weeks. I didn't. Are you saying there was an earthquake?"

"I don't know how else to explain it, but it wasn't the young man's fault. Something unusual happened. The tray flew into the air and I'm certain he did nothing to cause it."

The manager turned to see diners, obviously angry, starting to rise. Others were complaining to each other while dabbing at spots of sauce with their napkins.

"I'll take you at your word, Mr. Weeks." Another server entered from the kitchen and caught Peter's attention. "Melissa," he called. "Help me take care of our guests."

As they hurried to sooth tempers and minimize the damage, Jordan told Nancy, "We need to talk. Let's step outside."

He placed a fifty on the table to offset the cost of the appetizers and drinks, then made for the exit with Nancy beside him.

"Mr. and Mrs. Weeks," the manager hailed, obviously distressed. Glancing back and forth between them and the couple he was dealing with, he asked, "Is there anything I can do to make amends?"

"Don't worry, Peter. You'll see us again." Realizing he

was still hungry, Jordan added, "Once you've had time to sort things out. Maybe in half an hour."

As they stepped onto Paradise Drive, Nancy turned and repeated, "What just happened?"

"That's what I've been talking about."

"That was Warren," she declared, stating the obvious. "I know it was. I distinctly heard him." Jordan nodded. "But that's impossible," she insisted.

"I agree."

"How could… ?" Nancy stopped speaking and glanced back at the restaurant, as if she were trying to revisit the event.

"That's what's been driving me crazy all afternoon," replied Jordan.

He attempted to smile, but once again, he was starting to sweat—something not at all typical, even though it had already happened twice. He fumbled for his handkerchief, then remembered where he had tucked it. He blotted his face, then lead Nancy the hundred or so yards into town. He was intending to take her on a walk around Tiburon's downtown, a task that required no great effort. A loop that ran along Main Street, then turned right at the post office onto Beach, right again on Tiburon Boulevard and back to where Paradise Drive ran into Main, would take the average tourist or window shopper half an hour to negotiate at a leisurely pace. It would provide enough time for him to clear his head and to return his stomach to a state that might tolerate food.

Part way down Main Street, Nancy began, "We never should have allowed them to go walking, especially to the Tenderloin. Warren had far too much to drink. If we had been thinking—if we had any regard at all for their safety—we should have insisted they come with us, then driven them to where their car was parked."

Jordan nodded. "That's what I keep telling myself. I feel like such an idiot," he said and Nancy squeezed his hand.

They were turning past the yacht club's entrance when wind gusted out from its parking lot. Dust swirled in the intersection until the motes began forming themselves into a transparent specter. When its shape became distinct enough to see, Nancy clung to Jordan arm's.

"Jordan! Do you see what I see?"

Clutching his wife in return, he nodded and gasped, "It isn't possible."

Squinting, she observed, "He seems to be smiling."

5

A flood of emotions overtook Warren when he saw how many mourners were assembled. Until this instant, he hadn't realized how many people cared enough about him to set aside their daily affairs and drive all the way to San Mateo County to honor his memory and pay their respects. It shamed him that he was rarely moved enough by some friend's or relative's passing to act as this assembly had and it embarrassed him all the more when he realized he would never have the opportunity again. The presence of so many family members, friends, clients, and business associates brought him to a moment of loving kindness… until his eyes traveled to the congregation's center and came to rest on his son-of-a-bitch partner. The sight of him rekindled Warren's mission and the reasons that drove it.

When Warren first returned to the world of the living, the possibility of confronting Jordan was all he considered: a simpleminded plan to express his anger over what he had learned and what had been stolen. But now, amid the almost countless array of tombstones, the living hearts beating, the constant intake and outflow of breaths, drove home the finality of his predicament. His soul demanded justice and the need overwhelmed him.

What, then, would satisfy him? Jordan's death would certainly be part of it. At the moment, he could not say what the rest might be, but once he had summed up the things he required to obtain satisfaction, was there anything he could do to achieve them?

Bright enough to realize this opportunity was unique, he wondered about the extent of his abilities and how me might employ them. Like many of the others he had grown up with, Warren had heard occasional tales of ghosts and spectral hauntings. He wondered, assuming they had any foundation in fact, would he now be limited to rattling teacups and making eerie apparitions? Worse still: what if he could not do as he intended, but only passively observe? After all, changing his location, both in the afterlife as well as back here on earth, had been his single accomplishment. In order to achieve the satisfaction he was seeking, he needed to do more than simply observe, but to this point in time, there was no indication he could accomplish anything more. If that were in fact the case, it would be too pathetic to endure. That realization might have been enough to make someone less determined, less persistent than Warren, give up and return to an eternity of doubt and frustration. Reminding himself that he had never accepted any thoughts of limitations or failure before attempting every strategy imaginable, he revisited his plan.

Merely expressing outrage, as he had intended to do during their meeting on Monday, now seemed ridiculously inadequate. After he had done so, where would that leave him? Jordan would still be free to make his getaway. Even if Sabrina and Michael alerted the SEC's Division of Enforcement, could the authorities actually force Jordan to surrender what he had transferred to the Seychelles without a prolonged investigation or courtroom battle? Supposing Brandi were still willing to accompany him after their children's demise, could they still leave the country unimpeded? Warren expected they could.

And then there was Nancy. He didn't know her well enough to understand why she no longer desired any marital intimacy. But since he didn't dislike her, if he were able to take any action against Jordan, it would be bound to affect her as well. Warren wasn't sure that hurting her was what he desired, even though Nancy could eventually recover. He decided he would do whatever was necessary to set things straight.

Determined to learn his abilities' extent or limitations, Warren began to experiment. He started small, trying to kick dirt into the excavations in an attempt to draw attention and possibly create a little concern. However, even though the soil was loosely mounded, his foot passed through without any effect. Not even one of the tiniest clods so much as shifted. He considered tugging some of the mourners' clothing, but abandoned the idea when he realized that whatever he accomplished in that regard would be indistinguishable from the flutters caused by the afternoon breeze. He tried another approach.

"Hey people, I'm back!" he shouted.

Not one of the mourners reacted. Not a head raised. No one turned to look or shifted stance. He was trying to understand this failure when he glanced down at himself and saw… nothing. Even though he could feel all of his limbs, even though the torso they sprang from felt real and substantial, Warren saw not a trace. Were these perceived body parts like the phantom limbs that amputees describe? From what Warren understood, after an amputation certain sensations persisted long after the limb had been removed. Amputees describe an itch they cannot scratch or a phantom nerve pain. And though he experienced no discomfort, he could feel every part of the body he once possessed. When Warren tried to speak, he could feel his throat tense as his lips and tongue moved to form syllables. But with all of the parts of his body gone, was it any wonder no one could hear?

At some point, he became aware of a clamor around him: random words, entire sentences, people sobbing. Yet, when Warren looked around for their source, he could discern no correlation between these noises and the mourners' activities. At one point, he heard Sabrina going over her plans for tomorrow morning. Brandi's mother, Karen, broke into a series of rants and accusations that named Warren as the reason for her grandchildren's death and her daughter remaining in critical care. And though he carefully watched, like a movie whose audio track was out of synch with the video, their mouths and gestures failed to correspond to their words.

All at once, the truth came rushing in and he realized he was hearing their thoughts. That, in turn, sparked an idea how he might contact them. To test his theory, Warren approached Jordan and his friend started at his proximity.

That's interesting, thought Warren after seeing Jordan react, unsure at this point what had prompted it. Let's see if we can talk. *Jordie*, he said, thinking the name instead of speaking it.

Jordan's head came up and he glanced all around.

"Dear?" Nancy inquired. "Is something wrong?"

Warren spent the next several seconds toying with his partner, delighted he could now communicate.

It's all right, old friend. I just wanted you to know you haven't seen the last of me. Take care, good buddy. I'm back.

"Back?"

Like I told you before, we have some unfinished business to take care of.

Warren could not have been more pleased. He had caught his partner's attention and had elicited a response. That no one else had reacted, not even Nancy, who was standing next to him, made Warren pause to consider why that might be. Was it because he had directed his thoughts only at Jordan and at no one else? He was also perplexed over his failure to affect the soil at the gravesite. Deciding he would have to experiment, Warren grinned, knowing there would now be plenty of opportunities waiting. As in the case of coding software, he was certain that if he took enough time to dissect each of the elements, comparing successes with failures, he could sort this thing out. He had made contact with the living and that was the first step. He was confident he could master the next one as well.

As he ended his reverie, he spotted Jordan and Nancy rushing back to their car. Pleased with the way Jordan was panicking, he followed the pair home, watched Jordan pace around his living room, then followed the couple as they made their way to the neighboring restaurant. It amused him that walls and doors presented no obstacles. When the couple entered the establishment and Warren wanted to know what they were doing, desire became action and he was immediately inside with them.

He was musing over the way his incorporeal existence permitted previously impossible opportunities, when his thoughts returned him to the problem of interacting with objects. While, on one hand, physical translocation was easy and telepathic communication likewise, the issue of affecting material objects still eluded him.

It occurred to Warren that all of his present abilities involved his intent. The degree to which he was able to focus on any particular problem determined the extent of the resulting effect. At the graveyard, he had approached the matter of disturbing the soil with the same nonchalance he would have employed when he was alive—no real focus, just kick and be done with it. Considering what it had taken to remove himself from the Tunnel of Light, he now suspected that had he applied the same degree of mental effort back in Colma, it might have produced a superior result. Deciding that this had to be the missing element, after he had obtained Jordan and Nancy's full attention by speaking directly to their minds, he put all of his focus into an upward thrust from beneath the waiter's serving tray.

Wow!

Although Warren had been hopeful, he had not really expected he would be able to accomplish anything more than cause the tray to slip from the waiter's hand. He certainly didn't expect to send it and all of its contents flying. The result made him jubilant and suggested that he had only scratched the surface. He decided he was going to toy with the couple a while longer, the way a cat plays with a mouse, before he put the fear of God into them.

As he followed Jordan and Nancy into downtown Tiburon, Warren considered what his next move should be. In addition to wanting them to hear him and witness his power, he decided it was necessary that the two also see him. Passing the dock from where the Angel Island ferry departs, he was looking for a way to manifest when the wind from the bay blew several scraps of paper toward him. An idea began to germinate, and he willed himself to be an obstacle. As Warren had hoped, the debris blew around him in a manner that outlined his torso and a concept formed as to how he could put this phenomenon to use.

He waited until Jordan and Nancy were approaching the yacht club's entrance. Situated as it was at the bend in Main Street, dust and scraps of paper tended to accumulate where the road turned and the wind eddied. Today's collection had not been swept away yet and Warren decided that enough might be present to help him create the desired effect. Jordan and Nancy were deep in conversation, steeped with recriminations over Friday night's tragedy, while the breeze was creating a whirlwind. He was delighted when he found he could augment the air's velocity by focusing his will. As the mini-storm strengthened, drawing dust motes and debris into its funnel, Warren entered the vortex and, much to his delight, discovered the effect was as he had hoped. When the couple noticed and Nancy grabbed Jordan's arm, Warren grinned, experiencing newfound power and malevolence.

"Jordan! Do you see what I see?"

"It isn't possible."

"He seems to be smiling."

I'm ba-ack, Warren taunted, repeating a line from a movie.

"Wh-what do you want?" stammered Jordan leaning toward him, as if trying to see him more clearly.

You know what I want.

"I don't."

Liar.

That got Jordan's attention. Directing his thoughts solely at Jordan, he asked, *Do you want me to lay it out in black and white so that Nancy has a better idea of what kind of bastard you are?*

"Really, Warren," Jordan replied, "I think there's been a little misunderstanding."

Making his thoughts perceptible to them both, he snapped, *If you don't cut the crap, Jordie, right here and now, I'm going to start being specific. Do I make myself clear?*

Jordan nodded vigorously.

That's better.

"What's he talking about?" asked Nancy, furrowing her brow.

"I'm not exactly sure," Jordan lied. "But I have an

idea." Turning to Warren, he said, "It isn't necessary to bring Nancy into this. Can we discuss this in private?"

Deciding he had obtained sufficient leverage, for the moment at least, Warren believed he could afford to be magnanimous. *Of course, good buddy.* He grinned. *How 'bout at the office tomorrow morning?*

"Sure. That'll be fine."

"Hun?"

"It's no big deal," Jordan told Nancy, "if it's what I'm thinking. A little misunderstanding is all."

"He seems very upset."

"I'm sure I can straighten this out with a little conversation."

"You're sure?"

Jordan patted Nancy's hand.

"I'm positive."

Let's hope you're right, Warren replied, thinking solely at Jordan. *Understand, buddy mine, you're going to have to do more than just explain things.* When Jordan started to reply, Warren added, *Let me worry about the details. You just go on with your day... good buddy.*

... ...

Back in their living room, Nancy insisted, "This sort of thing doesn't happen."

"I know."

Having decided against returning to the restaurant but still feeling hungry, they had prepared grilled cheese sandwiches and one of their favorites—canned tomato soup seasoned with the juice of half a lemon, a pinch of oregano and a sprinkling of tellicherry pepper, washing down their meal with a Napa County table-quality sauvignon blanc—not exactly gourmet, but nonetheless satisfying. They were halfway into the nearly two liter bottle and were starting to unwind.

"I don't believe in shared delusions." Nancy took a generous sip and swallowed. "You saw him. So did I. That means Warren has returned, no question about it." Turning from the window to stare at her husband, she asked, "So what's this thing between the two of you he was talking about?"

"I'm not sure… "

"Don't give me that crap!"

"Nan… "

"You partner returns from the dead… " Nancy paused, took a few breaths and shook her head. "I can't believe I'm saying this." She downed the rest of the glass, then, intending to set it on the coffee table, she inadvertently placed part of its base on the edge of a wadded linen napkin. When it tilted and threatened to topple, she reached out to stop it, but struck it instead with her fingertips, sending the glass and its contents flying. Nancy gasped. Mercifully, after landing on the carpet the glass didn't shatter. "Shit! I think I've had too much to drink." She exhaled, dropped onto the loveseat and took a moment to gather herself. She ran her hands through her hair, looked up at Jordan and asked, "Where was I?"

"You were asking… "

"I was asking about Warren's comments."

"Like I was telling you," said Jordan, "I think there's been some kind of misunderstanding. All of last week, we'd been going round and round about which direction we wanted to take the company: whether to open another satellite like the one in Tiburon, or whether to expand elsewhere with a full blown operation—either in San Jose, or maybe even Los Angeles. Warren was adamant that we should acquire a space in Century City. I argued that would be spreading ourselves too thin, at least until we had a few more years under our belt. On the other hand, I felt opening a second major branch close to the one in San Francisco could dilute our client base. Eventually, I suggested we let the matter cool and sit on it."

"It sounded more serious than that."

"Lately, Warren's been getting emotional. I think running this business was starting to be too much for him. I've been sniffing around for someone to take over the bulk of his duties and maybe he got wind of it."

Nancy nodded and after a moment replied, "I suppose that would explain it." Turning to face him, she asked, "You weren't planning to get rid of him altogether, were you, after all he had done to get the firm up and running?"

"Nothing like that. I was just thinking of taking some of the weight off his shoulders. You saw how he's been drinking."

Nodding again, she observed, "That last night together was certainly embarrassing, watching Warren get sloppy in front of Brandi and the kids and all." Cocking her head, she asked, "Do you know how she's doing?"

"I've been thinking about phoning her."

"Why don't you?" Nancy glanced at her wristwatch. "Do you think seven thirty's too late?"

"I doubt it. It's only an hour or so past dinner and I think this is still visiting hours."

Nancy rose to retrieve the glass, but stumbled as she rounded the table. She caught herself by placing one hand on its surface, then, supporting herself, looked up and smiled apologetically. She hadn't told Jordan about the Valium she had taken to calm herself before settling down to eat. Taking time to insure she was steady, she drew herself up gradually until she was fully erect. She took two careful steps, bent, picked up the glass and rose slowly until she was once again upright.

"Are you all right?" asked Jordan.

She grimaced. "A little shaken up is all. I'll be all right," she assured, smiling but failing to disguise her insobriety. Giving up the attempt, she said, "I think I'm going to retire. Let me know how Brandi's making out, will you, dear?"

She stopped at the top of the stairs and turned to face him. Holding onto the bannister, she asked, "What's your take on Brandi's mother?" When he didn't respond, but cocked his head and sat waiting, she elaborated. "I can understand how she'd be upset, even reluctant to engage in a little conversation. But her recoiling the way she did when all I was trying to do was offer her a little support… I can't get it out of my head the way she reacted, like I was carrying the plague or something."

"Her reaction surprised me, as well. Warren appearing the way that he did made me forget about it until now. But now that I think about it, it was a little bizarre."

"Do you think something's wrong with her?"

"Like?"

"I'm not sure. But I'm thinking there was something more to it than just… well, grief." She started to head downstairs, then turned her head and said. "I'm wondering if that might be part of what went wrong between Brandi and Warren."

"I don't think so. I'm pretty sure it was his drinking."

He was about to say, "Brandi told me so," but caught himself in time to avoid saying anything that might link them.

"Just a thought," she said, then continued downstairs.

Their house was built to follow the hillside's contour. The living room, kitchen and dining room, as well as Jordan's office, were on the uppermost floor, with the guestrooms, the master bedroom, and adjoining bathrooms on the floors below. Jordan waited until she was well down the stairs before reaching for his cell phone. Device in hand, he tried to decide to which hospital's emergency room the ambulance might have taken her. California Pacific Medical Center would have been the most likely candidate because of its proximity, so he called there first, only to learn they had no record of a Brandi Holmes. The next one that came to mind was San Francisco General. The switchboard operator quickly determined that Brandi was indeed in their care and had since been transferred from the Emergency Room to the Intensive Care Unit. She connected him. When he asked if he could speak with her, an unfamiliar voice responded, "This is Nurse Regina Watkins. May I ask who's calling?"

"This is Jordan Weeks."

"Are you a family member, Mr. Weeks?"

"No. I'm... "

"I'm sorry, Mr. Weeks. Only family members or people Ms. Holmes has specifically authorized may speak with her at this point in her stay."

"I'm a close friend. Would you be good enough to ask her... ?"

Jordan heard Brandi in the background. After a muffled exchange during which Jordan suspected Brandi was covering the receiver, Nurse Watkins said, "Ms. Holmes has authorized you to speak with her. I'll hand her the phone, but please keep this brief. Her condition is still compromised."

"I understand."

When Brandi answered, she sounded weak, her voice tremulous.

"Jordan?"

"Yes, Baby. How are you doing?"

To Jordan's surprise, she laughed.

"They've got me so drugged up, I can hardly tell."

"Do you hurt?"

"Yeah. I know they're trying to keep the pain under control, but yes, I do. They were giving me something called dilaudid, I think. Anyhow, I'm not thinking too clearly." Brandi giggled. "What were you asking? I remember. You wanted to know if I hurt. I do," she repeated. "Partly my neck where he cut me, and my face where he and the other sons of bitches punched me."

Jordan had heard only secondhand reports as to what had happened on Eddy Street. Surprised by this revelation, he asked, "Who cut you?"

"The man, the one who… " Brandi paused and took in a deep breath that sounded like a sob. " …put a knife to my throat." She raised her voice. "He tried to kill me, Jordie. He actually cut me. And when I broke free, those bastards beat me." This time she really did cry. "Nurse!" he heard her address the caregiver, "No. I'm all right. Please let me talk." Jordan visualized Watkins trying to take the phone away. After a pause, during which there was a second muffled exchange she continued.

"They're gone, Jordie. Robbie and Rebecca. They were only children. I don't know how I can go on without them."

"Baby… "

"I couldn't be there when they were… " She made a choking sound and Jordan thought she might be suppressing a sob. She paused for a moment, then asked, "Was it nice?"

"Was… ?"

"The ceremony. Was the ceremony nice?"

"Yes. It was. Everyone was there. Your parents. Everyone you know."

"That's good. They shouldn't have been alone. Not then."

"Who do you mean?" he asked.

"Why, my babies. They shouldn't have been alone."

Although the sentiment was nice, he thought her comments irrational enough that he ought to test her disposition.

"Sweetie, when do you think you'll be well enough to take that trip we were planning? I think a change in scenery will do you good."

"Oh, no, Jordie. I couldn't leave them alone. I need to stay with them."

She broke down again. Almost immediately, Nurse Watkins came on the line. "Mr. Weeks, I have to terminate this call."

He had no time to object before the connection went dead. The nurse was right, of course. If Brandi's condition had been compromised before he called, it would be even more so now. He hoped it was the drugs she was taking that made her talk like that. He would have to wait until she wasn't under their influence before he brought up the subject again. He intended to phone periodically to determine if they had moved her from the ICU to a private room before he actually visited. In the meantime, a few other matters demanded his immediate attention.

First, he would have to cancel their reservations for the overseas flight and the hotel in Hamilton. He rose and headed toward the computer. Best to take care of both while he was still thinking about them. Next, he would have to manufacture some kind of alibi to explain away whatever Warren might have gleaned about him and Brandi. As he dropped into the deskside chair, he paused and asked himself what might Warren have actually learned? He had to assume that Warren knew everything, hard as it was to imagine how he might have done so. If that were the case, explaining the intended getaway to Warren would certainly be more difficult than what he'd concocted and spoon-fed to Nancy minutes earlier. The truth was, for the present he couldn't come up with anything that sounded even remotely plausible. He tossed the issue aside, deciding to let his subconscious work on it. Over the years, he had solved several knotty problems in his sleep. If he didn't wake up with a solution this time, he would just have to improvise. After all, Warren was dead. What could a dead man do? Jordan frowned when the vision of what had happened in the restaurant returned. Wondering if that explosive event presaged even greater possibilities, he pressed the power button and waited to log in and start working.

He had just opened his browser and was searching through his bookmarks when he thought he heard a scraping sound behind him. Raising his eyes from the monitor, he was starting to turn when he noticed certain portions of the living room reflected across the window pane against the outside darkness. Seeing nothing out of the ordinary, he was about to return to the keyboard when the same sound repeated and he noticed something happening in the reflection. Had the wine glass moved? He rotated the chair, expecting to see nothing unusual. As if only to prove Jordan wrong, the glass slid from one end of the coffee table to the other, wine sloshing against its sides when it halted.

He paused for an instant, gripping the arms of his chair, before rushing to kneel beside where the phenomenon had happened. He stared. Although the glass was now stationary, the liquid within was still undulating, giving proof to the impossible. Jordan lifted his eyes and began searching the room for a hint of some other presence.

"Warren?"

No answer.

"Warren, I know you're here." When no reply was forthcoming, Jordan rose and placed his hands on his hips. He picked up the glass, downed a third of its contents and exhaled.

All at once, he remembered the open browser. He set down the glass and rushed back to the computer to see if he had exposed any incriminating evidence.

Good. He was still on the Home page and had not yet opened the airline's website. He turned around and called, "Are we going to play cat and mouse all night?"

Silence.

"You came here for a reason. I can wait until you show up at the office, if that's what you want." Jordan chuckled. "If you actually do decide to show," he added. Suddenly irritated, he added, "You goddam son of a bitch! You always were a coward."

I'm not a coward, good buddy.

Jordan jerked upright and he glanced around wildly.

I'm just having fun. You're having fun too, aren't you, Jordie? I know you've never seen anything like that before.

"You said you wanted to talk. You indicated we were

going to meet at the office, but since it appears you've grown impatient, let's talk." Spreading his arms, he turned at the waist, first one way, then in the opposite direction. Gesturing at the empty room, he stated, "It's just you and me."

Sure. Let's start with this. What does Nancy know about you and Brandi?

Jordan's eyes flicked toward the stairwell. Deciding that Nancy had probably fallen asleep as soon as her head hit the pillow, he returned his attention to Warren. Feigning ignorance, he asked, "What do you mean?"

Don't play stupid. Does she know about the plane tickets?

Jordan thought he was ready for anything, but this brought him up short. His mind was racing to come up with an answer when Warren asked, *Does she know about the bank accounts in the Seychelles?*

"How... ?"

...did I learn about that little maneuver? That's something for me to know and you to find out, as the saying goes. I will ask you this, though. What will you do when I tell her? You'd better hope that nobody else gets wind of it.

Always uncomfortable with finding himself on the defensive, Jordan parried with a lie. "I was about to say, 'How do you know that's not my retirement account?' I'll tell you right now, someone's fed you a whole lot of bull."

Have they now? I can still see the Barnham and Whittelsby Bank report of wire transfers starting three years ago all the way to the present as if it was still in front of me. Would you like me to recite all of your account numbers? It's pretty funny. In my present state, I have a photographic memory.

Warren's tone shifted from glib to angry. *The amount*

of money you've been moving is way more than both of us earned ever since we started. You're going to hurt a lot of good people. That doesn't bother you at all, does it?

Shifting to a more formal tone, while still refusing to concede even an inch of ground, Jordan asked, "If I admit to it—just to keep you happy, understand?—will that make you go away?"

I'm not going anywhere. I'm planning to stick around until I've taken care of all my unsettled business... Warren sneered. *...and that includes you. Maybe I'll even hang around afterwards. Can't say for sure. I haven't made up my mind yet.*

More than anything, Jordan wanted the last of the wine. But since retrieving the glass might be taken as a sign of weakness, he restrained himself. Instead he replied, "I'd have thought you would have wanted to be with your children."

LEAVE MY KIDS OUT OF THIS!

Extending his arms in the direction from which Warren's voice seemed to be coming, palms facing outward, Jordan replied, "Hey, bud. No offense intended. I only wanted to say how surprised I am that you would want to waste your time over me."

If I were you, I'd start worrying about what I intend to do next.

Before Jordan could answer, he felt something cold pass through him, chilling him to the core. With that, he felt abruptly alone. He wasn't certain, but the room felt different and he thought Warren might have gone. He glanced around the living room for any indication he might be mistaken. Finding none, Jordan retrieved the wine glass, sat down on the sofa and stared out the window, glad Nancy had remained sleeping.

6

"Good morning, Mr. Weeks."

"Good morning, Allan," Jordan answered, pleased as always with the receptionist's style: pressed cotton blend shirt, pleated linen slacks, Italian designer shoes, handtied bow tie and an obviously expensive haircut. Too many people, he mused, dismiss the importance of one's appearance as an antiquated concept. Yet clients' perceptions of a successful brokerage house, Jordan realized—glad that Allan understood it, too—begin with what they see the moment they enter.

"That was a touching ceremony," Allan said as he lifted his hands from the computer's keyboard. He cocked his head and swiveled his chair to look more directly at Jordan. "Are you feeling better today?"

"I am. Thank you for asking."

"Pardon me, if I'm being too personal."

"Not at all," Jordan assured.

"We're not used to you arriving this late, so naturally we assumed… anyway, Rebecca has started rescheduling today's appointments. Hope you won't mind."

"I appreciate your consideration, but please ask her to speak with me before she changes anything else. I'd like to have enough of my day still intact to keep my mind off of… "

He waved his hand in a series of circles and left the rest of the statement dangling.

Allan reached for the intercom. "Yes, sir. I'll get right on it."

"Also, tell her that I'd like her to have everyone assemble in the meeting room, after New York closes."

"Everyone? Do you mean the support staff as well?"

Jordan nodded.

"So this is not going to be the usual weekly meeting?"

Jordan shook his head. "I have something else in mind. And will you have her come to my office as soon as possible?"

"Of course, Mr. Weeks. Shall I have someone bring you some coffee?"

"Thanks, but no. I'll grab a cup on my way upstairs."

When Jordan logged on to his computer, he was pleased to find that one of the morning's appointments was still on the schedule, as well as most of the afternoon's. That was reassuring because he felt it unlikely that Warren would be so bold as to make an appearance in the presence of anyone who was not party to his personal grievances. Consequently, the more Jordan was occupied, the less time Warren had to annoy him. At least, that is what Jordan hoped and he moved on to other matters.

A visit to all of his bank's websites showed that all the funds were still intact, although he could not imagine how Warren could do anything to affect them. It was then he remembered the airline reservations, something he had been too distracted to take care of after Warren had gone. Brandi's condition was one situation he could not afford to ignore, and he hoped she would be of sound enough spirit to travel before much more time passed. He knew that the firm's financial situation was sure to unravel sometime soon, and he could not afford to be around when it did. He recalled an old investment firm, located in Tiburon's downtown back in the 1980s. One of its principal officers had absconded with the retirement accounts of several local residents. The FBI managed to track him down almost a decade later. But by the time they found him holed up in Mexico, he was riddled with cancer and hoping to live out the rest of his days before the money ran out. Jordan didn't intend to be found. He had hatched an elaborate scheme involving multiple forged passports for all of them, Brandi's children included. After fleeing to Bermuda, their next stop would be Canada, then Germany. They would take a series of flights, hip hopping around the globe, changing identities as they went, eventually arriving in Micronesia. There they would stay until he felt they could safely assume their eventual lives and new identities in a more civilized location. The money would also take a circuitous trip through various banks, with each of the accounts closing behind them. Things still could go wrong, but he was as sure as he could be that he had planned well enough to avoid any mishaps. And while he hoped Brandi would join him, if she declared that she was either physically or psychologically unable, he wondered if he could afford to leave her behind. She knew more about him than he was comfortable with, but he felt it unlikely that she would betray him if he was forced to go without her. Besides, she only knew about the first leg of their journey. She would only learn each subsequent segment as his scheme unfolded. Still, since loose threads made Jordan nervous, he decided he would check back with the hospital on a regular basis.

"Mr. Weeks?"

His head came up and he saw Rebecca standing in the doorway. She was wearing a cream colored summer weight suit and camel colored suede flats.

"Are you all right?"

He ran his fingers through his hair and wondered how he appeared. He had lain awake the better part of the night, despite his attempts to forget Warren's visit.

"I'm fine," he said, forcing a smile. Then, remembering why he had asked to see her, he told her about the meeting. "Will you postpone my lunch with Morgan until tomorrow and see if my 2:00 appointment is willing to bump up till twelve? I'd like to make sure I'm free by 1:00 at the latest."

She glanced at her watch. "Matt Breitenbach will be here any minute now. Do you still want to see him?"

"Please. Ask Allan to notify me the minute he arrives, then send him straight up to see me."

Consulting her iPad, Rebecca asked, "Do you want to keep any of the appointments that are calendared for this afternoon?"

He thought for a minute, torn between his need to remain occupied after the meeting concluded and a desire to leave the office and think. Changing his mind from what he had expressed earlier to Michael, he said, "No. You were right when you decided to cancel them. I should be ready to give my full attention to everything starting tomorrow."

"Very well, sir."

Jordan reached for the cup on his desk and took a sip.

Hello, good buddy.

Jordan spat coffee all over the desktop and Rebecca gasped and stepped back. She tucked the iPad back under her elbow and examined her suit. Once she had assured herself it had not been harmed, she stared at the cup he was holding and asked, "Is something wrong with it?"

Jordan shook his head, too shocked to speak. He set the cup on his desk and wiped his mouth with the back of his hand.

Rebecca screwed up her mouth and said, "I'll see if I can find some paper towels," then rushed to the door and gave a backward glance before disappearing into the hallway. Jordan opened the desk's bottom right drawer and retrieved a box of facial tissue. He blotted his face, his hand, then dabbed at the front of his shirt.

You'll need to get a grip on yourself before the word gets around that you're crazy.

Jordan glanced around, believing he could hear Warren laughing. In the same instant, he realized how futile his attempt at tidying up had been. Wadding the tissue into a ball, he hurled it into the waste basket.

"How long have you been here?"

Long enough.

"What's that supposed to mean?"

Easy, good buddy. If you don't start speaking more softly, people are going to think you've started talking to yourself. Warren chuckled.

Unable to decide which way he should be facing, Jordan looked directly in front of him, as if Warren were standing there. "All right, now that you're here, what do you want?"

I'm trying to figure that out myself. I mean, I know what I want in general terms, but how I'm going to make it happen is where I'm still sorting out the details.

You see, whenever I heard people talk about ghosts, which I grant you wasn't often, I used to think that, whenever they appeared, they somehow knew how to do what all ghosts are supposed to. But they don't. At least, I don't.

Pardon me if I make myself comfortable, said Warren.

The in/out box slid and clattered onto the floor. Jordan leapt from his chair and retrieved it. He collected the half dozen or so scattered pages from the floor and put them back inside. "What do you think you're doing?" he demanded, a second before Rebecca reappeared with a roll of paper towels.

"Beth gave me this," she announced as she entered, then stopped and stared.

To explain what he was doing, Jordan retrieved a facial tissue and pretended to be wiping the desktop. He replaced the in/out box, half expecting he would have difficulty doing so because it would somehow collide with Warren. He was relieved when that didn't happen.

Oops! That was naughty of me, wasn't it?

Jordan ignored him. "Great," he said to Rebecca as he tossed the piece of tissue into the waste basket and reached for the towels she was holding.

Her iPad toned and Rebecca glanced at it. "It's a text from Allan. Mr. Breitenbach has just pulled into the parking garage."

"Give me a couple of minutes to finish this."

"I'm happy to help," she told him.

So am I, added Warren.

Fearing what Warren might do next, Jordan gave an almost imperceptible shake of his head, warning him not to do anything more, and was glad when Rebecca failed to notice.

"That's all right," he said. "Cleaning up will give me the time I need to compose myself. Greet Matt when he arrives and make him comfortable. I'll let Allan know when I'm ready to see him."

"I could tell him you're not feeling well and reschedule him."

Jordan shook his head. "He's a good client. I'll manage. Thanks, though."

We'll see how good a client he still is when your house of cards collapses.

Rebecca studied the desk and frowned at the remaining drops of coffee. Before she could offer her assistance again, Jordan said. "Please. This won't take long and I need something to do." He smiled. "I know it's not very boss-like, but honestly, I'd rather take care of this myself."

She nodded and smiled. "I'll empty the pot and brew a fresh batch."

Nothing was wrong with the first batch, but he made no attempt to contradict her. "Thank you," he said, and left it at that. "Will you please close the door when you leave? I'd like to have a few minutes alone."

"Of course." After giving Jordan and the office one last look, she smiled again, then shut the door behind her.

"You son of a bitch!" Jordan snapped when he felt Rebecca was no longer within earshot.

Me?

"Couldn't you have waited before… ?" He left the question hanging as he gestured at the remaining mess.

You're the son of a bitch, good buddy. You're the one who's been scuttling the ship. You're the one who's about to ruin this firm and leave all of our employees jobless, not to mention our clients who won't see this coming until it's too late. You'll go down in financial history with Bernie Madoff.

Jordan resumed wiping things dry, trying to prepare himself to see his client.

In the meanwhile, I've been trying to figure out how to stick it to you. I've thought about killing you whenever I get a better understanding of exactly what I can and can't do, since no one could convict me… let alone suspect I was the one who'd done it. But I think making you suffer is a better solution, for now at least.

"How exactly are you going to make me suffer? By haunting my home and office?"

Well, to start with, I think you should know about the nice conversation I had with Nancy after you headed off to work.

"You wouldn't dare!"

I not only would, but, like I said, I already did.

Jordan stopped cleaning. "What did you tell her?"

Pretty much everything: your affair with Brandi, your offshore bank accounts, the trip you're planning. Now I'm wondering how much of a home you'll have to return to. Jordan curled his hands into fists and his face and body grew rigid as Warren continued. *It's what you deserve. When were you planning to tell her? When were you planning to tell me, if I hadn't died? Don't bother to answer. I already know.*

"You're enjoying this, aren't you?"

Do you mean the part where my children were murdered, or the part where my wife was fucking my partner and so-called friend?

"You brought this all on yourself. You could have left the kids at home. You could have let us give you a ride. For that matter, you could have gone light on the booze."

I suppose I'm responsible for your greed.

"It's not that simple."

Not that simple? Aren't you wealthy enough? If you're not happy with your marriage, file for a divorce. Community property laws wouldn't hurt you. Half of your kind of rich is still richer than Midas.

"Mr. Breitenbach is here," the intercom announced.

Jordan sighed. He asked Warren, "Is there anything else you'd like to tell me?"

A few things, like: Have fun getting your head on straight when you talk to our employees this afternoon. Try to sound encouraging as you get ready to stick a knife in their backs. The same with your client. Oh, yes. Watch out for yourself. I promise, the fun has only started. Warren chuckled. *'Bye for now.*

With that, Jordan pressed the Reply button and said, "Thank you, Allan. Give me two minutes, then send up Mr. Breitenbach."

… … … … …

Despite Jordan's attempt to sound upbeat, the company meeting had been more difficult than he had imagined. He had outlined a plan to reorganize the firm in the wake of Warren's passing, fielding questions about who would assume the various responsibilities, all the while searching their faces in an effort to determine which employee or employees might have betrayed him. The reality was that most stock brokers would have made good poker players—certainly better than he had been earlier this afternoon—and he came up empty-handed. He hoped they would assign his lack of enthusiasm to yesterday's funeral, although he knew at least one or two would know the presentation for the sham it really was. Like it or not, he would have to continue this charade right up to the very end, hoping word would not leak before he escaped.

••• ••• ••• ••• •••

He turned the car onto Paradise Drive, hoping to find a few hours' respite from his difficulties, assuming Nancy would not confront him the minute he stepped inside. Fifty yards below his house, however, he slammed on the brakes. At the foot of his driveway stood several suitcases, half a dozen boxes, and his computer with all of its cables still attached. A neighbor walking her Doberman gave them a curious look as she and her dog were forced to step off the sidewalk and into the street. A few seconds later, when she passed his white Mercedes, she peered through the windshield and stared. He recognized her as someone he had greeted on half a dozen occasions. The smile Jordan presented did nothing to diminish her frown as she and her animal continued past.

Damn Warren all to Hell!

A sheer wall of rock rose skyward from the road's western boundary. A curb and sidewalk, but no parking lane, rimmed the street on the opposite side. With nowhere to park and no way to pull into his driveway, he rolled the passenger-side tires onto the sidewalk and killed the engine.

"What the hell do you want?" demanded Nancy when she opened the door and saw him standing with his hands folded in front of him. Smeared mascara showed what she had been going through.

"Can we at least talk?" asked Jordan.

"I have nothing to say to you. You can talk to my attorney, for all the good it will do." Her eyes flicked toward his belongings. "Let her know if I've forgotten anything."

"But, Nan… "

She slammed the door and Jordan heard the bolt click. He sighed and turned to stare at what she had left him, knowing it would take two or three trips to retrieve it all. Two five-star hotels near the city's financial district came to mind as places he could stay.

7

It was an odd experience, thought Warren: not needing to sleep, not having his limbs ache or his mind grow dull while his thoughts became less coherent, less crisp, sixteen to eighteen hours or even longer into the day. When he was alive, he often considered how much more he could accomplish if it weren't for the loss of so much time, week in, week out, month after month. He remembered a few friends who seemed to manage nicely after only five or six hours of sack time. Not this boy. If Warren hadn't managed to get in eight or nine, his performance suffered and he didn't feel right. Now, however, in this new existence, he didn't grow tired and he used this energy, coupled with his ability to translocate at will to the fullest extent.

It now came to him that it might be interesting to drop in on Brandi. Jordan's phone call told him where to find her and he willed himself to the hospital. It didn't take long to locate her room and, in a matter of minutes, he was beside her, studying her features by the glow of the medical equipment's digital displays.

Brandi was as pretty as he remembered. Even with her uncombed hair spread across the pillow case, even with tubes and wires running into her, even with the lingering contusions from the beating she had taken, the curve of her lips, her upturned nose and prominent cheekbones made him admire how lovely she was, even now, at her least presentable. He moved around the bed then hovered over it, taking his time as he studied her. At one point, her lips moved and he brought his ear close to them, hoping he could hear what she was saying. He thought he could make out most of her words, smiling when he heard her mention the names of their children. At the same time, he was relieved that she hadn't spoken Jordan's. When her lips quivered and he thought she might be crying, a note of sadness struck. He had always loved her, always would. Her infidelity cut deep and the thought of what he would eventually have to do to her cut even deeper. Even so, he sighed, then reached out and touched her.

Brandi's eyes came open and she put her hand to her cheek. She hauled herself onto her elbows and peered around the room as she drew up the covers.

"Hello?" she called, looking puzzled at the way her breath condensed in the chill of Warren's presence.

Bringing herself fully upright, she tried to pull the covers to her neck. But the combination of the bed's construction and how tightly the nurses had made it, rendered the act impossible. Releasing her grip, she glanced around the room, hugging herself and rubbing her arms with her hands.

"Is anybody here?"

Warren wondered if he ought to reply, curious as to how she might react to a ghostly apparition. He decided against it. He expected that Brandi's condition was still compromised and he wanted her to be in good health and fully recovered when he finally presented himself. Whatever else he might be, he was not one to take advantage of one so fragile. Nonetheless, he decided to use this opportunity to set the stage for his appearance. He moved toward a table near her bed that had a vase of flowers on top of it. He rotated the vase half a turn clockwise. The scraping sound it made caused her to look, so he turned it again. After a pause, he turned it another time.

"My God!" she gasped.

Warren stopped what he was doing, deciding it had been a successful demonstration. Now, he would have her attention whenever he needed it. Cat and mouse was an ancient but satisfying game, provided one didn't play to the point it became tedious.

When Brandi started crying and fumbled for the call button, Warren reached out and examined her thoughts. He learned she wanted a nurse to bring her a sedative, proving his tactic had worked. Her fears and worries would keep her occupied for the present, hopefully enough that she'd have little energy to spend thinking about Jordan.

With that problem out of the way, he decided to search for the thugs with whom he still had unfinished business. The clock on the wall told him this was about the time of night when the catastrophe had occurred on Eddy. Knowing old habits die hard, he headed for the Tenderloin, suspecting he would have little difficulty locating the ones who had set this all into motion.

… … … … …

Carlos released the tourniquet he had fashioned from a pair of shoelaces. He depressed the plunger and sighed as the narcotic took effect. His body sagged for several seconds before his head came up he handed the syringe to Robert.

"Whoa, dude," gasped Carlos. "That was more than I expected."

"Too much?" Robert asked.

Carlos shook his head. "Almost. It's good, though." He peered around the cluster of garbage cans, behind which they were sitting, and looked toward the street. Aside from the flash of headlamps and the rush of tires spinning beneath the passing automobiles, there were only two pedestrians. They appeared too engrossed in conversation to notice anything else, so he leaned back and said, "What did they say was in that shit?"

"Fenta-something," replied Robert.

"Fentanyl," Kevin clarified. "It's supposed to give it a boost."

"Tha's fer fucking sure," replied Carlos, starting to slur his words.

He had been squatting when he injected himself, and now he fell backwards, landing on top of the asphalt with his head canted against the adjacent building's foundation. He placed his hands on the ground and made an effort to rise, then abandoned the attempt. His two associates, sitting cross-legged beside one another, studied him for a moment, then returned to the task at hand. Robert began drawing the next dose into the hypodermic. After glancing at Carlos, who was by now at best semi-conscious, Robert drew in only half of what he had intended… then a little more, trying to gauge how much might be too much, as opposed to what would provide the desired high.

"You think he OD'ed?" asked Kevin.

"Dunno," replied Robert, holding the syringe up to the glow of a streetlamp as he began depressing the plunger to expel the remaining air.

"What'll we do if… ?"

"He'll be all right."

Kevin frowned as he studied Carlos. "You sure?"

"Prob'ly," Robert assured, flicking the syringe with his middle finger. He nodded in satisfaction when several droplets dispersed.

"You want this?" asked Kevin, offering the tourniquet.

Robert shook his head. Probing the inside of his left

elbow with his fingertips, he answered, "I can still find a vein or two."

Hello, boys.

The pair's heads came up. Even Carlos reacted by raising his own and staring skyward through unfocused eyes.

Nice night for a party.

"Did you hear that?" whispered Kevin.

Nodding in response as his friend clambered onto his feet, Robert lowered the syringe and set it onto his thigh. He watched as Kevin placed his hands on one of the garbage cans' lids and leaned forward to examine the space behind them, then gazed toward the now empty street. Kevin squinted, scrutinizing the alley's murky shadows. Seeing no one, he shouted, "Who's there?" Met only with silence, he looked at Robert and said, "Motherfucker's going to be in trouble when I get my hands on him."

BANG! The lid from the can next to Robert rocketed skyward. Wrapping an arm around his head for protection, Kevin ducked… then thought to look up before the lid fell to earth. "What the… ?" he cried and hurled himself to his left scant seconds before it struck the asphalt where he had been standing.

The crash brought Robert to his feet with his eyes and mouth open. In his panic, he stumbled. His foot landed on something and he heard it crunch under his weight. Glancing down, he spotted the syringe's shattered cylinder. "Fuck!" he said as he widened his stance in an effort to stabilize himself. When he bent to examine the syringe's remains, another lid shot upward. And another. With his arm still extended toward the spilled narcotic, Robert jumped back while twisting his head to determine the missiles' trajectory. The two disjointed acts caused him to lose balance and fall backward. He landed on his hip and cried out in pain.

Kevin, now in a crouch, his arms spread for balance, was looking for somewhere safe to stand.

One lid struck Carlos squarely in the belly. He sat up, becoming suddenly alert. Placing both hands on the pavement, he pushed himself to a sitting position. Responding to the metallic sounds issued by the oscillating lid, he turned to look as it came to rest beside him. Without removing his eyes, he struggled onto his feet, then shuffled to a spot next to Roger.

"Guys?" he pleaded. "What's happening?"

Where did you get your drug money this time?

The three looked around to see where the voice was coming from.

Who did you beat? Or did you murder somebody else?

"We didn't… " Kevin began before Robert cut him off with, "Shut up!"

Moving to the ally's center, Robert demanded, "Come out where we can see you." He stood there for several seconds, turning to see if someone appeared. There was no immediate response. The sounds coming in from the street were muffled and hollow, transformed into dull, indiscernible echoes by the brick and concrete that walled in the alley, and there was only silence in the minute that followed.

Finally, Kevin declared, "This is weird," and his partners nodded.

Their reactions delighted Warren. But now that he had frightened them, he could not decide what his next course of action should be. His initial thought had been to murder the three men outright—an act he had recently figured out how to perform. That, however, would cut short any pleasure a protracted revenge might provide, so he set that thought aside for the present. Further, when the time eventually came for him to act as their executioner, he wanted to be sure they understood the reason for their deaths and why they needed to be agonizing. And agonizing they would be, for it was important they suffer.

Warren wanted know what these sons of bitches had done to his family. He had heard Robbie and Brandi scream. It still puzzled him why Rebecca had remained silent. He could only imagine what these three had done to that sweet little girl. Needing to understand these things better, so he could provide an appropriate punishment, he decided to let them live until he could find some way to extract this information from them.

You haven't answered my questions, he told them.

"Who are you?" shouted Kevin.

Warren shoved him, putting the full force of his intent behind it. Kevin flew backward, sliding on his back fifteen feet across the rubble strewn asphalt.

I'LL BE THE ONE ASKING THE QUESTIONS! shouted Warren, with so much force they all covered their ears.

Carlos told Robert, "Hey, man. Like I'm out of here." Turning on unsteady feet, he began heading toward the alleyway's opening.

You're not going anywhere until I say you can.

One of the cans where they were sitting toppled, then rolled in front of him, blocking his escape and strewing rotting garbage. Carlos feinted to his left, but the garbage can duplicated his motion. A dodge to his right was similarly matched. The addict stumbled and dropped to his knees while the can wobbled in front of him. Hands on the pavement, Carlos looked over his shoulder at Robert. Sounding as if he was about to cry, he pleaded, "What's going on?"

Eyes darting everywhere, Robert held out his hands and asked, "What do you need to know? I'll tell you anything."

Why did you attack my family and why did you murder my children? Why did you murder ME?

"I never… "

On Eddy Street.

Robert started to shake his head before his eyes widened and a look of comprehension settled over him.

Yeah. That.

"Th- th- that was you? It can't be. This is impossible."

After all this, are you really that stupid?

"Shit," Robert muttered under his breath, then clenched his lips.

Warren thundered, *WHY?*

Kevin was the first to reply. "Hey, man, we'll do anything to make it right. Honest."

You CAN'T make it right. You fucked up. The damage you did to me and my family can't be fixed. Do you really think you can bring them back to life? That's the reason behind what I'm about to tell you.

"But… "

I'm not going to explain why what you said just now is stupid. But understand this: you are all going to pay for what you did and it's going to be painful. It's not going to happen now. And don't bother to ask when. It will happen when I'm ready for it to happen. My rules. My timeline.

In the next instant, they all were inexplicably aware he had vanished.

8

"No, Mr. Weeks," said Michael. "The company's database is password protected."

"Including its financial information?"

"Especially the financial information."

"So only a limited number of people can gain access."

"Yes, sir."

"Can you give me a list of their names?"

"I certainly can. How soon would you like it?"

"How long would it take?"

"A couple of minutes."

"In that case, I'll wait right here for a printout."

In fact, Jordan already understood everything Michael was telling him. Although he was determined to get to the bottom of who had unearthed his financial dealings, he could not afford to make his suspicions obvious, hence the charade.

He understood that the reason his activities had been uncovered is that he had conducted all those transactions from his office, rather than somewhere inaccessible to the rest of the firm. If he could have engineered it, he would have preferred to have performed all of those transfers on his home computer.

It wasn't because he didn't try. In fact, he had made several attempts to gain remote access. But despite his best efforts, he remained unable to hack through the firm's firewall, so his only choice was to execute them all within the network.

True to his word, Michael returned in a matter of minutes. The list came down to exactly one dozen names, including his own, culled from the company's seventy two employees. Jordan didn't expect any particular name would stand out. He had simply expected it would be a good place to start. And, in fact, none of them did. None had an obvious axe to grind, so he expected it would take a bit of sleuthing to unearth the one he was looking for.

"There aren't very many. Couldn't you have just told me?" asked Jordan, staring up from the single sheet of paper.

"I wanted to make sure I didn't miss anyone."

"I see," replied Jordan, returning his eyes to the faces staring back from the list he was holding. "Thanks for your diligence," he added.

Michael continued. "You will notice I divided the list into two groups. The two at the top, Warren Holmes and Jordan Weeks, who have a specific reason to access that information—our accountants and certain attorneys. The second group consists of their clerks and administrative assistants, people whose access is necessarily restricted."

"I also see that the ones you've listed are people who work at this location. What about the Tiburon office?"

Michael's eyes widened. "I'm sorry. My bad. Give me a second. I'll be right back."

"Don't bother. Only four people in that location. Sabrina is probably one of them. Who else?"

"Actually, Sabrina doesn't have any access at all." Jordan's eyebrows went up and Michael added. "The only one

84

who does is Melissa."

Jordan removed a pen from the caddy on Michael's desk, then glanced up, saying, "Pardon me. May I?"

"Of course."

Jordan added her name to the list, then returned the pen to where he had found it.

"Mr. Weeks?"

"Yes?"

"Do you think there's been some kind of a breach?" Michael asked, catching Jordan off guard. Had he not asked that particular question, Jordan would have passed him over without any further consideration. But by lingering on the issue, Michael had moved himself to the top of the list. Jordan paused for a second to study the accountant and was met with an unwavering gaze and a placid expression. Before his confusion became obvious, and in the event Michael was not the one who had discovered what he was up to, he hurried to come up with an appropriate answer… and lied.

"No, I don't," he said, making an effort to keep his tone even, "It's just that, while we're in the process of restructuring, I want to examine various individuals' responsibilities to see how our resources might be better employed. This is the first item that came to mind." His explanation sounded hollow and he knew it. Fortunately, Michael didn't seem to react.

Jordan spent part of the morning deciding if he should interview the suspects directly and, if so, whom he should speak to first. He also wondered what would be the best way to approach them, since overt questions would necessarily disclose more information than he would have preferred. Unable to arrive at a satisfactory solution, his next thought was to simply watch and wait. He had not expected that approach would unearth anything useful, but just before midday,

Sabrina dropped by the headquarters and went directly to Michael's office. Ordinarily, her visit would not have drawn his attention, since this was a weekly event. He was about to go on with his business when she glanced back over her shoulder, eyes dancing everywhere, then entered and shut the door behind her, taking another peek through the opening before the shutting the door.

Why should she care who's watching? Jordan wondered, followed by, *And what is there about this meeting that needs to be kept private?* Torn between believing he was just being paranoid and suspecting these were obvious clues, he decided to err on the side of prudence and keep an eye on them.

A little after lunch time, thoughts of Brandi began to intrude. A phone call to the hospital revealed she had been moved from the ICU to a private room. Armed with her room number, Jordan went down to the parking garage, then drove to see her. When he arrived, he found the door to her room had been left ajar, so he peered inside. He found her alone and apparently sleeping. He extended his hand and tapped on the door with his fingertips.

Her eyes opened. She touched her cheek and her head came up. "Hello?" she said, and he wondered if a nightmare had awakened her. He watched her struggle with the covers as she attempted to sit. When she rubbed her arms as if she were cold, he attributed it to her weakened physical condition. But when she gasped, "Is anybody here?" then gazed at something beyond his field of vision, he wondered if she might be hallucinating. When she continued to stare, then gasped, "My God!" he wondered if he should construe this as a sign her sanity had deteriorated, especially in light their recent conversation.

He decided he needed to test this possibility and entered her room and smiled when their eyes connected. His thoughts mirrored Warren's, namely that she was the most beautiful woman in the world, even in this condition. Although he was shocked by the extent of her bruises and her two black eyes, he tried not to let it show.

"Hi, Baby."

She smiled… before her expression collapsed and she broke down crying. Without any thought to what he did next, Jordan rushed to her bed, took her hand into his and kissed it. Before he could ask what had brought her to tears, Brandi wiped her eyes with her forearm and said, "I can't stop thinking about them."

"Of course not."

He knew better than to ask how she was doing—that much was obvious—but the clock was ticking. If he was going to bring her along when he made his getaway, he needed to determine if the loss of her children, as well as her physical condition would allow her to come with him. The gash across her throat caught his attention.

Following his eyes, Brandi sniffed, then nodded and pressed her fingers against it. "It wasn't deep. It could have been deeper if I hadn't managed to break away. The doctors say it's healing nicely."

"I'm surprised you're alive."

"I jerked free just as he started cutting." She scowled and said, "One of the bastards who were with him caught me by the arm and the other one started punching me. He didn't knock me out, but I was confused for several minutes. By the time I started to think clearly, they were gone and Warren and the children were lying on the sidewalk." Her eyes widened and she grabbed his hand. Staring into his eyes, she said, "Blood was everywhere. I realized they were dead and I started screaming." She started to sob, then caught herself.

"Eventually some cops showed up and then an ambulance arrived. I'd lost some blood, but not enough to kill me. They said I was fortunate," she sneered, then chuckled. "Really good luck, wasn't it?"

Jordan reached out and touched her wound. "Does it hurt?"

She shook her head. "They've switched me to Vicodin. It doesn't make me as dopey as dilaudid, but I still wish I didn't have to take it. It makes me sleepy and I can't think straight."

"Are you able to get out of bed and walk around?"

"Oh, yes. I've been walking around the floor for the last couple of days. I have to."

"Have to?"

"If I had to stay in this bed, I think I'd go crazy."

Seizing the opportunity, Jordon suggested, "That's why I think it would be best if we both get away from here. You know, take a vacation. There are too many bad memories here and there are a few places I'd like to take you."

"Oh, I couldn't. The children… "

"Like you said a minute ago: they're gone." He lowered his voice and tried to sound understanding. "What are you going to do? Sit alone in the dark? Spend your time looking at old photos and crying yourself to sleep?"

"But… "

He touched a finger to her lips. "Normally, you're the most intelligent person I've ever met. You're great when it comes to assessing almost any situation and seeing what needs to be done. The decisions you make are generally sound. But in this case… Let's just say you need to put a little distance between yourself and this terrible thing that's just happened.

Please trust me. When the hospital finally releases you, go home, pack a few bags with a few things you can't do without, and let's go somewhere peaceful and beautiful. It doesn't have to be forever," he lied. "It just needs to happen now.

"Once you're in a better frame of mind, once your emotions have had time to cool down, then you can decide what you want to do with your life and where you want to be. For now, let your housekeeper take care of things while you take care of yourself. You can remember your children just as well on a nice sandy beach where the waters and the sky are blue and perfect, as you can in your bedroom with the shades drawn. Probably better, because your mind will be able to focus on all the good times you had."

A smile crept across Brandi's lips and she nodded. "You were always good at getting me to calm down after Warren got to be too much to deal with. You're probably right. I know I'll break down if I walk into one of their bedrooms. I'll phone Jessica and ask her to start packing my things. Mom can probably help her and drop in from time to time to make sure everything's taken care of."

"That's starting to sound like the girl I remember," encouraged Jordan.

"But just for a couple of weeks," insisted Brandi.

"Let's not get too far ahead of ourselves. We'll take it one day at a time. You'll know when it's time to go home."

Jordan released a sigh, realizing his plan might, in fact, be feasible. He was confident now he could take her to Bermuda. The next step was anyone's guess. *One day at a time*, he cautioned himself.

"Have they given any indication when that might be?" he asked. When she stared at him, he explained, "When they're going to let you go home."

She shook her head. "Not in so many words, but they've started making noises that lead me to believe I'll be out of here soon."

"Your neck won't bother you?"

"I don't think so. But I'm sure there will be *somewhere* in Bermuda where I can have it looked at if I need to."

"Of course," he said. *Best not to let her find a reason to change her mind. I've probably said too much already.*

He remained with her a while longer, discussing things like the quality of hospital food and the care she was getting. Before he left, he returned to the subject of the beach and bright sunny days to keep her mind focused on their future together. He kissed her good-bye and was entering the hallway when Brandi's mother emerged from one of the elevators. She was adjusting an armful of packages, probably intended for her daughter—when she happened to raise her eyes.

"Mr. Weeks!" she exclaimed, apparently caught off guard. She caught herself and asked, "How is… Nancy, isn't it?"

"She's fine, thank you."

Karen chewed her lip for a second, then ventured, "You left the funeral quite abruptly."

"I know. That was completely inappropriate." Jordan paused, realizing what he said next would color her opinion of him and how she would react when Brandi eventually disclosed her plan to run away with him—something he believed wouldn't sit well with her anyway. Even so, he tried to improve his chances by offering, "But it was a very difficult occasion for me. I'm sorry if I offended you, but I just couldn't take it."

"You were that close to your partner," she said, intoning the statement so it sounded like a question.

"And I loved his and Brandi's kids."

Karen nodded, and Jordan thought she might be reconsidering. Although she would certainly despise him once Brandi informed her about their planned getaway, he wanted to remove some of the edge at this point in their relationship, were that even possible. Incorporating the recent turn of events into the next thing he offered, while hoping the motivating factor would not become apparent until after she and her husband returned home, he improvised. "Nancy and I… How should I put this?… are on the brink of a divorce. That, coupled with what had happened, was more than I could bear. I have to apologize. Again, I meant no disrespect. Looking back, I realize I should have stuck it out. The funeral certainly wasn't any easier for you."

"No. It wasn't," she said, her tone turning sour. "It wasn't easy at all."

"Is there anything I can do for you and Mr. Burkhardt while you are visiting?"

"That won't be necessary. We have everything we need. If anything else *does* become necessary, Brandi will assist us." Her frown emphasized how unsuccessful he had been.

Still, he smiled and added, "I understand. Please remember, however, my offer still stands."

Without another word, Karen stepped around him and went in to see Brandi.

9

Warren believed the best way to thwart Jordan would be to follow him and stay close on his heels in order to be ready to take advantage of whatever opportunity presented itself. Consequently, a few days after the business in the alleyway, he found himself once again at Zuckerberg San Francisco General Hospital and Trauma Center, the juxtaposition of two conflicting styles of architecture: the original red brick structure dating back to the early 1900s sporting a brand new, white, high tech, earthquake-proof inpatient tower. As Jordan drove into the parking garage, then made his way to the hospital's reception desk, Warren sought out Brandi. When he discovered her, his initial thought had been to wake her and confront her with her infidelity. But since such a confrontation would do little more than satisfy his ego, and since his primary concern was to understand the quality of the pair's relationship and its survivability in the wake of a personal tragedy, he decided to restrain himself.

As he hovered over her bed, Warren simmered, containing himself while his partner attempted to coax Brandi into joining him. Her initial reluctance pleased him, since it demonstrated that their children were more important to her than her love affair. But when she finally succumbed to Jordan's persuasion, Warren's thoughts turned to what he might do to the Mercedes' braking system. Or, if that task remained beyond his capabilities, how he might alert the stockbrokers and investors that his partner was planning to flee since, from Warren's perspective, Sabrina's fantasy had always been a near impossibility. He had suspected from the outset how unlikely it would be for the boys from the SEC to show up on Jordan's doorstep. Years before, he'd been told that the agency's enforcement officers were a group of attorneys who pursued offenders through court actions and filings, unlike the FBI, who might eventually be summoned to track Jordan down and arrest him. Yet, even given the remote possibility that such an event might occur, with all of the money hidden beyond their jurisdiction, it might be years, if ever, before the ones Jordan injured ever recouped even part of their losses.

Absorbed in his musings, Warren was unaware of Karen's arrival until she asked her daughter, "How are you doing, Sweetheart?"

"I'm fine, Mom," said Brandi and it pleased Warren when he noticed an edge to her voice.

"Darling, you don't have to lie. I know your heart is breaking."

Up until this moment, Brandi had been displaying some semblance of recovery. Suddenly, her lips quivered, her façade crumbled, and instead of a spoken reply, she split the air with a long keening wail. Karen took Brandi's hand into hers and stood helpless as her daughter's body convulsed. With each new sob, tears coursed in rivulets down her cheeks. Had it been at all possible, Warren would have cried as well. The rent in his soul had not yet even begun to heal, and he sometimes felt that, were he substantial, the hole in his heart would be so large the wind would blow through it, howling like the demon Brandi now seemed to resemble.

Minutes later, as Brandi began to calm down, Karen drew up a chair to her bedside. She offered in a tentative tone,

"I noticed that… What's his name? Warren's partner?"

"His name is Jordan," said Brandi, wiping her nose with a tissue.

"I was about to say that I noticed him leaving just as I was coming in," adding, after a pause, "I also noticed his wife wasn't with him."

Brandi sighed. "No. She wasn't."

"I didn't mean to imply anything untoward."

Brandi frowned at her and said, "Mother, you speak like someone from the last century. Please say what you mean."

"I'm sorry. I wasn't implying anything."

"Of course not." With that, Brandi pushed herself upright. Placing two pillows against the railing behind her, she propped herself against them. "Father isn't here with you either, is he?"

Karen turned her eyes downward. "No. He isn't."

"Should I read something into that?"

Looking up at her daughter, Karen opened her mouth, then hesitated. To Warren, she appeared to be struggling with what to say next. Then, in a voice tinged with indignation, she snapped, "No. You shouldn't. How dare you imply something is wrong with our marriage!"

"I wasn't implying anything. I just asked a question. But since we're on the subject, why isn't he here?"

"He has a conference call."

"He *always* has a conference call. Even before Robbie and Rebecca were born, it's been you and only you who's come to visit." Brandi drew her feet close to her buttocks and crossed her ankles. Wrapping her arms around her shins, she asked, "He couldn't even make time for his grandchildren while they were alive." Her voice cracked and she choked back a sob. "I took it in stride, but whenever you came to visit, the children were always asking, 'Where's Grampa?' How could he expect two little children to understand why he never came to see them?"

"It wasn't about them."

"Was it about me, then?"

Karen bit her lip and looked away.

She remained silent until Brandi asked, "Why won't you let me in? You know you can confide in me. My marriage wasn't perfect. In fact, it was falling apart long before… " She paused, then collected herself. " …that thing in San Francisco. Now that I think about it, yours has been broken for as far back as I can remember."

This new dynamic fascinated Warren and he realized Brandi was right. Mark had never accompanied Karen, so Warren had never met him. In fact, he knew his father-in-law by name only—no reputation, no anecdotes—as if someone was hiding some deep, dark secret. Now, he wondered how Karen would react to Brandi's relationship with a married man. He suspected that, if it appeared to have blossomed after his death, it might be less of a problem than if they had been trysting while he was still alive. An individual's morals are, after all, an unpredictable filter that may allow the identical act to be viewed as either favorable or unacceptable, depending on the circumstances under which it occurred.

As for Karen, he had always wondered about her numerous idiosyncrasies, starting with the way she dressed. Her attire was always too formal for the accompanying occasion and today was no exception. While most women would have worn something casual to a visit like this, Karen was wearing a matching charcoal gray jacket and skirt, a white silk blouse, three inch heels and a single strand of black pearls, making him wonder if she might be compensating for some unexpressed discontent.

"Can we leave it for another day?" said Karen.

"There is no other day," Brandi insisted. "You're always postponing real conversations. Today is all there is," she finished, the tone of her voice becoming gentle.

Karen's eyes flitted around the room, as if she were searching for some elusive thing. All at once, she erupted.

"I *hate* him!"

"Mother?"

"It's *we* who hold a family together. It's *we* who feel genuine emotions. It's women who know how to love, goddamn it!"

Now, it was Karen who was sobbing. Restricted by an electrical lead running into her torso, Brandi extended an arm in her mother's direction, but couldn't quite reach her. After a while, Karen calmed down. She and Brandi began conversing in a quieter tone. In an effort to hear, Warren came closer. But as soon as he was next to them, Karen shuddered.

"My God it's cold! Do you feel that?"

Brandi nodded. "I'm starting to feel ill," she gasped and slid under the covers.

A nurse was passing in the hallway, so Brandi called, "Nurse! Is something wrong with the thermostat?"

Their reaction to his proximity did not escape Warren's attention. As the nurse attempted to determine what the two were experiencing, he moved beside her as well. Her knees buckled and she wrapped her arms around herself.

"Do you see what I mean?" Brandi asked.

"I don't understand," the nurse gasped. "I've never felt anything like it. It shouldn't be this cold in here. I'll get someone to help me move you to another room."

Puzzled, but pleased by their reaction, Warren waited while the hospital staff moved Brandi to another room in same the wing. Once she had settled in, the two resumed their conversation.

"We need to get you home," said Karen. "I don't see why they keep such an old hospital operating."

"It's been thoroughly modernized. But you're right. I do want to go home and, actually, I've been thinking I'd like to get away."

"Someplace warm and sunny, I hope."

"Jordan suggested the same thing."

"That's the first sensible thing I've heard since Mark and I got here. Business and financial matters are all that most men care about… all your father cares about," Karen amended, her voice turning sour when she mentioned his name, and Warren wondered where she was heading. "Grandchildren, children and wives, the things in their lives that should matter most, are inconsequential. They are always less important than the things that can advance a man's career.

"You asked if the reason Mark never came to visit had something to do with you." Karen's mouth twisted into something ugly. "It was never about you, Sweetheart, just like it was never about me. Your father created a family in order to satisfy various social expectations. He had a family for the same reason he wears a Rolex, for the same reason he belongs to the country club."

Brandi put her fingers to her lips. "And that's why he came to the funeral" she said. She balled her hands into fists and crumpled the bedsheet. "So he could put on a show."

Karen nodded and managed a thin smile. "It's all a show."

"*We're* all a show," concluded Brandi and Karen nodded.

10

Two large, gray eyes filled Sabrina's dream. They stared at her, crowding out other images to the point she could think of nothing else. She recognized their shape and color and knew to whom they belonged. She opened her own and peered into the darkness. Pushing herself upright, she sensed that those other eyes were real and they were examining her.

"Warren?"

No response.

"Talk to me." It sounded crazy, but she said it anyhow. "I know you're there." Silence. "I can feel you."

Can you now?

Sabrina gasped, hesitated, then hissed, "Yes-s-s."

That's good. That's very, very good.

"What the Hell are you doing here?" she asked.

I want to talk to you.

She calmed herself and tried to deal with the impossible as rationally as she could. "I'm listening."

I need your help. When Sabrina cocked her head, but remained silent, Warren said, *I want to make sure that Jordan won't get away with it.*

"I'm already working on it."

You said you would, but I don't think that what you proposed...

"Michael and I have come up with another solution."

Have you now?

"The SEC has a whistleblower's website, and we're also looking into filing a Suspicious Activity Report through FinCEN." When Warren said that he wasn't familiar with the second option, Sabrina added, "The Financial Crimes Enforcement Network. It's a branch of the Treasury Department designed to deal with money laundering and similar crimes."

Like transferring investors' funds to offshore accounts?

"Exactly."

So he thinks they might actually show up?

"Depends."

On what?

Sabrina pulled the covers to her chin. The room's temperature had dropped with his arrival and the chill was starting to get to her.

"A number of things. Something he called 'resource allocation' was one of them." When Warren didn't respond, she assumed he was waiting for an explanation and said, "A combination of how serious they deem this particular crime to be, compared with how many agents are available to deal with it.

"When Bernie Madoff's sons phoned the FBI and told them the firm's asset management division was a massive Ponzi scheme, agents showed up the following morning and put their father in handcuffs. Of course, in that case, we're talking almost seventy billion dollars. In Jordan's, we're only talking several tens of millions, maybe a hundred million.

"Michael also thinks it depends on how high up in the firm the whistleblowers are. Madoff's sons ran pretty much everything, while Michael and I are somewhat farther down the food chain. In our case, Michael is pretty sure it'll depend on how thorough and compelling the information we give them turns out to be.

So maybe yes, maybe no.

"Pretty much."

I really wish you'd put more effort into it.

"Really? You wish… " Sabrina sat upright and searched the room, hoping to identify exactly where Warren was… standing? The term probably didn't apply. "If you will recall, I was the one who brought it to your attention. And now it sounds like you're completely unappreciative. Do you realize what will happen if I don't succeed?" Met only with silence, Sabrina explained, "I'll not only lose my job, but also probably my entire pension fund. Which, by the way, is exactly what will happen if I do succeed.

"Also," she said, "what happens if Jordan finds out what I'm up to? Do you think he's going to allow me to live? Any way you look at it, I'm screwed. So don't go sounding righteous to me, motherfucker!"

I doubt he will kill you.

"What?"

He's never done anything even remotely similar. I'm pretty sure you're safe on that account.

"Every killer has a first victim. You could have said the same thing about Ted Bundy or Jeffrey Dahmer at some point in time. The fact that Jordan has shown no compunction over harming others leaves everything else open to speculation."

Sabrina tore the covers aside. She reached into the closet for a flannel bathrobe and tucked her feet into a pair of slippers.

What are you doing?

"Since I'm totally awake and it's… " She glanced at the alarm clock's glowing, red digital display. " …almost six-thirty, I'm going to brew a pot of coffee."

She was emptying a pitcher of filtered water into the electric teapot when Warren said, *I need you to do a couple of other things for me.*

She stopped pouring and turned away from the counter in an attempt to face him.

"You have a lot of nerve."

I need you to talk to Brandi.

"Talk to her yourself," she snapped as she flipped the pot's switch to the on position, then returned the pitcher to the fridge.

I've tried.

"And?"

She doesn't seem to hear me.

"Doesn't seem to, or doesn't want to?"

I don't know. I can't tell. Whatever it is, she acts like I'm not there.

"Smart. That's probably what I should be doing."

Please, Sabrina. I need to get through to her.

"About what?"

104

To warn her about Jordan.

"She's a big girl. Let her figure it out for herself."

Look. I know I fucked up. There are a lot of things I could have done better, but I can't change them. Jordon's going to make her complicit in screwing our clients and I don't want that to happen.

Sabrina scooped three large coffee measures of ground medium roast into the stainless steel French press, then paused to consider.

"I don't either," she admitted. "You're right. That's big of you. So where is she?"

Then you'll help me?

"You really are slow. Yes, of course I will help you."

Thank you. The hospital is releasing her today. I expect she'll be home sometime this afternoon.

She set a mug on the counter. After looking through the pot's glass window and seeing that the water hadn't started boiling, she turned back to face him.

"I'm just not sure what I'm going to say to her. Something like, 'Hi, Brandi. I've been having a conversation with your spook husband, and he told me to tell you… '" She trailed off, leaving the sentence unfinished.

I know it's not going to be easy.

Sabrina snorted. "You think?"

I'm wondering if Nancy can help you.

"What makes you say that?"

We've been talking. When Sabrina cocked her head and furrowed her brow, Warren expanded. *So far, I've been able to talk to three people and know they've heard me: You,*

Jordan and Nancy. I'm hoping that you and Nancy together will be credible enough that maybe Brandi will listen.

Sabrina laughed. "Like, by myself, I just might be crazy. But it's less likely that the two of us share the same delusion."

Also, in case Brandi actually couldn't hear me, I showed her a few signs that she wasn't alone, when everything suggested she was. Warren explained the way he had manifested, adding, *If you'll let her know that you are aware of what happened to the vase when, by all rights, you shouldn't—you weren't in the room and no one else was either—I'm hoping that will convince her that you and I have spoken.*

Sabrina stared at the floor and nodded. Suddenly aware that the water was boiling, she reached for the pot just as its switch flicked off. Once she had poured enough water into the French press and pressed the grounds to its bottom, she filled her mug and savored the Seattle coffee.

Well, what do you say?

With her back still to the room, she asked, "Where does Nancy fit into the scheme of things?"

She knows about Jordan and Brandi. Sabrina's eyebrows went up, so he added, *I told her. Since then, she's thrown Jordan out, so I suspect she might be willing to accompany you when you go to pay your visit.*

"The fact that she kicked him out doesn't mean she's going to have any sympathies where your wife is concerned. If I was her place, I wouldn't go anywhere near the bitch."

What did you call her?

Turning toward the general direction of where she suspected Warren might be manifesting, she said, "Don't tell me you still have any feelings for her."

106

It was me who fucked things up. Not her. If it wasn't for me, Robbie and Rebecca would still be alive. She never would have turned to Jordan if it wasn't for my drinking.

"Well, there's that." She cradled the mug in both hands, sighed and stared out the window.

The sun was just rising, casting Raccoon Straits in shades of orange and purple. Richardson Bay was showing similar hues behind Belvedere Island and the town of Tiburon proper. Sabrina's view included both of them, as well as the Belvedere Tennis Club, the twin cities of Belvedere and Tiburon, whose boundary was indistinguishable except on paper, as well as tiny, white Old Saint Hillary's Church, the hillside landmark most people noticed upon entering Tiburon's downtown.

"Assuming she'll listen, what do you want me to tell her?"

Tell her we've talked. Tell her it's important that Jordan is all on his own.

"What if Nancy still feels some loyalty to him? I mean, they were married how many years? And this is a recent development. The fact that she threw the bum out doesn't mean she wouldn't take him back in if he suddenly returned and apologized."

Show her the plane tickets. If they don't convince her, explain how many people are going to get hurt. Bring some of the documents you showed me. Nancy is a decent human being. Even if she hates Brandi, I suspect that when she sees how many people Jordan is going to hurt... Hell! He's going to do more than just hurt them. He's going to ruin most of our investors to the point they'll never be able to recover. And if that's not enough, let her know how many of our employees Jordan is going to screw, yourself included.

Nancy likes you. She genuinely likes you. I could see, from the exchanges you two had in the downtown office, you both got along.

"Yeah. We did. And I like her, too."

So you've got that much going for you. See if you can work it to your mutual advantage. I'd go back and talk to her myself, but she has to see that it's coming from more than just me since clearly I'm biased. If she also hears it coming from you, that will add some additional credibility.

"All right. I'll give it a try. When do you think I should see her?"

Today might be good. You don't work weekends, do you?

Sabrina shook her head.

If she decides she's willing to help, the two of you can discuss when you'd like to approach Brandi. In the meanwhile, I have an idea how I might short-circuit Jordan.

"What do you mean?"

I'm still working out the details. It all depends on how well I've mastered my abilities. For the moment, let's just say you'll know if I've succeeded.

11

Nancy and one of her friends, a woman whose surname was synonymous with one of the nation's largest polling organizations, once lamented that, before they had moved to Marin County, they both had "real friends," people who would invite them over for neighborhood get-togethers or just for the hell of it. Since then, they agreed that all of the locals they had met—neighbors and social acquaintances alike—were only interested in spending time with people who could give them a leg up the social ladder, ones who could help them make their way to the top. And while they agreed their viewpoints might be skewed by their limited experience, both found it amusing, and at the same time annoying, that no one ever invited them over for a weekend barbeque or evening cocktails without something like a political fundraiser for a family member being part of the equation. Certainly, no one ever dropped by just to say "hello" or pass the time. Consequently, Nancy was surprised to hear a knock at her front door.

"Would you like me to answer it, Mrs. Weeks?"

"No thank you, Myrna," she told her housekeeper. Curious as to who might be calling, she placed her breakfast dishes on the counter.

"Sabrina?" said Nancy when she saw her standing on the doorstep. Sabrina nodded and offered a tentative smile. Nancy hesitated, then added, "So nice to see you. To what do

I owe the honor?"

"May I come inside?" Sabrina asked and Nancy thought she detected a trace of concern in her voice.

Although momentarily flustered, Nancy regained enough presence to remember the Southern hospitality she had grown up with. "Yes, of course you may," she managed, then added, "Please do come in." She glanced at the bundle Sabrina was holding, then smiled and stepped aside to usher in this favorite acquaintance. "So nice to see you."

Nancy guided Sabrina to the living room settee where she thought they could converse. "Myrna," she called.

"Yes, Mrs. Weeks."

"Have you finished with the master bedroom?"

"Not yet, Ma'am."

"Will you please take care of it, so Sabrina and I can speak in private?"

"Certainly, Ma'am," replied the housekeeper. "Just let me know when you'd like me to finish up the kitchen."

As Myrna headed toward the staircase, Nancy turned to her guest and asked, "Would you like a cup of coffee?"

Sabrina nodded. "Thanks. That would be nice."

When Nancy returned a few minutes later, she found Sabrina staring out the picture window. She placed the tray bearing a small silver pot, two china cups, and containers of sugar and cream on the coffee table. "The view always captures everyone's attention." she said.

"You're very fortunate," Sabrina replied and turned to face her.

"It's the primary reason Jordie and I bought this place." Then, moving a vase of roses to better accommodate coffee service, she said, "Please sit beside me," and started pouring.

Referring to the flowers, Sabrina said, "Such an unusual shade of… peach, isn't it? I've never seen anything like them."

"They're called Osianas. They're from somewhere in South America. There was a time when I could walk downtown and buy them at a stall in the Boardwalk Shopping Center. It's closed now, so I have to order them online and have them FedExed. Do you notice how fragrant they are?" Sabrina leaned forward and inhaled. "That's what drew me to them. Most varieties these days have all the scent bred out of them."

"They're lovely."

Nancy nodded as she replaced the coffee pot. "I always try to keep a bouquet or two somewhere in the house. That's one of the problems with this location: nowhere to grow a garden." Lifting the cup to her lips, Nancy paused, then asked, "But you didn't come here to talk about flowers, did you?"

"No. I didn't."

Nancy cocked her head and waited as Sabrina gazed out the window. After a moment, Sabrina lifted her cup, took a sip and said, "I need to talk to you about Jordan."

"I thought that might be it."

Sabrina spent the next several minutes discussing what Jordan had been doing and what his plans were with Brandi.

"I know all about it," said Nancy, not bothering to hide her disgust.

Cradling her cup with both hands, Sabrina nodded. Gazing directly at Nancy, she stated, "Warren told you."

Wide eyed, and taking care not to drop it, Nancy returned her cup to the coffee table. In a voice approaching whisper, she asked, "How did you know?"

"We've spoken."

"Have you now?"

"I don't know how you feel about Brandi, but… pardon me for saying so… " Sabrina paused. "Jordan shouldn't be allowed to get away with this."

"Meaning?"

"Well, everything really. He shouldn't be allowed to screw his investors and he shouldn't be allowed to take advantage of Brandi."

Nancy arched an eyebrow. "Do you know if he's been screwing Brandi?"

"No. I don't. But even if he has, I don't believe Brandi had any thought of hurting you."

"But she has, child. She's hurt me more than you can ever imagine."

"I can understand that."

"Can you?"

Sabrina turned her head, hesitated, then looked back. "No. Not really. I've never been married, or even been in a relationship for more than a couple of years. So, no. I'm being presumptuous. Pardon me."

Nancy smiled and placed her hand on Brandi's.

"I know you didn't intend it. But you have to understand, she's taken away the biggest part of my life."

"I believe Jordan's planning to leave the country in the very near future and take Brandi with him. Would you like to help me make sure that he can't?"

Arching her brows and caught off guard, Nancy

replied, "I would. But why would you care?"

"I can't change the fact that Jordan and Brandi have hurt you, but over the years I've gotten to know what kind of person you are. You're concerned about the people around you. What Jordan has already done is going to leave all of the company's employees jobless and ruin all of its investors, many of whom are your friends. I'd like to make sure he doesn't leave the country before the authorities have a chance to recover what he's taken."

"I couldn't keep him from cheating. What makes you think I can stop him from leaving the country?"

"I'm hoping he won't go without taking Brandi with him, and I'm hoping you'll help me convince Brandi to stay."

Nancy withdrew her hand. "You want me to *what*?" she gasped.

Sabrina leaned forward and fixed the woman's eyes with her own. In a tone approaching a whisper, she asked, "Do you care about your friends... the ones Jordan's going to ruin?"

"Well, yes. Of course I do."

"And the company's employees?"

"I suppose."

"Then please, if you can set aside your feelings about how Brandi has hurt you, if only for a minute, and help me convince her that the evidence I've brought... " Sabrina touched the package on the cushions beside her and Nancy followed the gesture. " ...demonstrates that Jordan is a sociopath and not the kind of man she needs to be with, I think we have a chance to convince her to stay."

While Nancy continued to stare at the brown, expandable file folder, Sabrina said, "I know this may be difficult, but if you will come with me, then, at the very least, you can help insure that the two of them are no longer together."

The assertion caught Nancy's attention. When she raised her eyes, Sabrina continued, "I don't know what feelings you may still have for Jordan, but I firmly believe that you and I have a solid chance at convincing Brandi not to go."

"What's in the package?" Nancy asked.

12

"We released her this morning," the nurse explained, so Nancy and Sabrina drove over to Brandi's house in a neighborhood close San Rafael's Dominican University.

Shortly before noon, they arrived at a terra cotta colored, three story residence. It had a Spanish tile roof, and was located halfway up a hill, partly hidden from view by stands of eucalyptuses and poplars. It was an established community, made up of large, custom built homes constructed in the 1940s, '50s and '60s on relatively narrow lots with the houses set back from the street.

Sabrina parked her car and the pair made their way up a brick and mortar path running through lush, terraced gardens. They announced their presence with a wrought iron knocker fastened to the seven foot high, hand hewn, polished oak front door. They were still recovering from the climb when the housekeeper answered. Although Nancy was still nearly breathless, she mustered a smile and greeted her with, "Hello, Jessica. Is Brandi home?"

The housekeeper studied her face for a moment, then broke into a grin when recognition struck. "Mrs. Weeks, it's so nice to see you! I apologize. It's been so long since you've been here, I almost didn't recognize you. To answer your question, Brandi came home early this morning." She glanced at Sabrina and nodded to acknowledge her presence. Returning her eyes to Nancy, she said, "She'll be so happy to see you. Won't you please come in?"

Two half-flights of stairs led the party to the living room. Half way up, Sabrina was struck by an oil painting on the wall at the top of the first landing with life-sized depictions of Warren, Brandi, and their children. It was a formal portrait. Warren was dressed in a dark blue suit and Brandi, standing next to him him, was wearing what appeared to be a scarlet silk gown. Robbie and Rebecca standing in front of them, were dressed identically with their parents, except that Robbie was wearing shorts, and Rebecca had on a pair of white socks under her black, strapped slippers.

Jessica, who was following just behind her, volunteered, "This house will never be the same again."

"I suspect you're right," Sabrina replied, turning to look at her. "How is Brandi handling it?"

"She seems to be coping," said Jessica as they continued up. Just as they were completing the last of the stairs, she offered, "You know her, then."

Nancy laughed. "I'm sorry. I forgot to introduce you. It must be the old lady in me and the walk leading up to the house. Jessica, this is Sabrina. She works at the Tiburon office and is one of the people who keeps the firm welded together. Sabrina, Jessica plays pretty much the same roll in this household."

As they were exchanging pleasantries, Sabrina surveyed the living room. In one corner, prominent amid the Persian carpets and antique furniture, the likes of which Sabrina had only seen in museums, stood a large, black, grand piano. Finding it hard to associate musical talent with Warren, Sabrina gestured toward it and asked, "Is that Brandi's?"

"Oh, yes," Jessica enthused. "Before the… " She paused. " …tragedy happened, she was rehearsing for a house concert." When Sabrina's eyebrows went up, she explained, "Brandi is a classically trained musician. She's been given offers to perform with the San Francisco Symphony." She lowered her voice when she added, "Mr. Weeks didn't want her to join it. He thought it was beneath her dignity, but he finally agreed that she could perform for a small audience of friends and neighbors."

Sabrina and Nancy exchanged glances and Jessica's lips tightened, obviously uncomfortable with having made the disclosure. Her eyes traveled from Nancy to Sabrina, then back again. When neither of them commented, her expression relaxed and she gestured toward a sofa. "Please have a seat. I'll tell her you're here."

As Jessica hurried upstairs, Sabrina said, "That's something I wouldn't have expected."

Nancy nodded. "I knew about his drinking, but I didn't realize he was so controlling. Jordie never mentioned it."

Sabrina slipped the leather bag and its incriminating documents from her shoulder and leaned it against one of the sofa's armrests. She took a place between the document case and Nancy and the two sat in silence, inhaling the pervading scent of sandalwood.

A few minutes later, Brandi called from somewhere above. "Nancy?" They turned to see her descending the staircase and frowning. "It's so nice to see you. What brings you to San Rafael?"

"The hospital told us they released you and we wanted to see how you're coming along," answered Nancy, a partial lie at worst.

"Much better, thank you," Brandi replied as she reached the staircase's foot.

They both rose to greet her. While Sabrina had not

actually met her, she had seen her drop by both the San Francisco and Tiburon offices on earlier occasions and had overheard her conversing with Melissa and Warren. Something moving above caught her eye, and she glanced up to see another woman descending. Brandi followed her gaze and said, "Mother, you remember Nancy, don't you?"

"Of course," Karen acknowledged, inclining her head in an inquiring manner. "How is your husband doing? Much better, I hope."

If Nancy had detected the hint of hostility in Karen's tone, Sabrina was relieved when she didn't show it. Instead, Nancy replied, "He's fine, thank you," without bothering to add any details about their separation.

As her mother continued to descend, Brandi finally acknowledged Sabrina's presence. Looking toward her, she said, "And you must be… "

"Sabrina," she supplied, trying to keep her tone neutral. She was already expecting the conversation would be difficult, but if this discussion were to be productive, she wanted to diminish whatever emotional charge Karen had begun to introduce. As it was, her mind was already spinning through ways to keep the visit as brief as possible.

When Karen reached the living room, she paused, saying, "I'm afraid I must apologize and leave the three of you to your own devices. I have to run into town to pick up a few odds and ends."

She kissed her daughter on the cheek, then made her way out the front door. Once she had gone, Brandi turned to her visitors and asked, "Can I offer you something to drink? Coffee or tea, perhaps?"

Nancy dodged the invitation saying, "I'm afraid I wasn't entirely candid. There is something important we need to discuss. Is there somewhere we all could sit face to face?"

Brandi cast her a curious look, then suggested they gather around the dining room table. When Sabrina hefted the shoulder bag, Brandi's face darkened. An awkward silence followed until Nancy broke the impasse, smiling awkwardly.

"Hun, there's something we need to tell you about Jordie." Brandi's eyes widened and her eyebrows arched. She was starting to reply when Nancy explained, "We don't want him to hurt you."

Brandi's eyes rarely left the briefcase as the three pulled up chairs and arranged themselves with Nancy and Sabrina sitting opposite her. When Sabrina withdrew the expandable file folder and its stack of documents, she said, "You need to look at these." As she began sliding the papers across to Brandi, she explained each of their contents.

It took Brandi a full ten minutes to study them. When she had finished, she raised her head and stared at her guests. "Why would he do such a thing?"

"It baffles us, too," conceded Nancy.

Sabrina added, "We're hoping we can convince you not to go with him."

Brandi picked up one of the documents that reflected the interbank transfers. "How can you be sure these transactions aren't legitimate?"

"Michael assures me they're not," said Sabrina.

"Michael from accounting?"

Sabrina nodded, then explained how Michael had come across the information and why he knew that no one else was privy to it.

"We're going to notify the SEC, most likely Monday morning."

As Brandi's eyes returned to the evidence, now spread out across the table, Nancy told her, "We don't want you to spend the next several years running from the law."

"Warren doesn't either," Sabrina added.

Brandi's head came up and she stared at her. "What did you say?"

Before Sabrina had time to reply, Nancy explained, "We've both spoken with him. I know this will be hard for you to believe… but he's back from the dead."

"Now I know you're crazy," said Brandi. She slapped her hands against the tabletop and pointed toward the door. "Get out of my house!"

"Do you remember the vase in your hospital room and how it rotated all on its own, not just once, but twice?" asked Sabrina.

Brandi's jaw dropped and she stared at her. "How… ?"

Sabrina completed the question. " …could I know about that?" She paused for a moment, then answered, "Warren told me. He also told me how cold you became when he moved near you and how the hospital staff changed the room you were in."

Brandi became silent and her chest visibly rose and fell. Nancy and Sabrina waited for her to digest the information. After a minute, Brandi whispered, "Only mother and I know about that."

"Only you, Karen and Warren knew about that," corrected Sabrina. "And now we do, too. When you stop and think about it, there's no other explanation, is there?"

Brandi raised her fingers to her lips, slowly shaking her head. "Oh, my God," she gasped.

Nancy chimed in. "Do you remember how badly

Jordan behaved at the funeral? You know that's not like him. Jordie may be a lot of things, but he's not disrespectful on that kind of occasion. He certainly wouldn't have acted like that without a good reason. Haven't you wondered why he acted that way? Why he up and left without so much as a how do you do?"

Brandi nodded.

"Warren was talking in Jordie's ear and it scared the shit out of him. Even I didn't believe him until Warren appeared before us later that evening." Nancy spent the next few minutes recounting everything that happened, before adding, "You know the two of us. You know me better than Sabrina, but you certainly should know her reputation. Please ask yourself why we would want to make ourselves sound like a couple of loonietunes, if there wasn't something more behind it. Consider what Sabrina just told you about what happened at the hospital. Think about it," Nancy urged. "How could she have possibly learned about it except from someone who was there with you?"

Brandi replied in a monotone, "I was alone. There wasn't anyone."

"Then who moved the vase?" Sabrina asked.

Nancy and Sabrina waited while Brandi digested everything they had given her. She shuffled through the documents and ran her hands through her hair, trying, like Warren had done in the coffee shop, to come up with a better explanation than what the papers made undeniable. Eventually, she turned to Nancy. "Why would you, of all people, want to help me?"

"Hun, I have no more control over Jordie than I have over the weather." Nancy clenched her lips and said, "I have to admit, coming here wasn't easy. To be completely honest, I'm more concerned about the firm's investors than I am about you. And while my heart still has some feelings toward Jordie, I can't let him get away with this. So I guess it's more about my ethics than it has to do with my feelings."

"Now, *that* I can buy," Brandi admitted. "I think if you had given me any other answer, I'd throw the two of you out right now, with no qualms about it.

"The question now becomes, 'What do I tell Jordan?' I've already told him I'd leave with him. Do you think he'd be suspicious if I told him I've changed my mind?"

Nancy smiled. "We women are allowed to be fickle."

"No. Seriously. Jordan and I have always been open with each other. If I tell him I've changed my mind, I have to offer a reasonable explanation."

"Tell him your mother wants to spend some more time with you," suggested Sabrina. "You've just lost your children and she's lost her grandchildren. I can't imagine that's any easier on her than it is with you. Doesn't your bond with your mother run deeper than your feelings for Jordan?" Brandi nodded. "If you can't find a way to tell him you're backing out, then simply postpone it. Tell him you need another month or two, then maybe you'll reconsider."

"That sounds plausible enough." Brandi paused, then nodded. "All right, then. That's what I'm going to do. I'll phone him on Monday. The children were both born in May, so I'll tell him Mother and I want to celebrate what would have been their next birthday together and we can discuss our plans after that."

"Fair enough," said Sabrina. "It's entirely possible the FBI will have stepped in by then."

"The FBI?"

"Dear," said Nancy. "Jordie's dug himself a pretty deep hole."

13

Jordan peered through the conference room's blinds just as Sabrina walked out of Michael's office. Even though her visits were regular occurrences and he suspected there might be some sort of chemistry between them, there was something about this one and the two or three visits before, that had a different quality from the usual ones. While Sabrina generally greeted everyone within earshot with a smile and a gregarious exchange about what she and the office's employees were up to and how they were doing, now, as she closed Michael's door while silently mouthing something to him, she was uncharacteristically restrained. She glanced about, as if hoping she hadn't been noticed, then hurried to the elevators where she smiled tightly at the trader who was waiting for their doors to open. Her actions made Jordan worry if she was the one he needed to fear. Possibly Michael as well? These were two of his most valuable employees and he wondered if this wasn't just a case of paranoia. Fear, he realized, often results in errors in judgement and he prided himself in being able to set his emotions aside whenever he was conducting business. This, and his analytical mind, were the reasons he had risen as far as he had.

He had to admit, the only reason he had cause for alarm was that he was still within law enforcement's reach. If he weren't so obsessed with Brandi, he might have fled the country already, so why was he hanging back now? Sure, she was a great lay and someone he could talk to, but the world was full of intelligent, caring, and amorous women, so why was he so hung up on this one? He was rich enough he should have no trouble attracting any number of others. Women flirted with him almost daily, so why should he remain fixated on Brandi at the expense of his well-being in all other regards? Was it because she was his first intimate relationship in years that he had become so indecisive? He clenched his jaw and decided he needed to force the issue. Now that she was due to be released and in better health than the last time they had spoken, he would insist she commit to a date when they would depart.

Another thought struck him. If someone were to walk in unexpectedly, Jordan would be hard pressed to explain why he was standing in the dark, staring through the blinds and ruminating. Jordan drew them closed and flipped the lights on. He ran a hand through his hair and neatened his appearance. He was about to walk out and join his associates when the nearest of the chairs around the conference table slid out from under it, turned around to face him, then moved into his path and barred his way. The air grew cold and his breath condensed into a cloud when he exhaled.

"Warren?" he called.

Silence.

"Look. I don't have time for this bullshit."

He tried to push the chair aside, but found that he could not. He pushed harder, but it was as if someone had nailed it to the floor. When he put his entire weight against it and shoved, he still couldn't budge it. He tried stepping around it, but another chair moved into his path and blocked it. When he tried to step into the space between the pair and the conference room wall, a third chair began sliding out from under the table.

Jordan halted, trying to decide what his next move should be.

"If this is your idea of a game, I'm not playing," said Jordan, reflexively looking around the room but seeing no one. He turned with the intention of taking the long way around the table, but a fourth chair moved into his way and he began breathing hard. "All right, then. If you want to talk, I'll talk. What do you want?"

No response.

Since Warren wouldn't engage him and he found himself blockaded, Jordan climbed onto the tabletop. He was scuttling across it, intending to dash out of the room as soon as he was back on the carpet, when a chair flew directly at him, striking him in the face and knocking him back over his heels.

Dazed by the impact, it took Jordan a few seconds to reorient himself. Looking around, he found that he was still on the slab of polished hardwood, still kneeling, but bent over backwards. His thighs ached and his knees felt as if the tendons were stretched to the point they might tear any second. His nose hurt, and he also worried that his jaw might be broken. He probed it tentatively and was relieved when, although his chin was still throbbing from the impact, it accepted his touch without complaint. Something moist ran down his lip, then fell onto the tabletop. He wiped the moisture away and his sleeve came away smeared with red. When he tried to examine his nose, the pain was intolerable. Glancing down, he saw several more droplets spatter the surface. Realizing he needed medical assistance, he placed his hands against the table, pushed himself upright, then attempted to continue his crawl. Glancing behind him, he saw a chair with its four wooden legs pointing upward, likely the one that had damaged him. With no indication where Warren might be or what he intended to do next, he grasped the table's edge with both hands and started pulling himself toward it.

Warren's voice resounded inside Jordan's head. *You enjoy blind-siding people, don't you? Well, so do I. How's this?*

Jordan screamed and white light flared across his vision when another chair struck him on the kidneys. "Are you trying to kill me?" he cried.

Warren snickered. *Nothing like that, good buddy. That would be letting you off way too easy.*

"So wh- what are you trying to do?"

Why, injure you to the point you're completely incapacitated, of course, Warren replied, his words sounding as if they were coming from inside Jordan's head. *After that, I will let you recover. Once you've start feeling like your old self, I'll start all over again. That's my game plan.*

"You bastard!" Jordan cried.

Moi? Non, monsieur, it is you who are the bastard. I'm just giving you what you deserve.

Another chair began moving and Jordan screamed as loud as he could. "HELP! ANYBODY! HE-E-L-L-L-P!!"

No one's going to hear you, good buddy, and nobody's going to see. Remember how you objected when I suggested installing a surveillance system? "Too much money," you said. "When would we ever need it?" Warren laughed. *And I thought I was a tightwad. The only cameras in the building are out in the hallways and the reception area, and they wouldn't record me coming or going anyhow. They certainly aren't going to capture what I'm about to do to you now.*

Jordan did remember his objections, and he cursed himself for his lack of foresight. He also recalled that he had ordered the conference room sound-proofed when he had it constructed. Furthermore, now that he had closed the conference room's blinds, no one could see in. Unless he could get to a window and break it, he was all on his own with no one to help him.

"Look. What if I return the money?"

Oh, you're definitely going to do that.

Jordan nodded vigorously. "Absolutely. Please let me leave and I'll get on it right away."

What about Brandi?

"I'll stop seeing her."

That'll be nice. But how do you propose undoing everything else you two did?

"I… " Jordan couldn't answer.

That's what I thought. So the next question becomes, what should I do to you now… good buddy? As Jordan searched for a way to escape, Warren mused, half to himself, half to Jordan, *I need to do something that won't kill you, but will cause you to regret everything you've done until now. Maybe do something to your hands?*

Jordan buried them under his chest.

We shouldn't do that, now should we? Show them to Daddy.

Terrified over what might happen next, Jordan tried to curl into a ball. The effort was futile. He felt something grab one of his wrists and tug. When he tried to resist, Warren's tug tore the ligaments in Jordan's shoulder, leaving him unable to pull his hand back. Jordan screamed as Warren pulled his arm straight upon the tabletop.

"Please don't!" he begged.

Don't? Don't what? You don't even know what I have in mind… do you?

"No," Jordan whimpered.

Damned conference room doesn't give me much to work with. I was hoping to use something different, but this will have to do.

A chair leg slammed onto Jordan's right hand and he screamed. Before he could hide it underneath him, the chair came down hard once again, then another time. Several more strikes followed. Jordan screamed in agony and white light blinded him.

Minutes passed. Jordan gradually returned to consciousness. When he began to think more clearly, he twisted his neck to see if anything else might be coming. With his cheek still pressed against the tabletop, Jordan blinked hard, then blinked again to clear away the tears that made seeing impossible. When, at last, his vision began to clear and his eyes started to focus, he saw several holes in the table's polished surface near where his hand lie throbbing. The chair that was resting near the indentations started to rise.

Welcome back. Now it's time for the other one.

Before Jordan could protest, Warren tugged the other arm free. The chair soared over Jordan's head and beyond his field of vision an instant before pain exploded through that hand. The first blow was followed by a second one. Then another. And another. Jordan soon lost count. Once the blows ended, Jordan lay weeping for several minutes, staring at the places where his bones poked through the surrounding tissue. His hands were pulsing and he started to cry. Desperate find someone to help him, he drew his knees underneath him and rolled onto an elbow. Next, he swung his feet in front of him until his lower legs dropped off the table and he was able to sit.

He raised his hands and tried to assess the damage. Unable to see clearly, he wiped his eyes with a forearm, then looked again. He gasped. Every finger was twisted, deformed, and bloody. Mottled in various shades of blue, red, and purple, his hands looked like the claws of some unimaginable beast.

"My God." The words fell from his lips and he wondered if he would ever be able use them again.

He sat like that for several minutes until the pain in his lower back made him remember he had suffered other injuries. His face hurt, but with his hands so badly broken, he had no way to evaluate whether that damage was confined to only his nose and jaw. He was about to call out for help when he remembered that no one could hear. Desperate for assistance, he studied his surroundings to decide what his next course of action should be.

One chair lay on its side next to him and two of its feet were bloody. He glanced at the nearby gouges and his blood smeared in and around them. The chairs Warren had used to corral him were still sitting at odd angles in the space between the table and the wall where the windows were, making a path around that side of the table impossible. He decided to come down on the opposite side.

Once he had managed to stand, he found himself wobbling and unsteady. Taking deliberate steps in order not to fall and thereby need his hands to assist him, he made his way around to the conference room's door. He looked at the doorknob and suspected it would be impossible to turn. He decided that the windows were his only recourse. He needed to break them, but unable to wield any possible tool, he knew he would need to use his body, most likely an elbow. The blinds were still drawn and he realized their slats might protect him. Raising an arm and taking aim before turning his head away, he thrust its elbow through the glass.

"Help!" he cried. "Somebody help!"

14

The thing about Jordan's theft that drove Warren mad was the simple awareness that he might actually get away with it. His frustration was heightened by the possibility that there was little he could do to prevent Jordan from escaping justice. Although he had made Jordan, Nancy, and Brandi aware of his return, he doubted that an FBI investigator, whose actions are driven by what he can prove with concrete evidence, would accept any contact Warren might make with him as anything other than delusional. Even if the agent were to believe that the contact was real and he mustered enough nerve to tell his superiors, they would probably have him removed from active duty and psychologically evaluated.

Warren knew that if he were still alive, the FBI would probably regard whatever allegations he might bring before them as credible, since he was one of the firm's principal officers. But now that he was deceased, Michael and Sabrina were the only ones who could act on the behalf of the firm's investors and he wondered how the FBI might regard whatever allegations the two might bring to their attention. He suspected their first reaction would be to regard them as two disgruntled employees. Perhaps they would give their assertions *some* consideration, but probably not the attention they deserved, and that wasn't Michael and Sabrina's only problem. As Warren watched his partner spying from the conference room, he feared what Jordan might do to them once he finally learned it was they who had unmasked him. Would such a sociopath feel even a hint of restraint when it came to exacting revenge? He doubted it and wondered what he could do to protect them.

He was coming out of his reverie when he noticed that Jordan was preparing to leave. Deciding that this was as good a time as any to act, he slid one of the chairs out from under table and placed it in front of him, then turned it around to face him, in order to remind Jordan who was in charge.

Boxing him in proved easy enough, and it delighted him to watch his partner climb onto the tabletop. So much for his dignity. But now that Warren had reduced him to crawling, he wanted to do something more than merely humiliate him. Reminding himself that his first priority was preventing Jordan's escape—not just from this room, but from the United States of America—his mind began running through the various ways an able bodied man could flee and it came to him that he needed to insure that Jordan was not, in fact, able.

The conference room offered little by way of tools for Warren to work with. But since he had already been having so much success employing the chairs to create a blockade, he wondered if there wasn't some other way he could use them. All at once, Warren's thoughts returned to the alley, the trio of street thugs, and the impression he had made with the garbage can lids. It was a short leap from there to how he could employ the furniture. He immediately discounted blows to the head. Severe enough brain injuries could put Jordan into a vegetative state and he wanted to make sure Jordan wasn't oblivious to whatever legal consequences might befall him. Since there had been times during the course of their partnership when Warren had wanted to punch Jordan in the face, he wondered why not now?

Wham!

The first blow bent Jordan over backwards. He waited

until Jordan recovered enough to start moving again before striking him in the kidneys. Jordan's hands, however, padding across the tabletop, made even more inviting targets. Nothing Warren could do to them would be fatal. But if he injured them badly enough, it would be a long time before Jordan could use them to paw Brandi's exquisite body. He struck at them mercilessly, pounding away until the tendons were distended, the skin was torn and discolored with Jordan's bones protruding through it.

After he had caused what he believed to be sufficient damage, he smiled as the firm's employees began emerging from their offices. They huddled over him, wondering among themselves how someone could have caused so much damage, then gotten away unobserved. It amused him when Allan bounded up the stairs then, unconcerned about the blood that was staining his gabardines, pulled up a chair and helped Jordan into it. When the paramedics arrived, Warren watched as they strapped Jordan to a stretcher after he complained that his back hurt.

Content that Jordan would not be leaving the country anytime soon, Warren went out into the city to do a little soul searching. Returning to his children was still a priority, but with all of eternity left for him to join them, it became a less urgent matter than insuring he had settled all of his earthly grievances. Without a specific target upon which to vent his frustration, he found himself wandering aimlessly.

He had drifted out to The Great Highway to spend some time near the Pacific, where he could be free of the city's clamor, when something touched him. It felt like another mind, like some conscious entity. He attempted to identify it, but aside from the drivers who were making their way along the asphalt corridor, the occasional stroller on the beach, or the residents of the Sunset District's households, no other living being caught his attention, so he dismissed the occurrence as an imaginary figment.

As the sun began setting, Warren decided that he might like to visit North Beach and spend some time near its nightclubs and restaurants. However, rather than being uplifted by the glowing signs and the evening's festivities, he found the setting depressing. Never again would he be able to sample any culinary fare nor share a drink with friends. He would never again feel the evening's breeze against his skin while he dined at a sidewalk café or strolled along the city streets, laughing and joking.

He was lamenting these losses when a similar sensation to the one he had experienced earlier touched him again. When it began to linger, he leapfrogged from mind to mind, looking for its source. Just as before, however, Warren encountered only the living and this one felt… different.

Hello.

The simple greeting startled him. Both alarmed and excited, Warren searched for the one who had spoken.

I thought I'd lost you, said an entity Warren could not identify. *I've been so alone. Until you appeared, I was afraid I was the only rational soul here.*

The only rational soul? asked Warren.

All the other ones here are demented in one way or another.

Encountering someone else like himself was startling enough, but the possibility of others was disconcerting and made him ask, *How many are there?*

Dozens. I've never counted them, but over the years I've run into more than a few.

And all of them are demented?

I haven't met a sane one in the bunch, the entity

replied. *One of the craziest is a woman people call the White Lady of Stow Lake. She died some years before the San Francisco earthquake. The quake destroyed all of the records that might have documented unusual deaths or disappearances, so there's no actual information. Just a few anecdotal tales. As the story goes, she was in Golden Gate Park, talking with a friend, when she realized the baby carriage she had with her had vanished. As you might imagine, she was frantic. She looked everywhere. She ran around screaming as she searched for it, until, at one point, the obvious struck and she ran into the lake to save her baby from drowning. The poor woman never came out. It's best to avoid her,* the spirit cautioned.

Why? Is she dangerous? asked Warren.

The spirit snickered. *Do you mean will she kill you?*

Of course not, Warren replied, feeling embarrassed.

That's good, Dearie. The spirit sighed. *All I will tell you is stay away from Golden Gate Park if you don't want to end up as crazy as she is.*

You called her The White Lady, said Warren. *Why is that?*

That's how she appears when she materializes. She and her clothing appear to be entirely white.

Curious about the Lady's ability to manifest, Warren asked, *How does she do it? Materialize, I mean. I've only been able to do so once, and even then I was almost invisible.*

I think it comes down to intention, the spirit replied. *I've never wanted to appear to others badly enough, and nobody's ever noticed me. And while I'm not sure the Lady actually wants people to see her, per se, she is desperate enough to get people to help save her baby that she manifests to anyone who comes her way.*

Even though it's too late.

I don't think she realizes she's dead.

What? exclaimed Warren.

I told you she's crazy. She's so absorbed with her predicament that nothing else has impacted her awareness.

Warren remained silent for a while, digesting the information. Finally, he asked, *Can I ask you a personal question?*

Of course.

He hesitated, trying to find a diplomatic way to approach the subject. When nothing more diplomatic came to mind, he asked, *How did you die?*

The spirit laughed. *I was murdered.* Before Warren could ask what the spirit found so amusing, the spirit replied, *That's what they did to men like me.*

Men like you?

That's what they did to... The spirit paused. *...homosexuals.*

Warren gasped and felt the spirit back away.

Do you find me disgusting?

No! That's not why I reacted that way. It's just that murder... Warren paused before asking, *Did they convict the ones responsible?*

The spirit laughed again. *Why would they? In those days, it was just like hanging nig... Pardon me. I'd forgotten. I believe these days you call them African Americans. So, no. No great crime. In fact, no crime at all. No court in the land would have found them guilty. Actually, not much different from today, depending on what part of the country you're in. That's why I don't bother to manifest. I'm much happier this way than I was when I was alive.*

I can understand.

Since we're telling tales, can I ask about your death? asked the spirit.

Warren told him about the night in the Tenderloin and why he had left the Tunnel of Light. *Once I've settled a few scores,* said Warren, *I'm going back. I intend to get back to my children.*

Good luck on that one, Dearie.

What do you mean?

As far as I can tell, it's a one-way ticket. Once you turn down eternity to return to the physical world you're... Well, let's just say I've never met anyone who was able to go back.

No one?

Well... there might have been a few, maybe two of three. All of them expressed the same desire. At one point, each of them disappeared. But since I have no way to determine what happened after they'd vanished, I can't answer your question with any certainty. Perhaps they did. Perhaps they didn't.

Warren pressed. *So, it's not a no.*

It's not a no, the spirit agreed, but with a reluctant tone to his voice that caused Warren to persist.

Is there anything about them that would give some indication about... ?

About whether they might have made it? I will say that they were some of the best folks I've ever met. They weren't what some people would call saints, but they were better than any of the rest of us.

Well, that's certainly encouraging, Walter declared.

Do you think someone could say the same about you? Is there some quality about you that might increase your chances?

Although Warren wanted to believe someone might make that assertion, but aware of the kind of person he was at the time he was murdered, as well as who he was becoming here, in the afterlife, he was forced to admit, *Probably not. Although I'm not a monster either.*

I don't believe you are.

That note of optimism caught Warren by surprise. *Really? What makes you say that? You don't even know me.*

No, I don't, the spirit agreed. *But your aura is bright enough that I won't put you in the same class as the Lady or any of the darker souls.*

I have an aura?

You do. Everyone does.

Warren found this statement surprising. *How can you tell? I can't see you at all, so I certainly can't see your aura.*

That will come over time. There is a period of adjustment for each of us. I suspect we couldn't have had this conversation much earlier. The fact you can't see me indicates you haven't been here very long.

Although he couldn't say exactly how long it had been since he had arrived, when he considered how much time should have elapsed between his death, the funeral, and the events that followed, Warren was forced to agree.

So, I'm probably stuck here.

Being "stuck here," as you put it, isn't so bad. Look at it this way: You'll never be hungry. You'll never be tired. You'll never feel any pain, at least in the physical sense. Emotions can be dreadful. The Lady's a prime example. But if you can keep your head about you while everyone else is losing theirs... Pardon me. It's been so long since I've been able to talk to someone who wasn't insane... I'll try to keep the bad jokes to myself. I have to tell you, there's very little by way of downside.

And what would that little bit be? asked Warren.

The downside is the fact you'll eventually have to deal with some of the darker souls. For example, there's Theodore Durrant. They called him The Demon of the Belfry back in the late eighteen hundreds. He raped and strangled two women for finding him unattractive, then left their bodies in the bell tower and library of the Emanuel Baptist Church. They hanged him on Alcatraz Island in 1898 and he's been prowling the city ever since. Although he mostly has it in for women, he can make your existence a living hell if you get on his wrong side.

The spirit enumerated several other ghosts Warren needed to avoid, before he ended the list with someone called Magnus.

Magnus what?

I don't know his last name. All I know is he committed a laundry list of crimes before his execution. The best advice I can give is to simply avoid him at all costs.

That isn't very encouraging, said Warren.

If you do your best to avoid them, Magnus and the others, they won't come looking after you.

And how will I do that? I was barely aware of you until just before we met and I haven't sensed anyone else.

That does pose a problem. You came directly at me twice today, so I simply assumed you wanted to meet me.

Warren shook his head. Then, realizing the spirit might

not be aware of the gesture, he said, *No. I ran into you strictly by accident. I wasn't aware of you until you spoke to me. By the way, what do I call you?*

My name is Bertrand. Bertrand Tolliver. And you are... ?

Warren. He started to tell Bertrand his surname, then thought better of it. As nice as Bertrand appeared, he was still an unknown quantity and Warren didn't want to give him any more information than necessary. He was about to ask something more about how to materialize, when Bertrand gasped. *We need to leave this place. Something evil is coming.*

Can we meet again?

Tomorrow, perhaps.

How will I find you?

Saints Peter and Paul's Church is generally safe. Meet me there in the morning, day after tomorrow.

All at once, Warren knew he was alone. He couldn't say why and he couldn't detect what might be coming. But believing what his newfound friend had told him, he decided he didn't want to find out the hard way. As for what he should do until then, since Jordan was going to need surgery, Warren decided to drop by the firm and learn what had happened to him.

15

Nancy dropped the phone and grabbed her purse and car keys. She dashed out of the house, failing to notice that the landline's receiver had cracked when it struck the Saltillo tiles.

What should have been a half hour drive to the California Pacific Davies Medical Center took longer than she expected. A CalTrans construction project on the Golden Gate Bridge forced southbound traffic into a single lane along the center span for nearly fifty yards, creating a backup through the Robin Williams Tunnel that extended as far north as Rodeo Drive. She swore when she was forced to stop and banged the steering wheel with the palms of her hands. Refusing to submit, she squeezed the Mercedes into the space an inattentive driver had left open. She repeated that tactic, striving for every extra yard she could manage until she was able to breeze through the toll booths with the aid of her FasTrack electronic pass. Roughly ninety minutes after she had departed, she turned into the hospital's parking lot, swung into the nearest space available, and made her way to the lobby where she found Sabrina waiting.

"Why did they bring him *here*?" she demanded. "There are at least two other hospitals closer to the office."

Sabrina described the damage that had been done to Jordan's hands, explaining, "It was a good decision. Some of the finest hand surgeons in the world practice here." She went on to explain how one microsurgeon had repaired the hand of a youth who had been injured on a farm north of Novato. "A piece of equipment tore off his thumb. His father panicked and drove the boy to the hospital without thinking to bring it with him. Without a thumb, that hand would have been almost useless. In an act of genius, the surgeon removed one of the boy's big toes and fashioned it into a functioning, opposable digit. Almost complete nerve reconnections and one hundred percent tissue compatibility. The doctor was skilled enough and creative enough to work out a solution to a problem that might have baffled most other surgeons. *That's* why Jordan is here."

Nancy sighed and her body visibly sagged. "When can I see him?"

"I expect the surgeons are going to be working on him for several more hours. Why don't you go to the cafeteria? Get something to eat. Food will help calm your nerves. You might even run into Michael. We both followed the ambulance. He probably got here about the same time I did. I'll join you later."

"Please come. I hardly know Michael and I really need you for moral support."

Sabrina shook her head. "I'm going to wait here until Brandi arrives. Trust me. You'll find that Michael is easy to talk to."

Although Nancy had committed herself to working with Brandi, she was still trying to reconcile her feelings about the affair and the importance of their working as a team. However, the thought of Brandi being in the same hospital room with Jordan made Nancy cringe. She suspected it must have shown, because Sabrina said, "She loves him too and I'm not going to play referee." Before Nancy could reply, Sabrina explained, "Look, I understand how their relationship must hurt, but that's not my problem. I'm going to be contacting the authorities in a matter of days and I need Brandi to help keep Jordan from leaving. If you want to help me, you're going to have to set your feelings aside because they're only going to make matters more complicated than they already are. I contacted everyone who might be concerned and told them where he was taken. If anyone gets wind that you have an issue with Brandi, it's going to raise the kind of questions that are likely to make Jordan's actions public and I can't afford for that to happen. All that people need to know is that Jordan was injured."

Nancy apologized. "I'm sorry. You're right, just as you were on Saturday. Please join us whenever you're ready." She started to leave, then glanced at her handbag. "I almost forgot. There's something I want you to see." She paused and added, "It would be better if it was just the two of us."

Sabrina nodded. "Of course."

… … … … …

When Sabrina entered the cafeteria, she found Nancy and Michael sitting with their heads together. She walked toward them, making her way between the mostly square white tables where several other visitors were either eating or chatting. She also noticed half a dozen hospital employees, readily identifiable by the various shades of their blue or green scrubs, sitting among them.

"The room was a bloody mess," Michael was saying when Sabrina arrived at the large, rectangular table where the two were sitting. "Chairs were scattered everywhere. Some of them were piled on top of the table and there were gouges where Jordan's hands had been." When Nancy looked surprised, he explained, "There were bloody palmprints by the gouges. It looked like several people had ganged up on him.

"This is the crazy part: the security footage showed no one entering before Jordan went in and no one leaving any time after that." Michael started shaking his head as he stared into space, as if trying to envision how any of that could have happened. "I asked our security administrator to review all of the footage from both cameras as far back as last night."

"It's almost as if his attackers were invisible," Nancy suggested. All at once, her words struck home and she turned toward Sabrina.

Sabrina returned her stare and nodded her understanding. Instead, she replied, "That's crazy," and left it at that.

"I know," said Michael. He shoved back his chair from the table and told them, "My blood sugar's low. I'm going to get something to eat. Can I bring you anything?"

Sabrina shook her head.

"Thanks, Hun," said Nancy. "Not right now I'll grab something once my nerves have settled. Take care of yourself."

As Michael made his way to the cafeteria's stainless steel counter, where racks of potato chips were hung beneath the tray slide, Nancy reached into her purse and produced a folded sheet of paper.

"I wanted you to see this," she said. Handing it over, she added, "I discovered this while I was cleaning out Jordan's desk. I don't know if you can use it, but it looks like a list of passwords."

Sabrina unfolded it and studied the document. "It certainly does and the items on the right look like abbreviations for various websites. It's too bad he didn't write them out. When Michael gets back, I'll see if he can decipher them."

Nancy frowned. "Why would you want to show this to Michael?"

Sabrina looked up and clenched her lips. "I probably shouldn't have said anything… " She hesitated, then admitted, "But Michael is the one who discovered what Jordan was up to." Returning her eyes to the paper, she said, "If some of these turn out to be websites and any of the passwords can unlock Jordan's bank accounts, then you might have given us a way to recover our clients' money."

"I see."

A few minutes later, Michael returned with his meal and placed what looked like a healthy version of a tostada salad—a crimped, toasted tortilla shell filled with rice, arugula, beets, shredded cheese, guacamole, salsa, and sliced jalapeño peppers—on the table.

Nancy looked at it askance and asked, "Nothing to raise your blood sugar?"

"Watching my weight. Ten or so years ago, I was developing a six pack. These days, I've been working on a keg and I'd like to get rid of it." He patted his belly and grinned. "There should be enough carbs in the salad and sugar in the dressing to do the trick."

After he'd finished eating, Sabrina produced the document and slid it toward him.

Michael raised his brows and asked, "What's this?"

"Nancy found it in Jordan's desk. We think it's a list of passwords and websites. I'm hoping they can take us to his bank accounts."

"It's possible," he said as he studied it.

"Do you think you can make sense of it?" asked Sabrina.

Michael cocked his head. "Maybe. I'll have to think about it. You're right, though. The letters in the left hand column do look like they might refer to websites," he said, pointing to indicate. He looked at Nancy and asked, "Do you mind if I make a copy?"

She shook her head. "You can keep it. I don't have any use for it."

He folded the paper and folded it again, then tucked it into his breast pocket.

"Did… ," Nancy began. "Did the doctor say anything about how bad Jordan's hands are? I mean, did they say whether he'd be able to use them again?"

"No," Michael replied. When Nancy frowned, he explained, "I'm not immediate family, so he couldn't disclose any details. Why don't you ask him when he comes out of the operating room?"

A woman's voice interrupted them. "Hi, guys!" They looked up to see Brandi threading her way between the tables that were now starting to fill. "Mind if I join you?"

"Why don't you take mine?" replied Nancy, smiling thinly as she back her chair.

"Are you sure?" Brandi asked. "I can take the empty one."

"I need to stretch my legs," she replied. Turning to Michael and Sabrina, Nancy said, "I hope my little contribution turns out to be what you think it is."

16

It wasn't until the next day that Nancy was finally able to visit Jordan. The surgery—the first of what was expected to be several procedures—had been long and involved and Jordan spent most of the time afterwards sleeping. Shortly after breakfast, she came into his room and found him sitting upright and watching the local news on the television.

Standing just inside the door, she asked, "How are you doing?"

At the sound of her voice, Jordan turned his head and looked at her. His eyebrows went up and he stared for a moment, then touched a finger to the remote and the TV screen went dark.

Nancy looked at the hand and asked, "Doesn't that hurt?"

"It's uncomfortable," he answered, "but they have me so doped up I can tolerate using it." He frowned and added, "Pressing the control button with my finger is about all I can do with it."

She glanced at the television and said, "I didn't mean to interrupt. If you'd like, I can come back later."

"You're fine," he assured. "I'm glad you showed up. To tell you the truth, I wasn't really able to focus on what I was watching. It's just something to pass the time." He managed a feeble smile, then said, "It's nice to see you. I wasn't expecting you to come. I… " He left the sentence unfinished.

Instead of addressing his comment, Nancy asked, "Do you mind if I sit?"

He shook his head. "No. Not at all." He gestured toward a chair and said, "I hope you can stay for a while."

Nancy pressed her lips together, then said, "Just for a minute." She paused, looking uncomfortable. "There's someone else who would also like to see you."

"Christ!" he exclaimed and looked at the ceiling. "You have to believe me. I never thought the thing through."

After a moment of awkward silence, she continued. "I came here to tell you I've boxed up the rest of your belongings. Since I guess you won't be picking them up any time soon, I'll probably rent a storage unit."

He sighed and admitted, "That's logical. Look, I… "

"Don't bother to apologize. I'm here because I still have some feelings for you and hate to see you injured like this. But you also have to understand that our marriage over." She paused, then wiped away a tear with the back her hand. "I'm torn between wanting to know why, after all these years, you'd want to do such a thing, and… " Her tone grew bitter. " …not giving a damn." She looked away and clenched her lips. "I'm sorry," she said. "That isn't the reason I came." She looked at his hands and asked, "Have they given you any idea if you'll be able to use them again? Sabrina and Michael told me how badly they were injured, bones poking through the skin and all."

Jordan nodded. "The surgeons are optimistic." Holding them up and turning them to show off the plaster that was covering the surgeon's work underneath, he said, "I hope they're right." Managing a smile, he added, "I don't expect I'll ever be able to play the piano again."

Nancy frowned. "You never played… "

"I'm sorry. Bad joke."

Her expression relaxed. "I suppose it's good you still have a sense of humor."

"They're saying it will take somewhere around three months for me to recover from this operation. Then, depending upon the results, they expect to follow it with one or two more. I'll always have some metal pins in my hands, so I'll probably have some trouble passing through airport security."

Nancy frowned at the intended humor and changed the subject. "Warren's told me what you did with all of the money. Really, Jordie? Is that the kind of man I married? Please don't tell me you still plan to go through with it."

Jordan's face darkened. "I don't know what you're talking about."

"Cut the crap! Yesterday I… " She cut short her comment in time to prevent herself from mentioning the document she had given to Michael. Instead, she asked, "Don't you have any regard for anyone else? Don't you care about your friends? They've put their trust in you, and now you're going to fuck them over? Christ, Jordie! Don't you have a heart?" She turned away for a second, then turned back and stared at him. "Does Brandi know what you're up to?" When he didn't answer, she said, "Well, that tells me everything. I pity the poor girl. First she had to deal with a drunkard for a husband. Now she's thrown in with a thief.

"All of a sudden, I'm not jealous anymore. I'm not hurt, either. Good riddance is all I can say."

With that, she pushed back her chair and stormed into

the hallway. On her way to the elevator, she passed Brandi.

"He's all yours, Hun," she said. "Good luck." She paused a second, then added without looking back, "You're going to need it."

She wasn't aware that Brandi stopped and stared, nor that she remained watching until the elevator's doors shut. All Nancy could think on the way down to the lobby was that she would do everything within her means, now that she had complete control of both her and Jordan's bank and investment accounts, to bring the man to justice.

··· ··· ··· ··· ···

Brandi peered into Jordan's room and saw him sitting upright, propped against a pillow, looking pensive and staring out the window to whatever lay beyond.

"Baby?"

He turned and smiled when he saw her. He sighed, as if he were releasing some burdensome thought, and said, "Hi, Sweetie. Man, you're good to see! Come here where I can look at you."

She hurried to his bedside and was starting to embrace him when her eyes fell on his hands. She stopped and stared.

"It's all right," Jordan assured her. Reaching out he explained, "We just have to be careful."

Taking care not to hurt him, she leaned over the railing and slid her arms around and under him. Then, as Jordan rose to meet her, she drew him close and pressed her lips against his. They kissed for several seconds until, with a sudden convulsion, Brandi broke down and sobbed. She lowered him carefully, making sure not to hurt him, then cried for several minutes. Once she was able to control herself, she brushed her hair from her face and wiped her eyes with a forearm. "I've been so worried," she told him.

"You had good reason to be," he said.

"How did it happen?" she asked. "Michael and Sabrina told me some ridiculous story about Warren and I almost believed them."

Jordan grimaced. "Did they now?"

She nodded and asked, "So tell me, what really happened?"

He stared into her eyes for several seconds, then replied to her question with one of his own. "And if I also told you it was Warren, what would you think of me?"

She cocked her head and stared back as Jordan responded with, "I'd like to tell you something different—that a disgruntled investor took out his frustration on me, or that some criminal did this—but, I'd be lying. You're going to eventually hear that the security cameras didn't show anyone coming or going, and… " He sighed. " …there is a reason."

"Warren," she said, almost inaudibly.

Jordan nodded, then affirmed, "Warren. I don't know how he did it, but he's returned from the grave and he's pissed off at me for God only knows why.

"Of course, that's not what I'm going to tell the doctors or the authorities, for that matter, if someone thought to file a police report. I'll probably say that someone I've never seen before broke into the office and attacked me for some unknown reason. If they ask about the security cameras, I'll probably suggest they malfunctioned. Unfortunate, but they'll have no other choice but to believe me. I'm certainly not going to tell them what actually happened. They'd put me in a nut house."

"But you think *I'll* believe you." Phrased as a statement, it sounded more like a question.

"I haven't a clue. I certainly hope so. If you don't, then you'll have to make up your mind whether you want to stay with me or not."

Brandi moved away from the bed and started pacing, avoiding Jordan's eyes. After a minute, she stopped and said, "Nancy and Sabrina came to my home right after I got out of the hospital. They told me you stole some of the firm's money, that Warren told them about it. They said that he wants you to pay for what you've done."

Jordan furrowed his brow and asked, "You don't believe them, do you?"

"About Warren or the money?"

"About the money, of course. Do you really think I would do that?"

"Right now, I don't know what to think," she admitted. "This is all very crazy."

"So, why are you here?" Jordan asked, and his voice had an edge to it. "If you think I'm some sort of criminal, why the *hell* are you wasting your time coming to see me?"

"Jordie… "

"If you're so goddamn sure I would do *anything* like that, then you can walk out that door right now," he said, pointing toward it.

Brandi clasped her hands in front of her and her knees started to buckle. "I'm sorry. Please forgive me. I didn't mean it like that. It's just that, now that my babies are dead, I don't know what to think about anything."

She started to cry again, so Jordan said, much softer now, "Come here, baby." Extending his arms, he told her, "I'm sorry, too." She returned to the bedside and leaned over the railing. She rested her head on his stomach and sobbed. Jordan

152

placed a hand on her head and said, "This is all very crazy. Between the drugs and what's happened to my hands, I'm not myself either.

"If you and I are going to make it, we have to remember how things were between us before all this shit happened. These are emotional times and we can't let our emotions get the better of us. I love you, and you have to believe it. You also have to believe what I tell you, or everything's going to fall apart." He sighed, then added, "Let's take it easy and forget all the poison the others have been putting into our heads. The only important thing is how we feel about each other, and the fact that, deep in our hearts, we know we can trust one another."

Brandi lifted her head and looked at him. "Then the thing about Warren… ?"

"Unfortunately, that part is true." He raised his hands again. "Here is the evidence. Everything else is hot air. Nancy is upset about our relationship, so I expect she'll say anything to drive a wedge between us."

"And Sabrina?"

"Nancy has probably poisoned her mind as well."

Brandi hugged him and said, "Thanks. I needed that."

"You're still planning to go away with me, aren't you?"

"Is that even possible?"

Jordan clenched his lips and nodded. "I'll find a way to make it happen."

17

Well, that didn't go as well as I would have liked, thought Jordan. He had almost spoiled whatever chance he had with Brandi by losing his temper and he was grateful she didn't leave when he told her to. After having engineered his plans so successfully, he realized how close he had come to throwing it all away just for the sake of some satisfaction over his need to be right. Granted, the damage Warren inflicted had left him physically damaged and on the ragged edge emotionally, but if he couldn't control himself any better than he had a few minutes earlier, it could cost him dearly and he resolved not to repeat it.

He examined his hands and the sight of them drove home his predicament. The surgeon had explained that the plaster casts and bandages encasing them would come off in another ten days, to be replaced by removable braces so he could bathe with assistance. He had strict orders not to try to grasp anything for the first two months, until the tendons had healed. Ongoing physical therapy would be followed by successive operations.

Jordan exhaled. He knew he could not afford to remain in the United States with the law closing in. He would need to contact Rebecca and ask her to conduct online searches for surgeons in multiple countries who were capable of continuing what this surgeon had started. Searching multiple countries would send investigators down several false trails. But since one of those trails had to be legitimate, it would eventually put the authorities hot on his heels—hopefully later than sooner. He had not anticipated adding this level of complexity to his getaway, but it had become unavoidable. Another problem was that he could not carry his or Brandi's luggage. Hell! He couldn't even open a door. The one redeeming element was that he had sufficient financial resources tucked away in his bank accounts to get around those obstacles, so maybe, he considered, he could complete his plans after all.

Hi, good buddy, said Warren, interrupting his reverie.

"You again. Haven't you done enough to me already?"

Oh, but I'm just getting started. You really upset Brandi, didn't you?

"How long have you been here?"

Long enough to hear you lie to her. How long do you think her love's going to last once she finds out what a bastard you are?

"You're a great one to give advice."

Watch out, or I'll find some way to fuck with the two of you.

"Your fucking things up is the reason we got together in the first place."

A nurse stuck her head through the door and asked, "Are you all right, Mister Weeks?"

"I'm fine, Nurse. I just got bored lying here with nothing to do and started talking to myself."

"Would you like me to turn on the TV, or maybe give you something to help you sleep?"

Relieved by her interruption, and at the same time

irritated that the world wouldn't leave him alone, he said, "No, thank you. I'll just lie here and vegetate, if you don't mind."

"Not at all, Mister Weeks. But while I'm here, let me examine your chart."

"Fine by me," he said and sat back while she went about her business.

Once she was gone, he told Warren, "I suppose you're still here."

Not for long. I have better things to do. I just thought I'd drop by and check out my handiwork. Make sure you're still alive but incapacitated.

Jordan had no desire to inform his ex-partner about the scheme he was hatching to leave the country as close to his original schedule as he possibly could. *Wealthy invalids everywhere hire people to help them get around, to take care of their needs*, he told himself, *so why shouldn't I?* Buoyed by the knowledge that he could short-circuit Warren's intentions, he settled onto the pillow and began working out the details.

… … … … …

Directly to the north across Filbert street, stood cathedral-like Saints Peter and Paul's Church with its rosette window and crucifix-topped twin spires. A group of Chinese women were practicing tai chi in Washington Square while North Beach's pedestrian and vehicular traffic was settling into its post commute level of activity. As Warren waited for Bertrand Tolliver to appear, he watched the women exercise, admiring their graceful and practiced movements and enjoying the morning's tranquility.

Bertrand was running later than Warren expected, so his focus started to drift. At one point, a distant white flicker in the sky caught his attention, then vanished. He was about to dismiss it as something imaginary when, a few seconds later, it reappeared closer than before. He realized it was assuming the outline of a person and seemed to be approaching at a high rate of speed. Alarmed, he attempted to get out of its path, but the form collided into him, if such a word as "collide" could be applied to an immaterial being such as Warren.

What are you doing here? the thing demanded. *This is _my_ church!*

Before Warren could react, he found himself lifted skyward, high enough that the streets spread out like a three dimensional map. The presence buffeted him, sending him back and forth in all directions.

How dare you intrude? it cried.

Helpless and terrified, unable to defend himself, Warren tried to escape, but found he could not. He was wondering what was happening and what he had done to provoke such an attack when a second presence collided with first one. Freed by the impact, Warren watched as the two specters grappled, hammering at each other with fists before tearing into each other with claws larger than any living animal's. Mouths opened and fangs appeared. What initially had looked like two human beings, now assumed the forms of two grotesque beasts, acquiring horns and tails, then a row of large triangular scales along their spines. Legs wrapped around bodies and fangs bit into necks. When Warren happened to glance at Washington Square, he saw that the people below seemed oblivious to the battle that was raging only yards above the treetops.

Afraid to keep his attention diverted for too long, lest the battle move in his direction, Warren was relieved to see that the entity who attacked him was starting to recoil from the second one's attacks. All at once, as quickly as it had appeared, the first specter broke free and fled into the distance, soon becoming a white fleck in the blue morning sky before disappearing altogether.

Tolliver's voice interrupted Warren's reverie. *That was certainly unexpected,* Tolliver panted.

Warren whirled and saw the remaining monster transform into the shape of a middle aged man, possibly in his late thirties or early forties. His hair was thinning and his belly was starting to paunch.

Bertrand? gasped Warren.

At your service.

What... What just happened? Warren asked. *What was that... er... thing?*

That was someone who associates his demise with the Roman Catholic Church, Tolliver replied, *and with this building in particular,* he added, inclining his head in the direction of nearby Saints Peter and Paul's.

But you said this place is safe, said Warren. *The church, I mean.*

Generally speaking, it is.

Generally speaking? replied Warren. *What does that mean?*

In a reassuring tone, Bertrand explained, *The world is a dangerous place. When you were alive, you had to deal with traffic accidents, murders, and fatal diseases. And while they always posed a threat, most of the time they wouldn't have affected you. It's the same way now, but newer dangers have taken their place.*

Like eternal damnation, Warren suggested.

Well, yes and no. Being condemned to remain in this world, without any hope of ever returning to the Tunnel of Light could be viewed as one form of damnation. Although certain spirits have disappeared from time to time and never reappeared, one might conclude that they did, in fact, return to the Light.

You said that the last time we spoke. I'm still bothered by what you told me… that nobody knows for certain where they had gone.

How is that any different from when you were alive?

What do you mean? asked Warren, not at all sure he liked what he was hearing.

People died, didn't they?

Of course they did.

And no one knew what happened to them once they were gone?

No, conceded Warren.

So did you live in constant fear of what would happen to you, once you were gone?

Of course not.

So I don't see what the problem is.

Warren sighed. *I guess you're right, since you put it like that.* Considering how to broach his next question, he decided to ease into it. *Something else concerns me. The day before yesterday, you said this place is safe. That suggests that certain places are dangerous.*

The afterlife does indeed have certain dangers, like what happened just now, but they're all understandable, said Bertrand. *They are the direct result of what happened to the spirits in their previous lives.*

Like the Lady, Warren suggested.

Like the Lady, Bertrand agreed.

160

Does that explain what happened now?

Indeed it does. In the early nineteen twenties, when Saints Peter and Paul's was under construction, a group of terrorists set off a series of dynamite blasts, trying to destroy it. When the police arrived in time to prevent another explosion, they shot and killed a member of the group its associates called Ricca. And while Ricca has appeared from time to time, he has never threatened anyone... until now. I can't explain why he's taken such a disliking to you. You weren't a priest in your former life, were you?

Surprised by the question, Warren replied, *No. Why would you ask me that?*

Since Ricca seemed to have it in for the Catholic Church, I'm trying to form a connection between you and the Holy See. Whatever the reason, he certainly doesn't like you.

Bertrand's tale troubled Warren. Until this very moment, he had believed he was the next best thing to God Almighty. He had felt invincible, almost omnipotent. Just by thinking about it, he was able to appear anywhere he chose. Nothing, he believed, could harm him. Now, he was anything but sure of either himself or his surroundings. This morning's event had left him shaken and afraid because of Bertrand's description of threats by various entities Warren could not perceive.

Why can I see you now when I couldn't earlier? Warren asked.

You're coming into yourself. You're acquiring new skills, Bertrand explained. It's like when you were a child. *As each day passes, you're able to do something you couldn't have done the day before. There's so much more lying ahead that you still don't understand—like what just happened now—at least, not for the present. I don't mean to offend you, but using the same analogy, you're like a child who asks questions whose answers he's not ready to receive.*

In fact, Warren's initial reaction had indeed been to take offense, until he remembered his earliest attempts at performing tasks he now considered simple. The world to which he had returned, while seemingly familiar, was both strange and daunting. Things in his former life that would have been easy to perform, were suddenly impossible, while the heretofore impossible was delightfully easy. He resolved to do what he did best in his previous life: he would be patient as he worked through whatever problems he encountered, glad that he now had someone to explain them.

Another question arose.

Why me? When Bertrand furrowed his bow, Warren repeated. *Why me? Why did you decide to help me, a total stranger?*

Hah! laughed Bertrand, before the joy in his voice vanished. *You haven't become dangerous yet, at least not that I can see. Just like you, I am alone here. I prevailed against Ricca…* his voice darkened… *this time. There may come a time when I cannot. I need a friend who will help me when I am in danger, the same way I protected you now.*

Startled by the implications of Bertrand's declaration, Warren asked, *Do you believe I will ever become someone like Ricca? For that matter, will you ever pose a danger to me?* He paused when another troubling thought arose. *We're dead, Bertrand. How can anything harm us?*

In a somber tone, Bertrand replied, *The world you knew in your previous existence grounded you and kept you sane. There were enough reinforcements to your mental stability because you, like everyone else, mirror your environment.*

When Warren furrowed his brow and looked at him

askance, Bertrand explained, *Let me give you an example.*

In the late nineteen seventies, Bay Area resident, Patricia Hearst, daughter of the newspaper tycoon, Randolph Hearst, was an ordinary rich girl living an ordinary rich girl's life until a terrorist group called the Symbionese Liberation Army kidnapped her and held her hostage. They raped her and tortured her until, after weeks of captivity, she eventually identified with her kidnappers. She did so, because following the path of least resistance—in other words, mirroring her environment, rather than fighting it—helped keep her sane. So much so that, at one point, when the SLA robbed the Sunset District branch of the Hibernia Bank on Noriega Street, surveillance footage showed Patricia clad in a khaki, military style uniform, a black beret, and holding an automatic rifle as she guarded the bank's entrance. Eventually, the members of the SLA were shot and killed in an FBI shootout. After conducting a lengthy crime spree of her own, Patty was eventually taken into custody. She was tried for bank robbery and sentenced to thirty-five years in prison. President Jimmy Carter commuted her sentence and she was eventually pardoned by Bill Clinton, after which she returned to her previous lifestyle, which she has maintained ever since, once again mirroring her environment as we all do.

Consequently, because you and I live in a world where all the ones like us are crazy and dangerous, we run a serious risk of becoming like them. I'm hoping you and I can provide enough mutual reinforcement that we will maintain our sanity and, more important, our civility.

How do you explain people whose actions run against the majority? asked Warren.

I can't. I'm not a sociologist, so perhaps my theory is flawed. I guess I've managed to remain as I am because of my previous life. My existence as a homosexual male ran contrary to what society expected. To do that, I had to be strong. I have to be strong now, if I'm going to retain my sanity. I'm just not sure I can remain strong enough forever. That's why I reached out to you.

Unsettled by Bertrand's revelations, Warren left Washington Square to ponder their implications. Their conversation lingered as Warren dwelt on how uncivil he had already become. Deeply disturbed and lost in thought, he wandered over San Francisco's downtown, past 555 California Street—what used to be called the Bank of America Center—around the Transamerica Pyramid to ever loftier heights, eventually circling Salesforce Tower with no other thoughts than to see the city's lights spread out beneath him and to distance himself from the living, breathing population of this place he had previously known so well. No longer a part of it and now out of his element, he wondered if he had made a mistake by returning to Earth. He had to ask himself if, once he had accomplished all of his intended tasks, was he truly stranded, destined to remain forever apart from his children and the ones he loved? His conversation with Bertrand Tolliver seemed to suggest it. In fact, the revenge he intended to exact on Jordan and Brandi and the rest seemed hollow if the way back to the Light became forever unattainable. If that were the case, what would he do then? He couldn't imagine an existence as a purposeless phantasm, destined to haunt the places he had known while never being part of them. Yet what other alternatives were there? Doomed to explore the world as an observer, never as a participant, what joy would there be in, say, a visit to Paris if its culinary delights were beyond his reach? Purchasing anything in Tokyo's Ginza district, or another city's marketplaces would be impossible. So what about visiting parts of the world that many of the living dream about? Climbing Mount Everest was all about the journey. Once at the summit, his enjoyment of the view would be short lived at best. Part of the attraction of a boat trip up the Amazon was, in large part, sharing the sights and sounds with one's companions, friends he would never have. In fact, most of the things people found enjoyable were largely attractive because of the difficulty of obtaining them. Since he could go anywhere by simply willing it, he realized the joy of visiting these places would not endure after years, or even centuries, in a world he could never again call home.

18

It was the kind of night Warren used to relish: warm enough for strollers to dress in shirt sleeves and a clear, starry sky with a full moon to illuminate the world beneath it. His mind drifted back to another one like it a few years earlier, when a friend who, in his Santana 22—a beamy little racing sloop that took off like a rabbit at the slightest hint of a breeze—took Warren and two other friends for a moonlight sail. After gliding past the San Francisco skyline with its skyscrapers' windows glowing like fireflies against the darkening sky, they crossed over to the Olympic Circle where they tied up at the Berkeley yacht club, then marched to an elegant restaurant that was perched at the end of a neighboring pier. Although the four were dressed in the waterproof, yellow, foul weather gear that sailors habitually wear on San Francisco Bay, the restaurant's host conducted them to a table at the dining room's center where they attracted the attention of the fashionably attired. They all ate it up, grinning like schoolboys who had stolen the contents of their parents' cookie jar, because they knew it was the height of envy to be able to sail here, rather than drive as the rest of the diners had done. Warren knew he would never experience anything like it ever again because now, unable to feel the air's temperature or the wind blowing past, he felt like a spectator encased in glass.

If that wasn't depressing enough, with each passing day, Warren's preoccupation with Brandi continued to grow.

He hung around her house as a way to be close to her. As he waited for Jordan to recuperate, he found himself continually peering in. He watch her bathe, then towel herself dry, before deciding what to wear. He watched the movement of her lips as she savored the food Jessica had prepared for her, wishing he could taste those lips again. His fixation was less about her relationship with Jordan than his personal failure to keep Brandi as his own. He knew it was his addiction to alcohol, coupled with his inability to master it, that had driven her away. As far back as he could remember, he had always been in charge of his life. But whenever this inanimate substance beckoned, he answered, and his lack of control tore at him. Alcohol had become the focus of all his activities. Toward the end, there hadn't been a minute in which the thought of having a drink didn't pop into his mind. It had cost him not only his free will, his honor and dignity, it had also cost him his wife and children. Now that he thought about it from a less selfish point of view, it had also cost his children their chance to grow into the wonderful people he knew they would have become, given half a chance.

The thought of alcohol as a drug turned his mind to another kind of substance and the trio shooting up in an alley. Those were the murderers who had put him here. Something had to be done about them and he decided it had to happen now. If he had a fist, he would have pounded it on the rooftop where he was perched. Failing that, he decided to see how much pain he could inflict on the trio and how he could prolong their suffering.

Willing himself once more to the Tenderloin district, Warren started to search. Since he had already been inside each of their heads, he was now able to recognize their thoughts and separate them from the others around them, the way a friend's voice often stands out from among the other guests at a party.

The first one he noticed was Carlos, the most inebriated of the three on that previous occasion. He was now in a dingy, two room apartment with bed sheets draping the windows in an extended stay hotel on Eddy Street. Faded brown wall paper, curling at the edges and printed with what might have once been a floral pattern, revealed the green painted plaster hidden underneath. A layer of smoke hung across the room in which a gaunt, pale skinned man, probably in his late 20s, dressed in a sagging undershirt and dark gray trousers, was sitting on a broken down tan sofa. Deprived of his olfactory sense, Warren was unable to determine the contents of the hand-rolled cigarette the man was holding. Although he suspected, from the way the man pinched it between his thumb and forefinger, that it probably was marijuana.

"No fucking way," the man was telling Carlos as he exhaled. "Cash up front or you're shit outta luck."

"Hey, man. You know I'm good for it," Carlos replied, then pleaded, "But times are tough."

"Do I look like I'm Donald Fucking Trump? Come up with the money or get out of my face."

Amused by Carlos's predicament, Warren decided to toss in something unexpected.

Having problems are we, Carlos?

The intrusion snapped Carlos's head around. Eyes wide and mouth agape, his knees bent and threatened to betray him as he glanced around in search of the one who had spoken.

Sucking air around the joint he was holding, the man on the couch grinned as he asked, "Hey, dude. Are you trippin'?"

"No, man," Carlos gasped as he started to cower. Palms outward, as if he were trying to protect himself, Carlos insisted, "It's a spook. Don't you hear him?"

The man on the couch started to laugh, but coughed instead, reacting to the smoke he was trying to keep inside. "Dude, you're cracking me up," he croaked as he began to recover. "You're totally paranoid. Are you sure you're not high?"

"Man, I'm telling you, it's a spook."

"You're nuts."

When Carlos shook his head, Warren asked, *Shall we show him?*

"What do you mean?" Carlos whimpered, an instant before Warren lifted him from the floor and slammed him into the wall beside the smoker. Carlos shrieked and Warren released him. He slid to the floor, crying out again when he landed hard beside a stack of pornographic magazines.

"What the fuck!" the man shouted and tossed the reefer aside as he scrambled to the armrest farthest from Carlos. He failed to notice that it landed on an exposed section of stuffing.

Carlos stared at him, pleading with his eyes and responding in a whisper. "Jus' what I told you. It's a spook."

What did you do to my daughter? demanded Warren.

Carlos glanced around frantically, trying to determine where the voice was coming from. "What d'you mean?"

Just before that son of a bitch killed me, my daughter was screaming. What did you do that made her scream?

"I didn't do nothing."

LIAR!

"Honest, man. I… "

Tell me what you did or I'll make you wish you were

dead.

Carlos thought for a moment, then replied, "It was Kevin. He's always been talking about how he likes doing little girls, so he started messing with her. Y'know, with his hand 'n' shit."

And you just <u>watched</u> him?

"What did you expect me to do?" Carlos answered as his eyes searched for the one who was grilling him. "I had to keep you under control. If you want to blame anyone, blame Robert. He was the one who started feeling up your wife."

He <u>what</u>?

"He put a knife to her throat so he could do what he wanted, but she wouldn't have none of it. She started screaming, so Robert panicked and he cut her."

Looking around, but seeing only Carlos, the man on the couch started to lower himself. "Who the fuck are you talking to?" he asked.

You chicken shit son of a bitch! shouted Warren. *I'm going to throw you out the window.* Then, seeing the stuffing starting to smolder, he calmed himself. *On second thought, I have a better idea.*

The man on the couch noticed it, too. "Holy fuck!" he cried. He leapt from the sofa and ran to the adjoining room, reappearing a few seconds later with a glass of water.

Warren moved an end table into his path and the man ran into it. Unable to change direction or adjust his step, he toppled forward, his hand lost its grip, and the tumbler shattered against a wall, showering the floor with water and shards of glass. Barefoot and off balance, the man landed where the fragments were. He cried out when he landed on one, then cried again when he attempted to rise. Lifting one knee, he plucked out a bloody triangle. He looked at it, then flung it aside. Remembering why he had come from the kitchen, he glanced up and saw the flames that were forming.

"Holy shit!" he cried.

He climbed to his feet, then, removing another piece of glass from his foot, he dashed back to the kitchen.

"I gotta go," said Carlos.

I don't think so, Warren replied.

When Carlos started heading for the door, Warren lifted him and hurled him once more into the wall. Carlos rebounded, landing upright, and grabbed his arm.

"I think you broke it," he cried, doubling over and grasping his shoulder. He looked toward the exit door, then back at the flames. Seeing that the coach was largely engulfed, Carlos begged, "Man, please. I really gotta go. If I stay…"

Yes. I know. You will die.

Just then, the man reappeared, wearing a pair of unlaced sneakers and trying to pull a jacket over his shoulders. When he raised his eyes, he noticed the flames and halted. They were licking at the ceiling and the section of carpet between him and the door had also started to catch. He tightened his mouth and frowned, then started running toward the exit… before he ran into resistance.

"What the…"

Warren lifted him and threw him next to Carlos. While Warren didn't hold a particular grudge against this one, he decided he didn't much care for him either. The man gasped when he landed. He tried to stay upright, almost losing his footing as he bumped into Carlos. One arm was still halfway into a sleeve, and now he couldn't extract it. He started to complain, but coughed due to the spreading layer of smoke and gasped, "We need to get out of here."

"We can't, man. He won't let us."

The man stared at him and demanded, "You crazy?"

"No, man. It's like I was sayin'. It's the spook. He won't let us leave."

The man looked toward the way out of the apartment and saw that the flames had become an impenetrable wall. Putting both hands to his head, he blurted, "I almost forgot! There's a fire escape." He went to a window and began struggling with the latch. He turned back to Carlos as he started to panic. "It won't budge."

Carlos ran next to him and tore off one of his shoes. Looking at what was rapidly developing into an inferno he shouted, "Get back!"

The man did as he was instructed and Carlos, covering his eyes with a forearm, swung at the window with all of the force he could muster. The glass shattered. When the man came forward and started to climb through, Carlos said, "Wait a second," and started using his shoe to clear away whatever shards remained stuck in the sill.

"That's good enough," the man said after a few seconds. "Let's get outta here." He peered through the opening and look down. "This is the one," he confirmed and began to step through. Abruptly, he flew forward, shrieking as he sailed into space.

Like the man said, Warren remarked. *He's outta here.*

Moving back from the window, Carlos demanded, "Man, did you have to do that?"

Warren laughed and said, *That's the kind of guy I am. Then again, you really didn't like him that much, did you?*

"No, man. But… "

Are you ready to meet your maker?

Carlos looked at the window. "I can't die like that."

I'm not planning to do that to you.

"So you'll let me climb down the fire escape?"

I'm sorry, but no. I have a better idea.

Carlos must have realized what Warren intended, because faced with the glowing furnace on his right, he started running for the window. A blow to his midsection hurled him away and into the center of the room. Landing hard, he shrieked and started to sob as he grabbed at the arm Warren had injured only moments before. There was a loud pop, as the resins in something made of wood exploded and Carlos jerked his head toward it. Warren could barely distinguish the sofa's outline through the engulfing flames, and he knew Carlos couldn't either.

Eyes wide, Carlos pleaded, "I can't stay here."

Oh, but you must.

"Please, man," he begged, his sobs turning into great, heaving convulsions.

'Please?' Warren asked, unable to conceal the glee he was feeling. *Wasn't that what my children said when they were begging for their lives?*

Carlos nodded vigorously. "C'mon, man. Ya gotta let me go."

I can't do that.

"I'm sorry, man," he screamed as the heat started searing his flesh. "Ya gotta believe me. I'm real sorry. I won't never do it again."

That's good, Carlos. Real good. It warms my heart that you're finally repentant.

19

Warren went into the night. Still caught up with what he had done to Carlos, he was unaware of the sirens approaching, unaware of the fate of the others who lived in that extended stay hotel, especially those now trapped on the floors above the rising flames. His only concern was finding Kevin.

It didn't take long. He found him in the same alley as before, crouching behind the row of garbage cans. But unlike the last time, Kevin was alone, gripping one end of the tourniquet between his teeth and the other end with his left hand as he depressed the plunger with his right.

Warren came close and said, *Feels good, doesn't it?*

Kevin's head came up and his teeth released the belt. He glanced toward the street and the space behind him.

Does it make you feel good the way a little girl does?

Kevin withdrew the needle and sighed. As the drug started taking effect, the hand holding the syringe fell onto his knee and opened. The device dangled from his fingers for an instant, then dropped onto the asphalt and rolled away, before coming to a stop. His eyes glazed over and he smiled.

"Yeah," he admitted. "Kinda."

When his eyelids started drooping, Warren shouted,

WAKE UP, GODDAM IT!

Kevin's entire body tensed and his eyes came open. Placing both hands on the pavement, he struggled to sit upright.

That's better, said Warren. *I want you to appreciate what I intend to do to you… as limited as that appreciation's going to be.* He was more than a little disappointed that his handiwork would likely not provide as much pain as he wanted due to the narcotic, but no matter. He would do it anyway.

"Who are you?" Kevin slurred.

Warren ignored the question, responding instead with one of his own. *Do you remember that night on Ellis Street when you molested a little girl while one of your friends kept her father from stopping you?*

Kevin grinned and nodded.

I've been wondering, Warren continued. *What happened to the little boy while you were playing with his sister?*

Kevin chuckled, "That was easy. I held him with my other hand." He chuckled again. "He thought he was tough. But I showed him he wasn't strong enough to do anything about it. It wasn't hard." Kevin's mouth tightened and his voice grew angry. "Except when the little bastard bit me. Then I showed him what I could do with my fist and he started crying like a baby."

Warren bit back his anger and struggled to control himself. If he was going to do this properly, he needed to remain calm enough to calculate what his next actions should be. And because the narcotic would dull Kevin's senses, he needed to be certain that what was to follow was as excruciating as possible, and that would require thoughtful calculation.

176

You're pretty tough, aren't you?

Kevin clenched his lips and the corners of his mouth turned down. "Baddest ass in the neighborhood."

Tougher than Robert?

"That pussy? Shit! He can't do anything without at least two other dudes to help him."

Is that why you and Carlos were there?

"Fuckin' A." Kevin rubbed his face with his hands and said, "If he didn't have a solid connection, I'd 'a' been someplace else."

Like at Carlos's friend's on Eddy?

Kevin snorted. "Yeah. Right. Like if I wanted something that'd been stomped on. I wouldn't be surprised if he cuts some of his shit with Drano. The dude's such a crook he… "

Let's get back on track. I believe we were talking about you.

Kevin stopped speaking, but his mouth remained open. Warren suspected he wouldn't be able to hold the addict's attention forever, since the attempt to goad him had taken him down a different path from the one he had intended. Hoping to obtain a full admission of guilt, he tried a different approach.

That little girl wasn't the first one you diddled, was she?

Kevin appeared to be nodding off, but this question brought him back to the present. He smiled and cocked his head, as if remembering.

Care to tell me about it?

"Too hard. There were so many."

How many, would you estimate? When Kevin furrowed his eyebrows, Warren prodded. *Go ahead. Take a wild guess.*

"Couple dozen, easy."

That many? I'm impressed.

Kevin boosted himself a little more upright and asked, "Do you want me to tell you about some of 'em?"

While Warren was encouraged that he had hit upon a subject that kept Kevin from sliding into unconsciousness, he was finding the topic increasingly distasteful.

Maybe another time. I'm curious, though, about what happened on Eddy Street. If you'll remember, I had my back turned, so I couldn't see what you were doing.

"You missed a lot." Kevin paused to think, then said, "While I was having fun with the kids, Robert starts feeling up your old lady." He chuckled. "That really pissed her off."

Which thing? What you or Robert were doing?

"Both, I think. But mostly me." Kevin giggled. "She starts coming after me, so Robert grabs her and puts his knife to her throat. That's when the bitch starts hollerin'. I see people comin' up the street an' I think Robert saw 'em too. We knew they would see us. That's when he tells us to cut 'n' run." Kevin started laughing. "Get it? Cut? Anyhow, we couldn't afford to stick around. So, Carlos did you, I guess. Robert finished your wife an' I finished the kids."

Fait accompli, thought Warren. *Now, to finish Kevin.*

Kevin laughed again. "This is weird. I'm talkin' to a dead guy."

Very astute.

Warren began studying his surroundings, looking for

something with which he might perform an execution, when he noticed a small, square mirror lying on the ground a few feet away. On it lay a tiny pile of white powder and a collapsible hunting knife was lying next to it. The knife, he felt, would be perfect for what he intended, but he didn't believe the skills he had thus far developed would permit him to open it. He decided to see if he could persuade Kevin to do it for him.

I see you got lucky.

"How's that?"

You scored half a gram of cocaine.

"Full gram," Kevin corrected. "I like the way it adds to the buzz."

That's pretty expensive stuff.

"Yeah. Especially when it's almost uncut like this shit."

How can you tell?

"You take a tiny bit an' drop it in a glass of water. If it all disappears, it's absolutely pure. There was only a little bit of something left over when I tested this batch just before I bought it, so I could tell it had only been cut just a little."

I see. I'm a little naïve about these things. Would you mind telling me how you... uh... how do you get it into your body? Do you shoot it up?

"Hah! No, dude. I snort it."

Do you think you could show me how?

"Sure. I was just about ready do to a couple'a lines."

Kevin, who had been sitting cross legged, put a hand on the asphalt, swung his legs out from under him and arrived in front of the mirror kneeling. Although he nearly fell forward when he reached for the hunting knife, he was able to extend a hand and place it on the ground to brace himself. When regained his balance and was again kneeling upright, he depressed the release on the hunting knife's handle and extended the blade with his other hand.

Is the knife sharp?

Kevin nodded and said, "My daddy taught me how to use a whetstone, and I always keep one in my pocket." His voice turned sour. "That's the only good thing that son of a bitch ever taught me." After a moment, his breathing calmed and he was starting to say in a more even tone, "What you need to do now is chop it up carefully… " He halted mid-sentence when Warren willed a gust of air to disperse the powder into a cloud that disappeared into the darkness.

"What the fuck!" shouted Kevin. He dropped the hunting knife and patted the ground around the polished glass square. He raised his head and whispered, "It's gone."

No shit, replied Warren.

Putting his plan into motion, Warren retrieved the knife and shoved Kevin face down onto the asphalt. He pressed the tip of the blade against Kevin's neck, firmly enough to draw blood. When Kevin cried out, Warren ordered, *Don't fucking move or you're a dead man*, the addict responded with a series of rapid nods. Before Kevin could do anything else, Warren turned the knife so the blade's edge was pointing upward, then ran it under the collar of Kevin's shirt.

Let's see how sharp it is, he said.

With that, he yanked it upward. When it successfully cut through the collar, he ran it edge upwards along Kevin's back, slitting the shirt all the way to his waist.

Attaboy, he said. *You weren't lying. You've done a great job maintaining it.*

He set down the knife, then tore the fabric apart. He regarded the exposed hairy back, replete with pimples, and added, *God, you're ugly.*

Warren picked up the knife again. This time, he turned the edge downward.

I won't lie, he told Kevin. *This next part is going to hurt like hell.*

He ran the blade from the bottom of Kevin's neck, a quarter of an inch deep, all the way to his waist. Kevin screamed and Warren made a similar horizontal cut from shoulder to shoulder inscribing a T. When Kevin drew his knees up, then placed his hands under his shoulders, preparing to run, Warren forced him down, then severed an ear.

Try that again and I'll cut off the other one. After that, I'll cut off your nose. Keep trying to run away from me and I'll mutilate you so badly even your mother won't recognize you... motherfucker.

"I'm sorry," cried Kevin.

That's what Carlos said, but it didn't save him. Tonight, you're going to pay for those things you and your buddies did on Eddy Street and I promise you this: if I decide not to kill you, you're going to wish that I did. So start saying your prayers, because tonight, live or die, you're going to Hell.

Warren began a leftward, horizontal slice just under the skin, starting where the T's vertical line ran into the crossbar. Then, because he had found that visualizing himself performing an act, as if he were still in a corporeal state, helped him do what he intended, he cut away a flap of skin large enough that he could have grabbed it. When he envisioned himself closing his hand around it, the flap buckled as if he were holding it. He was intending to tear it away, but when he attempted it, he found that the skin adhered to the underlying tissue. He decided to assist the act by continuing to undercut as he pulled, smiling as the flap of skin he created came away. *This is for Robbie*, he cried. With a jerk, he tore the skin to the left and downward, peeling it until he had exposed the underlying muscles and tendons.

Kevin screamed and started to rise. Then, covering his remaining ear, he dropped back and begged. "Please!" His body quaked as he broke into sobs. "I won't do it again."

Bet your ass you won't, Warren said, then sneered, *As if your ear is more important than the rest of you.* He made a similar incision into the remaining skin on the right side of Kevin's back. *This one's for Rebecca*, he cried as he tore away that flap as well.

Kevin's shrieks were now continuous. As blood began oozing, Warren flipped Kevin over. When the exposed muscles came into direct contact with the dirt and loose bits of rock overlying the pavement, Kevin howled, "Oh God! Please stop! Please stop! Please stop!"

Warren inserted the blade into the skin just above Kevin's sternum, level with the bottom of the collar bones. In a calm, even tone that Warren knew Kevin could still hear—words he was inserting directly into his thoughts—he stated calmly, *This is for me and Brandi.*

… … … … …

Drunk with his ability to inflict harm with impunity on those who had wronged him, Warren went searching for the trio's leader. The absence of Robert's thoughts in the neighborhood soon indicated he was elsewhere. And though Warren's passion gradually cooled, his determination to hurt the one who had refused to allow him and his family to pass without incident kept him searching in ever widening circles until he found him in a sports bar on Divisadero Street.

Although Robert's thoughts were loud and clear, he wasn't in the barroom where all of the red leather seats were occupied. Warren drifted through the late night partiers to the book-lined back room, where people were playing foosball and nine ball. A few seconds' search found Robert, decked out in a sportscoat and slacks, standing near a corner alcove beneath a spotlighted painting of palm trees. He was talking to a woman who appeared to be in her early forties, perhaps half a decade older than Robert. Her faded blonde hair sported an inch and a half of outgrowth and the dress she was wearing had seen better days. Another man, dressed in the same style as Robert, was handing the pair two mugs of beer and Robert began regaling his companions with some sort of tale.

"Chuck," Robert was saying, as he lifted the mug to his lips, "I was just telling Myra about a couple of really hot stocks."

Disinterested in hearing about what was probably a scam, Warren was wondering what he could do to Robert in a place packed with so many people who might come to his assistance. Disappointed that he could not exact the intended revenge, and deciding a better place and time would eventually present themselves, Warren passed through the brick wall beside them, satisfied by what he had thus far accomplished.

20

Early Monday morning, shortly after W&H Limited opened for business, Sabrina shoved the front doors open and strode past the reception desk.

" 'Morning, Sabrina," called Allan, as her heels resonated across the polished marble floor. "You're here earlier than usual."

She turned her head and tossed him a smile, offering no explanation. When the elevator opened onto the second floor, she spotted a crew of workmen replacing one of the conference room's windows. Not bothering to knock, she entered Michael's office and found him working on a spreadsheet. Lifting his hands from the keyboard, Michael pivoted his chair and smiled.

"I have some promising news," he told her. "Pull up a chair." Once she was sitting beside him, Michael toggled to a different spreadsheet that displayed three columns of characters. "I've transcribed some of the information from the paper Nancy gave you. The column on the left shows several possible websites. I haven't had time to confirm any of them yet, except this one," he said, gesturing toward a group of characters. "I Googled what I thought they represented and was given a link to a bank in the Seychelle Islands."

Sabrina asked, "What led you to that conclusion?"

"It started with a hunch." Michael opened one of the desk's doors, and took out a piece of paper. "This line's 'BW' reminded me of the private banking firm, Barnham and Whittelsby. A search showed me they do indeed have a branch there."

"Impressive."

"Dumb luck," he countered. "Their name came up in a conversation I had with a colleague a few days ago. I gave it a shot and… Voila!" He went on to explain, "Now that I have one possible lead, I'm studying the other character groupings."

Sabrina cocked her head and asked, "Since we already know that the Seychelles are where he's moved most, if not all of the money, why not simply Google 'Banks in the Seychelles' and see if that produces any other matches?"

Michael chuckled. "That was probably too simple for my complex mind. I'll get right on it."

"You've left a lot of the spaces blank," she noted.

"I haven't filled in all of them in yet, because I'm still trying to decipher Jordan's shorthand, but I'm reasonably sure of the ones I've filled in.

"The second column proved to be the easiest. It shows Jordan's user names. You'll see that most of them involve his email address. I thought he'd be smarter than that, but the fact that he isn't makes me reasonably confident that I'll be able to decipher the rest of the document, or, at least, most of it."

Sabrina shifted her eyes from the computer display to Michael. "You should be working for the FBI or CIA."

He smiled, then turned back and continued. "The third column shows Jordan's passwords. Most of the ones I've figured out contain references to various aspects of his life. Take this one."

He pointed to a line that read, Me&Nan4EVR$. Below it were cells that read, MeNNan4EVR$ and MeandNan4EVR$.

"These are the three most plausible combinations of characters I could infer from this line." He indicated an entry on the paper .

Sabrina snickered. "No mention of Brandi?"

He shook his head and said, "That's probably because he started setting up these accounts three years ago and he and Brandi have been an item for less than that."

She nodded.

Michael went on. "You'll also notice this line is complete: website, username and password. I was about to see if it worked."

"And…?"

"I'm a little nervous. Because if I'm wrong, I'm not sure how many false attempts I can make before it locks me out. In that case, the bank will email Jordan password reset instructions the first time he tries to login and finds that he cannot. He'll immediately understand that someone has tried to access it and he'll change the passwords on all of these websites, at which point, all of this information," he gestured toward the paper Nancy had given them, "is worthless."

"But you at least have to try," Sabrina prompted.

Michael nodded. "Yeah. I know." He propped his elbows on the armrests, interlaced his fingers, and rested his chin against them as he stared at the display. After another few seconds, he took in a breath, exhaled, and sat upright. "You're right. I have to try." He flexed his back and said, "Cross your fingers."

He launched his internet browser and pasted the Barnham and Whittelsby link, then hit Search. Almost immediately, the bank's website was in front of them. Michael amended the link by adding /login, hit Search again and the login screen appeared, requesting Jordan's username.

He turned and looked at her.

"Go on," she said.

Michael toggled to the spreadsheet application, copied Jordan's email address, then toggled back, pasted it into the appropriate field and clicked Submit.

"You should know Jordan's email address by now," she said, frowning. "Why not just type it?"

"Copying and pasting avoids typos."

She nodded.

The website took them to a second page that required him to enter Jordan's password. Moving rapidly between applications, Michael copied, then pasted the first password on the spreadsheet. But when he hit the Submit button, the website wouldn't accept it.

"That's one down," said Michael.

Sabrina nodded and said, "Try again." When Michael bit his lip and hesitated, she said, "One incorrect entry is normal. You know that as well as I do. Even a second false entry isn't likely to lock you out. People do it all the time."

"But a third one… "

"That hasn't happened yet. Which password do you want to try next?"

He switched to the other application and stared at the remaining possibilities. When he sat frozen, Sabrina said, "At this point, it doesn't matter which one you choose."

"But if I pick the wrong one… "

"Then you'll close the browser window and try again tomorrow."

"But… "

"And if you fail again, you'll start Googling other banks. If you find another candidate, confirm their website, and work on the password for that one." She touched his arm and said, "We're not in a hurry. If it takes you another few days… another week… "

"Jordan might leave the country by then," Michael fretted.

"That's right," she said. "You might not be able to crack any of them. In which case, we go back to Plan A."

"I thought this was Plan A."

Sabrina shook her head. "Plan A was notifying the SEC. Which is exactly what we're going to do next, whether or not Plan B is successful."

Michael, turned back to the computer, rocked in his chair for several seconds, then nodded. He reentered the earlier user name, then selected the next password combination, copied and pasted it and tested to see if it worked.

"Wow!" Sabrina exclaimed when the screen presented them with a series of bank accounts, each one of a different nature. She turned to see Michael gripping the armrests with his jaw hanging open.

"You've done it."

"Yeah," he whispered. Then, in a louder voice, he added, "Kinda cool, dontcha think?"

"Kinda cool," she repeated.

When Michael eventually turned to her, he asked, "What do you think we should do now?"

"I can think of a couple of possibilities."

"Such as… ?"

A knock, followed by the sound of someone manipulating the door latch brought Sabrina's head around. Out of the corner of her eye, she saw Michael moving quickly. The door swung open and Cameron, from the marketing department, poked his head inside. He was opening his mouth to speak when he noticed Sabrina.

"Hi, Sabrina," he said, then looked back to Michael, just as Michael was saying, "Except for Marin County."

His unexpected remark caused her to turn in his direction. She saw that the computer monitor now displayed the spreadsheet he had been working on when she first came in and Michael was pointing at row of numbers near the top. The spreadsheet was large enough that it took up the entire screen, effectively covering whatever windows might otherwise have been visible behind it.

Michael glanced at the newcomer. "Good morning, Cameron. What can I do for you?"

"Aaron just announced that he's calling for an emergency meeting in the boardroom at ten o'clock."

"That doesn't surprise me. Tell him I'll be there."

Cameron nodded, smiled briefly at Sabrina, then retreated into the lobby, pulling the door shut behind him.

Sabrina glanced back at Michael. "That was some quick thinking," she said. "But what was that comment about Marin County?"

"I didn't want us to look like two deer caught in the headlamps. Without knowing who was entering, or their relationship to Jordan, I had to say something that sounded like it related to the monitor display. Since Marin County's numbers were the third row from the top, it was the first thing that popped into my head."

"Pretty impressive," she said.

Michael brought the browser to the front and stared at the bank accounts. "Would you look at those totals?" he said.

"How much of our investors' money do you think they represent?"

"Somewhere between ten and fifteen percent would be my first guess."

"So the remaining banks… "

" … undoubtedly hold the balance," he finished for her.

Sabrina frowned. "Why wouldn't he just put it all in one place?"

"It's hard to say. My guess is that it's to prevent someone from doing exactly what you and I are attempting. A hostile party might take part of the money, but they probably wouldn't get all of it."

Sabrina sat back in her chair and said, "So, he's not so dumb after all."

"Either that, or he's simply paranoid," concluded Michael.

Sabrina nodded. "So what do we do, now that we're in?"

"You said you had a few thoughts on the matter," Michael reminded her.

"You're the money man," Sabrina countered. "I'd rather hear your ideas."

He thought for a minute, then said, "I'd like to keep a web archive, assuming the website will let me, in case we eventually lose access."

"I don't understand."

"If you ever want to preserve what's on a website at a particular moment," he said. "Go to your browser's File menu and select Save. All of the site's information on the page that you're viewing will be downloaded to your computer, assuming you have enough disk space.

"I intend to exercise the same sort of paranoia that Jordan did. Now that we've gained access, if, for whatever reason, we're locked out sometime in the future, we'll have a permanent record of at least this much detail."

"Great!" said Sabrina, "Then do it."

"The problem, for the moment, is where do we put it? If we save it to the firm's computer system, there's always the possibility that someone else will be able to access it."

"Including Jordan," she said.

"Exactly."

"So what do we do?"

"My first thought is to invest some of my own money into a brand new computer with a gigantic hard drive, then download everything here onto it."

Sabrina frowned and said, "But wouldn't that amount to theft?"

Michael nodded. "I'm no attorney. But my intuition tells me that once I've dumped this information onto my personal property, I can no longer prove that I'm working on the firm's behalf… "

" …or those of the investors."

"Yup," he agreed.

"So we're stuck."

"For the moment. The good part," said Michael, "is that, until Jordan changes his password, we can log in whenever we want. What I'd really like to do, assuming it's even possible, is to access all of Jordan's bank accounts, archive all the information to something that belongs to the firm… "

He broke off for a minute, then said, "If I can order a storage device, using the firm's money to purchase it, then find a way to install it without anyone else's knowledge, we can archive all of those websites onto that one, then encrypt it so that no one else can access it until we bring the SEC, or some other law enforcement agency, into the picture. Once we've preserved all that information, the next step would be to download all of the money Jordan has taken back to the firm's bank accounts. At that point, we can create new passwords that will deny Jordan the ability to ever steal it again… "

" … while preserving the evidence of his crime," Sabrina finished.

"Exactly. If we were to withdraw all of the money without having documented the evidence, we would still have the satisfaction of having thwarted Jordan's scheme, but he'd never see justice."

Sabrina grinned. "Can you do it?"

Michael nodded. "I think so. As the seniormost person in the accounting department, the LLC's Articles of Organization make me responsible for almost everything involving its finances. I believe that, if push comes to shove, I can present an argument that would justify the expense."

"So do we hold off going to the SEC?"

"For the moment. I think it would be wise to wait until we have everything else in place."

As Sabrina was rising to leave, she paused and asked, "What do you think the emergency meeting's about?"

"I suspect it's to decide what to do while Jordan's incapacitated."

21

What have you done?

Nothing.

Don't tell me "Nothing." What have you done?

I...

Your aura has changed. It's grown darker. You've done something awful. Tell me what you did.

After failing to deliver justice to Robert, Warren had returned to Washington Square where he hoped to locate his newfound friend and maybe gain insight as to how he could obtain eventual satisfaction. Finding him didn't take long and now Bertrand was confronting him with his crimes. Faced with these accusations, Warren wondered how he could describe the things he had done to Kevin, Carlos, and Carlos's friend, without going into all the gory details. In his past life, he had always been reluctant to own up to his flaws, like admitting he had a drinking problem——something minor when compared with these murders and the way he had committed them—even to Brandi, who had witnessed his drunkenness. Refusing to admit to his faults was one of Warren's two fatal flaws. The other was his quickness to anger. So, when Bertrand, who had until recently been a complete stranger, demanded that he recount his actions that would horrify all but the most insensitive, he found himself tongue-tied.

How can I trust you? Bertrand was saying. How can I count on you as a friend if you won't…

I avenged my children's murder.

Bertrand remained silent a moment before asking, *How were they murdered? Your children, I mean.*

Warren recounted the night on Eddy Street, sparing no detail about all the things Carlos and Kevin had done to them… as if their misdeeds would justify his own. He also described what had happened to Brandi and her subsequent condition.

They murdered you, as well, didn't they?

Yes.

I understand how tempting it is to seek justice, replied Bertrand. *On more than one occasion, I've considered finding the ones who murdered me and doing terrible things to them. The problem with seeking revenge is that, here, in the afterlife, your actions have long term consequences, and those consequences are the reasons the Lady and Magnus are stuck here. I don't want to find myself in their situation. My hope is to find my way back to the light as soon as the opportunity presents itself. You have already expressed the same intention, but now I'm worried you may have made your own return impossible.*

When Warren explained his reasons for having committed these deeds, Bertrand countered with, *Rail against it all you want. There's no court for you to turn to. I believe mankind invented the fantasy of standing before God in a final judgement as some sort of solace, some way to believe they will have any say in the matter. Unfortunately, no one does. You undoubtedly experienced what actually happens. You were drawn into the light, then made a decision to return to earth. Now that you've done so, every decision you make from*

196

that point forward determines whether or not you will be able to reverse that choice.

But… Warren began, but Bertrand would not be interrupted.

Murdering someone is a horrible act. There is little excuse, if any, that justifies it. You can rationalize all you want. Ultimately, however, how it impacts your future is beyond your control. All you can do now is hope that whatever extenuating circumstances might exist, will be sufficient to tip the balance in your favor. The only advice I can offer now is, be careful what you do from this point forward.

Let me ask you something, he said. *Are there any among the living whom you might help? Is there anything you can do to improve their situation?* As Warren paused to consider, Bertrand added, *I'd give it a great deal of thought if I were you, because helping the living is probably the only thing you can do that can improve your chances.*

Bertrand's statements shed new light on Warren's situation because, if what he said were true, whatever satisfaction he had hoped to obtain was now beyond his reach if he ever hoped to see his children again. The anger he felt for Robert would remain a thorn in his side, something that would prick him forever but something he could not remove. He wondered if he could learn to accept it. He also wondered if he could simply walk away from Jordan's and Brandi's betrayal as if it never had happened.

As for people he could help, the only ones who came to mind in his immediate circle were Sabrina and Nancy… and possibly Michael. He hoped that, given enough time, a few more names might come to him.

During the course of this conversation, Warren realized his perceptions were changing. He thought he caught his first glimpse of Bertrand out of the corner of his eye, but when he tried to look directly, the image vanished. Sidelong glances, however, revealed a man somewhat taller than he was and slightly overweight. He was unable to determine Bertrand's age, but Bertrand's voice indicated that he had been older than a teenager and not yet elderly at the time of his demise.

Shifting his thoughts to Bertrand, Warren asked, *What made you decide to return?*

Bertrand chuckled and said, *Anger. The same thing that brings everyone back. My life was perfect at the time I was killed. I'd started my own business—a small boutique—and it was doing well enough that I was about to open a second location. I had found a new lover, and it seemed as if it might turn into something permanent. My elderly parents had finally accepted who I am and for the first time in my life, my finances and all my relations were exactly what I wanted. He paused and the tone of his voice changed. Then that group of ASSHOLES came along and murdered me. They didn't know me. They didn't know anything about me except I was obviously gay.*

How could they tell? asked Warren.

Maybe it was the way I walked. From time to time, people commented on it. I tried to walk like a straight man. Heavens know I tried, but my body wouldn't cooperate. Maybe it was because my business was located at the edge of the Castro, even though, in the late 1960s, the district was still largely made up of white, middle class families and us gay folks had just started moving in. Anyway, one night after I had closed up shop and was walking to the Twin Peaks Tunnel, four teenagers surrounded me. They started pushing me and calling me "faggot" and lots of other obscene names. I tried to ignore them. I asked them to leave me alone, but they refused to stop.

At one point, I saw the trolley coming. The Muni wasn't using a light rail back then. I pushed one of them aside, hoping against hope that those punks would allow me to board. That was my fatal mistake… as if there was anything else I could have done that wouldn't upset them. They started shoving me back and forth between them, like I was some sort of ball and they were playing a game. The trolley pulled right up beside us and the doors opened. I needed to board it because it was probably the last one for several more hours. No one was exiting, so I know the operator had to have seen us. Then… Bertrand's voice cracked and Warren thought he sounded as if he was starting to cry *…the doors closed and the trolley started pulling away. I couldn't believe it. The man who was driving it had to have seen us. He just HAD to. But he left me there at the mercy of those thugs. There I was. On the platform, alone with the four of them. They started laughing and one of them punched me in the stomach. I doubled over and the rest of them started beating me. It went on and on and on until I lost consciousness.*

When I finally came to, I was floating in a… a void, I guess you could call it. You know what happened next. Probably the same thing happened to you. I couldn't go into the tunnel of Light. I couldn't just go inside and forget about what they'd done to me. I had to come back and…

The problem was, once I had been here awhile, I began to observe the other ones like me. I started to see what they had turned into. Someone else—she's gone now. Probably managed to go back—started telling me about all the other ones here. That's how I have some understanding of the way things are. And now I'm telling you. I'm hoping I can help you because, like I said, I'm afraid to be alone.

Warren said, *But they can't kill you.*

No, answered Bertrand. *But they can still do a great deal of damage. People aren't all that far off when they talk about Hell.*

Psychological damage, suggested Warren.

Not just psychological. It's not exactly physical either, Bertrand explained. *I don't know what you would call it, but I've seen one other… ghost, I guess you would say, who has been terribly damaged.* He released a curt laugh that Warren thought sounded as sad as when he had started to cry a few moments earlier. *I guess I've been trying to deny it. But, yes, that's what we are. Ghosts.*

Anyway, at one point, Magnus started injuring the one I was telling you about. He appeared to be doing real damage to the man's limbs. His arms and legs started looking broken and bent. I don't know how that's even possible considering… anyway, I don't want that sort of thing happening to me.

But now you're telling me about the revenge you were taking, Bertrand continued, *and I'm worried whether you're going to become like Magnus.*

I'm not a violent man, countered Warren, before he realized that, while that might have been true when he was alive, he couldn't say the same about himself now, so he amended his comment. *At least, not toward my friends. And I do consider you a friend.*

I suppose that should reassure me, replied Bertrand, *so, for the moment, I will accept your statement as genuine. You have to understand, though, it goes against my better judgement. It's only because I need someone who will help me the next time Magnus attacks that I consider it at all. I have to warn you, though, don't disappoint me or I promise you'll regret it.*

Are you threatening me? demanded Warren.

It's you my… Bertrand hesitated. *… friend, I suppose… who are threatening me. In the meanwhile, you*

*need to consider what you can do to improve your situation—
not only to increase your chances of seeing your children
again—but also because doing so will show me how genuine
you are.*

22

Let me know when to expect you, he typed, followed by, Regards, Jordan Weeks.

Just as he pressed the Send button, there was a knock at his door. He rotated his chair so it was facing away from the desk, then leaned forward and pressed against the armrests with his forearms in order to push himself to standing. When the peephole showed that his visitor was one of the hotel's bellmen, he used an elbow to press the door handle downward.

"You'll have open it yourself," Jordan called.

When the door swung open, the hotel employee cast a curious glance at Jordan's casts, then asked, "Where would you like me to put them?" He gestured toward the hallway and at a bell cart loaded with department store shopping bags.

"On the sofa, please," Jordan replied as he stepped aside to admit him.

Once inside, the bellman started unloading. Brandi followed shortly after, carrying two armloads of flowers.

"Hi, sweetie," she said, and planted a kiss on Jordan's cheek. "I think I got everything." When he cast a puzzled glance at the bouquets, she smiled and explained, "This suite needs a feminine touch." Turning toward the sitting room, she called to the bellman, "Can you please put the vases on the wet bar?"

He nodded, then retrieved two, large, etched glass vases from beneath one of the shopping bags that were still on the trolley and did as she requested. Brandi went to the adjacent dining area and set the bouquets on a table, not far from where she had indicated. Once the bellman had finished unloading, she handed him a tip.

"How's it going?" she asked Jordan as the bellman rolled the cart through the doorway and shut the door behind him.

"All right, I think. I hired an assistant and sent a confirming email just before you got here."

"And… ?"

"He's already indicated he could be here sometime next week. I asked him to let me know when he had a more definite ETA."

"What are his qualifications? I can take care of you to a certain extent, but if something happens… "

"Bryce is a trained EMT and, interestingly enough, he also works as a bodyguard. So I think he can handle just about anything that comes our way. Also," he added before Brandi could question him further, "there are three hospitals near where I expect to be staying."

"That's great! What about the reservations?"

"I was about to take care of them next. Hopefully, I can still arrange for first class airfare and a connecting suite in Hamilton."

"I can't wait to get away," she exclaimed. She threw her arms around him and Jordan was quick to spread his arms wide before she could complete the embrace. Brandi halted. "Oh my God! I almost… "

"You're fine," Jordan assured her, then drew her close while keeping hand contact to a minimum. He kissed her full on the mouth, savoring her taste and enjoying the physical contact.

When, at last, they were standing apart, Brandi asked with a wicked grin on her face, "Can we do anything else?"

He grinned and said, "I'm sure we can manage if we're careful. Although, for a while, you'll have to do most of the doing."

"Then, I'm going to have my way with you."

They spent the next several minutes enjoying one another before Brandi returned her attention to the floral arrangements and Jordon returned to the computer. He launched the internet browser and, once he found one of the websites he needed, he turned to Brandi and asked, "Will you please open my wallet and hand me the black card?"

The black American Express card to which he referred is something unknown to most of the public at large, being nothing they can apply for. Instead, the American Express company awards it to people it deems its best customers, based on their assets and income. With no spending limits whatsoever, the individual who possesses it can purchase literally anything—a Ferrari, a house, a private jet or luxury yacht—assuming the seller will accept it. And why shouldn't they? It's money on the spot, almost a cash purchase and the buyer doesn't have to be present.

After locating his billfold and the card he requested, she glanced at the computer display. "You're booking the reservations for next week?"

"I'd like us to get away as soon as possible."

"What about... Br... ?" she hesitated, struggling to come up with the man's name.

"Bryce," he supplied. Reaching for the piece of plastic she was holding, he said, "If something interferes with his departure, he can join us after we have arrived. We had a lengthy conversation, so I'm reasonable sure of his sincerity. I can always book him a separate flight if I need to."

Fifteen minutes later, Jordan announced, "That's it. Air and hotel reservations in place."

"So, we're really going. I can hardly believe it," Brandi exclaimed as she completed the second floral arrangement. She inhaled deeply and released it. "It suddenly feels as if a weight has been lifted and I can finally breathe again."

Inclining his head toward the shopping bags, Jordan asked, "What did you get?"

She paused for a moment to admire her handiwork, then went to the sitting room.

"All I could find in your closets were business suits and things that are suited for Bay Area weather. I wanted to see if I could find anything at all that would work in Bermuda." She opened one the bags and withdrew a short sleeved sports shirt. Holding it up so he could see it, she said, "Even though the stores are already stocking up for Autumn, I got lucky. What do you think?"

"Not bad."

She draped the shirt over the back of a chair, then, one by one, began displaying the rest of her purchases. "It wasn't easy," she said. "I think I stopped by every clothing store in town." Laying aside a pair of shorts, she added, "If you need anything else, we can finish shopping after we've settled in."

"You're an angel," he said, and came beside her. He was putting his arms around her when the air grew cold and a chill swept through him. Jordan shuddered and Brandi reacted as well, shivering and rubbing her arms to reduce the raised hairs and goosebumps. Jordan glanced around the room. "Warren!" he called. When he received no response, he called out again. "Warren! I know you're here." Silence. "This isn't funny."

Brandi frowned and asked, "Do you think that was him?"

"It's damn well not the air conditioner. Warren!" he shouted. "God damn it! Answer me."

After another minute without any sign that Warren was still present, Brandi asked, "What do you think he wanted?"

Jordan shook his head. "Whatever it is, I'm pretty sure we won't like it."

… … … … …

Locating Jordan hadn't proven difficult. Warren had selected a five star hotel situated between the financial district and Nob Hill and, in a matter of minutes, found his partner in a penthouse suite, staring at his computer and Googling for personal assistants and bodyguards. He found Jordan's diligence fascinating, as he alternated between websites that featured employment requests and his own employer internet account where prospective employees could log on and apply for a position. When an applicant responded, he would open their resumé and examine it. Most he deleted. But if one of them caught his attention, he would email the applicant a request either a Skype or Zoom interview. His questions focused on both their bodyguard experience and their willingness to help in matters related to his disability. And while most of the individuals who called themselves bodyguards shied away from working as a nurse, the few who did express interest also inquired about additional monetary compensation.

Although Warren knew from experience that Jordan

respected people who were financially motivated, it amused him when Jordan changed the tone of his voice when the topic turned to money. It was not that such an inquiry would have been inappropriate. It was just Jordan's obvious enjoyment at playing the manipulator that Warren found interesting.

Most of the applicants sounded like bouncers, so Jordan put each of them off, promising he'd get back to them. Things changed, however, when a man named Bryce Taylor appeared on the monitor.

"Tell me something about yourself," Jordan began, as he had with each of the preceding candidates.

"What would you like to know?"

"I'm looking for an experienced bodyguard. Tell me about your most recent client and why are you're no longer employed."

"A reasonable question," Bryce conceded. "She's the daughter of Cosa Nostra capo… " Jordan's eyebrows went up. " …and lives on Belvedere Island. Her father hired me, and I'd probably still be looking out for her except I'd started to have feelings for her—which is never good in my line of work—and also, she's so screwed up on drugs that it would have compounded the problem if I had stayed."

Jordan paused, then ventured, "I would assume you're fairly decent with weapons."

"I was a military sniper. In addition to the M24, I'm competent with a number of sidearms."

It must have been the quickness of Bryce's response that caused Jordan to hesitate, but after a moment he ventured, "Are you a decent driver? I mean, if I'm being pursued, could you… "

"I can handle escape and evasion, if that's what you mean. Not that it's necessarily relevant, but I'm also a pilot."

"Ah… what kind of planes can you fly?"

"Pretty much anything fixed-wing. The army trained me to pilot fighters. I've never flown cargo planes, but I expect you won't need that. Helicopters are a whole other skillset, so I don't fly those either."

There was another pause before Jordan asked, "If we need to take a commercial jet, how can you bring any weapons with you?"

Bryce chuckled. "The world is full of armed bodyguards. We carry special licenses that TSA recognizes. I'm allowed to bring weapons on board, but not ammunition. For that, a FedEx courier meets me on the other side of airport security and gives me my ammo. I load up in the men's room and, when I'm ready, I phone you to meet me in baggage claim.

"I have to ask, though, is this going to be part of my duties? Is there someone known to you who poses an immediate threat?"

"Why? Is that important?"

"It is," said Bryce. "When we start talking about money, we're also going to have to discuss hazard pay."

It was Jordan's turn to laugh. "No. There isn't. Not really. I was just curious. Actually, this is a new situation for me and, I have to admit, you're the first person I've interviewed who sounds like he knows what he's talking about.

"The thing that concerns me now is whether you're willing to help me with my day-to-day needs until my hands get better: things like opening the door, being my second set of hands."

He held them in front of the laptop's camera so Bryce could see what he was talking about and Bryce let out a whistle.

"Hand surgery?"

"After someone did a number on me," Jordan explained.

"So I have to ask you again, does he still pose a risk?"

"Possibly, but I hope not."

"Still, that adds to our discussion."

Warren could hear the alarm going off inside Jordan's head because of how expensive this proposition was becoming and he wondered if Jordan would still consider moving the conversation forward. Not that it mattered. Warren would deal with whichever person Jordan selected when the time came.

"As for your medical condition," Bryce continued, "because I've always understood the danger outsiders could pose to my clients, I trained as an EMT for five years."

"Because you were planning to become a bodyguard," Jordan supplied.

"Exactly, but to the right set of clients."

"Like your previous client and me."

Bryce nodded. "I know who you are. As for what else you need to know about me, I plan to retire before I reach fifty. I excel at what I do. If you decide to go forward, I will be happy to provide you with my work history, along with how to contact my former employers. You will find the history I provide is continuous, without any gaps that, if they were present, might be construed to indicate a dissatisfied client."

"Let's cut to the chase," said Jordan. "If I decide to hire you—contingent, of course, on the aforementioned resumé and its verification—how much are we talking about?"

Without missing a beat, Bryce replied, "Three hundred

sixty thousand dollars a year, divided into equal monthly payments of thirty K each, to be deposited into the bank account I specify one week in advance of each subsequent month."

Jordan stared into the computer's monitor. "And the hazard pay you mentioned."

"Assuming you sustain no serious injuries, an additional ten thousand dollars per incident, payable immediately afterwards."

"No *serious* injuries. What do you mean by… ?"

"If I need to push you out of the line of fire and you sprain an ankle, get bruised, or… " Bryce nodded in Jordan's direction. " …the condition of your hands become aggravated, but you're not hit, you're still alive, I won't consider those injuries serious—unfortunate perhaps, but not serious under this definition. In that situation, I've done my job. I've kept you alive, so I expect to get paid. This amount also assumes I haven't been wounded or injured."

"If you are… ," Jordan began.

Bryce, however, would not allow himself to be interrupted. "If you decide you're interested, I'll send you a contract that spells out all the details. If you find it acceptable, sign and date it, and I'll start working for you at once."

Warren was impressed. Bryce sounded like the professional Jordan was looking for. Apparently, so was Jordan. He provided an email address to which Bryce could send the PDF detailing his history. Upon its receipt, Jordan was able to contact two of the names listed in less than one hour after their conversation ended. Their glowing recommendations, as well as the reasons they gave for terminating their relationship, gave Jordan all the proof he needed that Bryce was the genuine article. He emailed Bryce for the contract and, once he had read it, he printed, signed and dated it, then returned it in color so that the blue ink of his signature would stand out. When a countersigned copy arrived, Jordan sent an email asking Bryce about his intended arrival.

Warren hung around long enough to understand what Jordan's plans were. He didn't intend that Jordan would actually be able to depart, but he wanted to make sure that Sabrina and Michael were able to relate his plans to the authorities in time to stop him. Once he had witnessed Jordan make the reservations, he had all of the information he needed.

… … … … …

Bertrand Tolliver was waiting outside the hotel when Warren exited.

Is that all you're about, Warren? Revenge?

I... I... Warren sputtered.

I expected more from you. As I told you before, I need a friend I can count on and, whether you believe me or not, so do you. If we're to protect each other from the darker forces, we need to control our impulses. I have as many dark thoughts as you—thoughts of wreaking revenge on those who wronged me—but I don't act on them. You need to ask yourself: how will harming those people affect my situation?

Warren could not answer, so Bertrand answered for him.

Trust me when I tell you it will do nothing. It will bring you down to their level and it will change your situation for the worse. Don't you want to see your children again?

Warren nodded, and was surprised when Bertrand seemed to perceive it.

Good, replied Bertrand. *You need to keep that in mind,*

because I promise you, if you don't, you will find yourself stuck here for all eternity.

You mean I won't go to Hell? asked Warren.

Bertrand laughed. *Isn't this Hell enough? You'll never participate in the lives of those around you. You'll never taste, smell, or feel any part of the world again. Remaining here, with no way out, will constantly remind you of how you failed to be eternally happy, of how you blew your only chance to go into the Light and be with the ones you love.*

Do you want to be stuck here with Magnus and the Lady? Do you want to be stuck here with me?

You're not so bad, countered Warren.

Thanks for that. But seriously, do you really want to spend all of eternity here?

Again, Warren didn't answer, so Bertrand continued.

This world, these people, won't be here forever. Don't you understand that? I don't know what we'll be left with when the human race disappears, when the sun finally burns out, but I promise you this: we'll be here to witness it.

Don't you get it, friend? We won't die with them. We're already dead. So whatever happens when this whole shebang finally ends—and I promise you, it's going to be a long, long time before it does, and you're going to be here to watch every minute of it—you're going to wind up in the dark and lonely aftermath. I'll tell you right now, I don't intend to remain here if I can avoid it. I can't help thinking there has to be something better than this, and I intend to do everything possible to get me there. So should you.

Bertrand had already discussed this, but not in such detail, and the full ramifications of Warren's actions were starting to sink in. As he considered the life he had lost and his current situation, his feelings were starting to shift. He had never been much of a father. In fact, Robbie and Rebecca had simply been part of life's furniture, like his college education, his career as a stock broker, his success as a businessman. True, he felt an affection toward his children and had enjoyed their company, but he had never really known them as people. So, while he did want to see them again, he was beginning to understand that his marriage had hinged solely around Brandi. She had been his real focus, always had been when he was alive. But now that there was evidence she might be falling in love with Jordan, whenever Warren thought about her, his anger started to simmer and he was beginning to ask himself if he had ever really loved her at all.

The fact was, Warren loved himself… always had. Now that he stopped to consider it, Brandi's love had merely served as validation of his actual worth as a human being. And while he had previously asked himself how he had ever deserved her, he now began to realize that this reservation sprang from a life-long insecurity.

In another moment of insight, he realized that none of this was exactly true either because, on that fateful night on Eddy Street, he had been willing to lay down his life for all of them. He would have, too, had he been able.

Why is it so complicated? cried Warren.

We're complicated creatures, answered Bertrand. *Very little about us is simple and straightforward. Morality isn't black or white and no one is simply good or bad. If it was just that simple, life wouldn't be so complicated and the decisions we face would be easier.*

Bertrand reached out a hand to touch him. When it passed though without sensation, Warren realized how much he longed for human contact.

23

"Mrs. Weeks is here to see you," the secretary announced as she ushered Nancy into Darryl Chapman's office.

"Thank you, Belinda," the attorney replied, rising from his chair to greet his prospective client.

As Nancy approached his desk, she became aware of the office's mahogany walls with matching mahogany bookcases, of two lampshades and an illuminated stained glass panel that had the look of Tiffany. The Persian carpet, which appeared to have originated in Qum, also spoke to Chapman's success. Although her friend in Tiburon had spoken highly about him, she found these trappings reassuring because she wanted to retain the finest lawyer money could buy.

"Thanks for setting aside the time," she said, extending her hand to reach his.

"Of course," Chapman replied as he completed the handshake. "So nice to meet you. Won't you please have a seat?" Once they were seated, he asked, "What can I do for you?"

"Mr. Chapman, I've come to talk to you about a few related issues involving investor fraud."

The attorney's eyebrows arched. "Shouldn't you be taking these matters to law enforcement?"

"It's my understanding that certain members of the firm that's involved are doing just that. I've come to see if you can help me determine if there is a way to address what I believe might be a civil side to the case."

Once Nancy had described all of the details, Chapman replied, "From what you're telling me, it seems we're talking about initiating a class action lawsuit. Are any of the affected parties aware of what's happened?"

Nancy shook her head. "Not yet."

"Then I think this matter is still premature." When Nancy frowned, he explained, "Until there are actual damages and I have identified the investor who will act as the primary litigant, typically the individual who has incurred the most losses… I take it you're not one of the affected parties." Again, she shook her head. " …there's nothing I can do." He smiled and added, "Feel free to contact me when the investors have been made aware of what's happened and are ready to initiate a lawsuit. If any of them want to pursue this matter at that time, I'll be happy to represent them." He started to rise, but when she pressed for more information, he also explained, "If the investors' funds have not been recovered by the time we've taken action, and if the firm lacks the resources to reimburse them, then I will have no choice but to go after whatever the firm has that's liquefiable. That includes all the firm's assets. From the way you've presented your case, I suspect you care as much about its employees as you do about the investors."

"I do."

"They will, in all likelihood, lose their jobs if the court rules in the investors' favor. I will also go after all of Jordan's assets. Are you two still married?"

Nancy nodded.

"Then you might want to consider filing for divorce before I initiate any proceedings against him. Should you fail to do so… " He cocked his head and looked into her eyes. " …you may find yourself penniless.

"You're a fine person, Mrs. Weeks. I'd hate to see you hurt as a result of your good intentions."

"I'm already considering doing so," she said. "Is there a divorce lawyer you'd care to recommend?"

"There is. Let me give you her number."

The drive home wasn't easy. Nancy's visit to Chapman had been unavoidable. She was not the kind of person who could turn a blind eye to an injustice perpetrated upon people she cared about, even if helping them wound up hurting the man she used to love. Twice, she had to pull her car to the curb because her vision had blurred and she needed to compose herself before she could safely reenter traffic.

When she was finally home, she went to her kitchen and uncorked a bottle of pinot grigio, then poured herself a glass and downed it. When the glass was empty, she poured a second that she could take the time to enjoy. Then, with nothing better to do, she opened her purse and retrieved the card Chapman had given her. Nancy examined what he had inscribed on its back. There, below the handwritten name, Julia Nguyen, was the number which, once she had dialed it, would change her life forever.

She lifted the phone's receiver from its cradle and wondered if she had the courage to call. She was still debating when her finger ran over something that didn't feel right. She turned the receiver over and spotted a crack. Curious how it got there, her mind slowly returned to finding it lying on the floor when she returned from the hospital. She chuckled. Then, resigned to accept the inevitable, she turned it back and began punching in the numbers 4-1-5-4-6-4-

Hello, Nancy.

Her hand opened and her fingers released it. When the receiver struck the tiles this time, a piece of gray plastic shot across the room and vanished behind a ceramic pot.

"Warren?" she gasped and glanced around the kitchen, before she remembered how futile that was.

None other. How are things between you and Jordan?

"How do you think?"

Sorry. I didn't mean to sound callous. I just know that if I was in your shoes…

"You're not."

Don't shoot the messenger. Before she could respond, he said, *I told you about what he had done because I care about you.*

"Really? Are you sure it wasn't because he was screwing your wife and you wanted to… ?"

That was part of it. I won't deny it. But you also have to believe me when I tell you it was also because of our history as friends.

Nancy picked up the glass, gulped down half of its contents, and gasped. "Look," she said. "I don't know why you're here, but I'd like you to leave."

I understand.

"Do you?" she said. Gesturing with a sweep of her arm to include the kitchen and the area beyond, she asked, "Do you realize how you ruined my life?"

I wasn't the one who ruined it. I just brought to your attention everything Jordan had been doing behind your back. You were going to learn about it eventually. Would you rather you were blindsided?

She took a smaller sip and replaced the glass, then leaned against the counter and admitted, "I suppose not."

Fine. And you're welcome. Since you've asked why I'm here... Nancy came upright. *Calm down. I'm going to leave in a couple of minutes. But before I do, I'd like to know if there is anything I can do to help you.*

"Such as... ?"

I got a look at the name on that business card. "Julia Nguyen, Family Law." If you're considering a divorce, you might want some evidence.

"California's a no fault State. Everything is divided fifty-fifty."

Fair enough. Even so, I suspect you might also like to know where Jordan hid all the money.

"Someone's looking into it. I believe they've already located some of what he's taken. I suspect they'll eventually have a handle on all of it."

Really?

"Really. So, unless you can offer anything else of interest, this conversation is over." Nancy grinned at what she considered to be the "pregnant pause" that followed, amused by the possible irony of what Brandi might be baking.

Are you interested in seeing Jordan brought to justice?

"I think the people who are recovering what Jordie has stolen will take care of that."

Michael and Sabrina have no idea that Jordan is preparing to leave the country. And even if they find out, they have no way of knowing where he and Brandi are going.

Now it was Nancy's turn to be speechless. She was not only surprised that Warren knew the two conspirators' identity, but also by his assertion that Jordan was preparing to fly the coop.

"He's too injured to go anywhere."

Do you have any idea how rich he is?

"Of course I do," Nancy countered. "Although he won't be for long."

I'm not just talking about the money he has embezzled. I'm talking about…

"I've already taken control of our bank accounts. He can't touch them."

Have you, now? Clever girl. I'm impressed. But still, until Michael and Sabrina manage to divert all of his foreign assets—even a part of which leaves him with significant resources—he will have enough funds available to hire people to help him. If he manages to escape, I know where he's going.

"I already know about Bermuda."

That's just the first leg. You don't know where they're going after that, do you?

Nancy shook her head.

Well, I do. He's already putting his plan into motion, but I can't do anything on my own to stop him. You can put the FBI on his tail if you'll allow me to guide you. So, again I'm asking, would like me to help you make sure Jordan gets what he deserves?

"Of course," Nancy replied as she reached for the wine glass.

24

"Good morning, Allan."

Preoccupied with something on his computer's monitor, the receptionist's head jerked up at the interruption. He managed to compose himself.

"Good morning, Mrs. Weeks. To what do we owe the honor?"

"Cut the crap," Nancy replied, diffusing the sarcasm with a smile.

"I'm sorry. I just… "

"I understand, Hun. But how long have we known each other? Your sugary personality is what our clients expect, but really… ?"

Allan bit his lip and grimaced.

Ignoring his discomfort, she asked, "Any chance Michael and Sabrina are in?"

"Michael's in his office. Sabrina isn't due until tomorrow. If you'd like, I can call her and let her know you'd like to see her."

Nancy shook her head. "That won't be necessary."

"In that case," he said as he reached for the intercom, "I'll tell Michael you're here."

"Thanks," she said and headed for the elevator.

When its doors opened onto the second floor's lobby, she ran through all of the things she needed to discuss, then went to Michael's office. She pressed the latch on the door and peered inside.

"Time to shit or get off the pot, Hun."

Michael swiveled his chair and returned an inquiring look.

"Jordie's getting ready to fly the coop," she explained.

"So soon?" he asked. "His hands are… "

"He's hiring someone to help him. How's it coming with the passwords?"

Michael smiled and said, "I've made more progress than I expected."

He rotated the chair halfway toward the computer and gestured at the monitor. Nancy saw that all but two of the lines that had heretofore been cryptic groups of characters were now replaced by the names of bank websites, followed by what appeared to be user names. A collection of upper and lower case characters, numbers, and special symbols occupied the end of each line and Nancy realized these were passwords.

"I can't guarantee that everything I've come up with is correct," he said. "But these results almost guarantee it."

"Sure looks like it. Does anyone else know what you're doing?"

"When was the last time you were dying to see what your accountant was up to?"

Nancy laughed. "Point taken."

"In the event of the occasional visit by one of the staff, I just toggle to a spreadsheet." Michael grinned. "One look at all of those numbers and their eyes glaze over and they immediately lose interest."

Nancy gestured toward the display. "What about the last two lines?"

Michael folded his arms and shook his head. "Except for those, this has been like cracking a code. Whatever characters I've deciphered began to reveal the broader pattern that, in turn, revealed a subsequent set of characters." He inclined his head toward the computer. "These two, however, leave me baffled. It's as if Jordan decided to use an entirely different coding system—something, I believe, that's completely beyond his capabilities—or else he forgot what he had been doing with the rest of them. Maybe he invented this set several months before or after he created the others. In any case, the scheme he'd been using doesn't seem to apply to the last two."

"Maybe there's not much money in those last two accounts," she suggested.

"Or maybe they contain the lion's share."

Nancy frowned. "What do you suggest?"

He sat back in his chair and said, "I'm wondering if you can look around the house to see if there's another piece of paper like the first one."

"I'll give it a try. Although I'm pretty sure I packed up everything when I threw the bum out. Finding the one I gave you was probably just a fluke."

"How much time do we have before Jordan leaves?" he asked.

"According to Warren, probably a week."

"Well, that's something in our favor," said Michael. "I'd really like to empty as many accounts as possible before

Jordan leaves. Unless, you have something better in mind, I'd like to get on it when Sabrina drops by. I'm afraid that, before he takes off, he'll start transferring money to other accounts."

"What makes you say that?"

"Nothing really. I'm a born pessimist. I tend to assume the worst will happen, then do what I can to prevent it. It probably comes from years of dealing with the IRS."

"That gives you as much as five days to do what you need to."

"Pretty much, although I might have even less."

"How's it coming with the SEC?"

Michael blew a stream of air between his lips. "Sabrina's discouraged. You watch movies and television and picture them strapping on guns and jumping into action."

Nancy laughed. "That's what I thought," she said. Then her tone changed and her expression darkened. "But you believe it isn't likely."

"That might happen when they're dealing with a drug lord like El Chapo," answered Michael. "But I don't think white collar crime gets the same amount of attention. She's filled out the necessary forms and is waiting to hear back, but as far as we can tell, nothing's happening yet. Maybe they're actually doing something and we'll learn what came down once everything's over."

"I hope this doesn't turn into some bureaucratic nightmare," she said.

"That's the reason I'm about to take direct action." He paused, then, giving Nancy a curious look, he asked, "Did Warren give you any idea what he intends to do if Jordan tries to leave?"

"He said he'd… ," Marking spaces in the air with two

fingers on each of her hands to indicate quotation marks, she finished …"'take care of things.'"

"Like he did in the conference room?"

"He wasn't specific."

Michael raised an eyebrow. "Are you comfortable with that?"

Nancy shook her head. "I'm very conflicted. On one hand, I want to see Jordan punished… "

"For having an affair with Brandi, or for embezzling our investors' funds?"

"Both. But I'm also afraid of what Warren will do. I don't want either Jordan or Brandi injured, but I can't actually say what I do want. I'd prefer it if Brandi could see what kind of man she's getting involved with and find someone else. If I had my druthers, I'd like to see Jordan develop a conscience and return all of the money on his own."

"That's not likely to happen."

"I know," said Nancy. She felt herself shrink under the weight of what was descending upon her, almost as if her body was starting to collapse into itself. She pursed her lips and looked away. "I don't want to see Jordie do hard time, either." She started to cry and Michael began to reach out to her, before withdrawing his hand and placing it on top of the one in his lap. After a moment, she reached into her handbag and took out a tissue. She dabbed at her eyes and managed to say between sobs, "I don't know how to make things better."

"I understand," said Michael. "I'd like that, as well. But now that we've started involving law enforcement, I think the only way to a better solution rests with Jordan. And I don't believe he's up to it. And since Warren is the loose cannon aboard this ship, all you, Sabrina, and I can do is look after ourselves and the investors. The rest is anyone's guess."

25

"Michael," Rebecca hailed through the intercom. "Matt Breitenbach is on 101. He's telling me he's unable to access his funds. Ordinarily, I would hand the matter to Jordan, but… "

"I understand," Michael replied, all the while thinking, *The shit's starting to happen.* "I'll take care of it."

Before reaching for the phone, he took a moment to decide how to handle it, not only because Mr. Breitenbach was one of the firm's biggest investors, but also because he was solidly connected. Until a few years ago, he had been on the San Francisco Chronicle's board of directors. He was also a friend of the man who had built one of the East Bay's largest real estate developments, the man whose name was on a street that runs through the Oakland International Airport—no small accomplishment, given the fact that two of the other streets are named after John Glenn and Neil Armstrong. Matt Breitenbach was not a man to be trifled with and could easily bring this firm to its knees.

"Mr. Breitenbach," he said, trying to sound upbeat. "This is Michael in accounting. What can I do for you?"

"You can give me access to my money."

Feigning ignorance, Michael replied, "I'm afraid I don't understand."

"For the last two days, I have been trying to make a withdrawal and your system tells me my account is empty. How can that be? Has somebody robbed me? I'm worried because, if someone has, there will be Hell to pay."

"This has to be some kind of glitch. I know very well your account has a significant balance."

"A *very* significant balance. And I would like to access it *now*," Breitenbach said, making no attempt to disguise his irritation.

"Yes. Of course you would. I'm not sure what the problem is, but if you'll give me time to look into it… "

"It's eleven thirty-eight. I'll give you exactly twenty-four hours to fix this," the man said, his tone growing angrier. "If I have to wait one minute longer… "

"You won't have to."

"I'd better not."

"As soon as this call ends… "

The line went dead and Michael knew he had to act quickly. He punched 9, to access an outside line before entering Sabrina's private number. Six unanswered rings brought up the greeting, "You have reached Sabrina Babich. I am either with a client or… " Without waiting to hear the rest of the recording, he hung up and dialed her cell. After two rings, she answered.

"Yes, Michael?"

"I need you here *now*."

Before she could ask why, Michael described the situation.

"I'm on my way," she said.

It was twelve-fifteen when the office door opened and

the scent of Lancôme's La Vie est Belle, Sabrina's customary fragrance, announced her presence. Without needing to look, Michael remained in his chair, studying the computer's display.

"Hi," he said.

"How's it going?" she asked as she pulled up a chair and sat down beside him.

"I'm reasonably confident that I've identified all of the banks and the correct passwords, but there's no way to be sure that I haven't fucked up until I try to use them."

"It's a little like standing at the top of a Double Black Diamond for the very first time and wondering if you have what it takes," she said.

Michael rotated his chair and stared at her. "You've actually done that?"

Sabrina nodded. "On my sixteenth birthday."

His eyebrows went up.

"Don't look at me like that." Her reply could have been mistaken for anger, but she softened it with a smile and Michael relaxed. "The woman who taught me how to sail, single-handed her Santana 23 across the Atlantic from Boston, and celebrated her twenty-first birthday in Liverpool. The following year, she won the single-hand division in the Trans Pac from California to Hawaii. When she wasn't sailing, she spent much of her time climbing rocks or racing downhill."

"As a skier."

"Yup."

"Ballsy," Michael replied. When Sabrina gave a questioning stare, he explained, "You're just so... uh... feminine."

Sabrina laughed. "Is there a contradiction?"

Michael grimaced. "I'm sorry. I… "

Rather than continue the thread, Sabrina looked past him to the internet browser and asked, "What are we waiting for?"

He offered a tight smile and said, "I wanted you to be here when I began."

"Well, I'm here."

Michael tightened his lips and nodded, then turned in his chair and placed his finger on the trackpad. He selected the first bank on his spreadsheet, then double-clicked the associated username, thereby copying it to his computer's memory. He then clicked the link that Google provided and held his breath as the browser scoured the internet. He exhaled when the bank's logon page appeared.

"Got it," Michael whispered.

He pasted the username into the appropriate field, before returning to the spreadsheet for the corresponding password. Toggling back to the website, he pasted what he hoped was the appropriate string of characters into the field marked **Password** and clicked the **Submit** button. A circle of dots rotated as the data made its way through the online network and the bank's computer digested what it had been given. Michael and Sabrina gripped their armrests until a new window appeared that showed the bank's logo alongside a title that read **ACCOUNTS: Bermuda, Canada, Germany, Micronesia.**

"Well, we're back," said Michael, " and everything looks like it did the last time."

"These aren't all of them, are they? Not all of the places he plans to visit?"

"I'm not sure. It's possible the other accounts he's set up—Canada, Germany, and Micronesia—will direct funds to various banks around the world. He's set it up so that, if someone were to stumble onto what he's up to, they won't be able to learn the full extent of his travel plans from just one bank. He's arranged it so that some of the funds should be waiting in Bermuda when he arrives. But if he gets to Hamilton and his funds aren't there, he can move on to Montréal, pick up what's in that account, then change the rest of his itinerary on the fly. It would then take him, max, a couple of hours to log on to all of the other websites, learn which accounts, if any, are still intact, then reroute whatever funds are still there to bank accounts that people—meaning us—have not yet discovered."

"That's some level of paranoia," observed Sabrina.

"Jordan didn't get where he is by trusting others… or being stupid."

"You're going to actually start transferring funds this time," said Sabrina.

Michael nodded. "I've been able to log in to all but the last two banks, so I think it's safe to begin. Once I've taken care of the first dozen, I'll start figuring out the last two."

"Everything's archived?"

He nodded again. "I spent last night hooking up the new computer."

"What happens now?"

"I need to learn how to make transfers from this website to outside bank accounts—ours in particular—then move those funds as quickly as possible. I've already changed the firm's passwords so Jordan can never access our accounts again. Then, I'll start working on the next bank. Once I've emptied all of the ones I can access, I have to make sure I transfer the appropriate amounts to each of our investors, starting with Breitenbach."

Sabrina started fumbling through her purse. Michael frowned. "What's up?"

"Are you hungry? I know I am. I suspect you haven't had lunch either."

He shook his head.

Sabrina replied, "That's what I thought. If you're going to think clearly, you'll need something in your belly. I'm thinking Chinese will be light enough you won't have to wrestle with brain fog."

"Good thinking."

"There's a restaurant at the corner of Washington and Stockton whose patrons are almost exclusively Chinese."

Michael smiled. "That's a solid recommendation."

"And they don't use MSG," Sabrina added. "It's one of my favorite places, so I always keep one of their menus with me. I'll phone in an order and pick it up while you get started."

Michael extended his arms, laced his fingers, and cracked his knuckles. "This is probably going to take several hours if it doesn't end up turning into an all-nighter."

"Wait! You said it would only take Jordan a couple of hours."

"And he's been at this how long?" asked Michael. "I'm a newb. Each bank is going to have its own transfer protocols and I don't know how long it's going to take me to learn each of them. Even if I have all of their user names and passwords right, I can pretty much guarantee I'll still be working when you return."

As she headed for the door, she looked back and told him, "Be back as soon as I can."

…… …… …… …… ……

Hands full of takeout bags, Sabrina nudged the door open with her shoulder.

"You can put it over there," said Michael, gesturing with his hand at a horizontal filing cabinet on the wall to his left while keeping his eyes on the display screen.

Curious at his focus, she did as he suggested while keeping her own eyes on him. "What's up?" she asked. "That's not the internet browser, is it?"

He shook his head. "I didn't have two of the necessary passwords so, rather than get locked out, I'm trying to figure out Jordan's bullshit coding system. Hopefully, I'll have something useful by tomorrow morning." He swiveled his chair and regarded the bags of Chinese food. "Well, at least the afternoon won't be a total loss." He rose to examine the goods that Sabrina had brought. "What do we have here?"

"It's Chinese Chinese."

When Michael didn't appear to comprehend, she explained, "They don't serve anything Western, no sweet and sour or chop suey or that sort of stuff. My favorite is their raw fish salad." When Michael frowned, she laughed and said, "It's not as weird as it sounds. I promise, you're going to love it."

She removed the metal handles from two of the carryout boxes and unfolded the cardboard into two circular dishes. "I forgot to ask if you have any silverware. Do you know how to use chopsticks?"

He nodded. "I'm an old hand," he replied, regarding the unusual fare with interest.

When they had divided the food into two roughly equal proportions and were beginning to eat, he asked, "Can you come back tomorrow morning? I'd really like you to be here, if only for moral support."

26

"How's it going?" asked Sabrina.

She pulled up a chair and sat next to Michael, placing a bag marked with the logo of a doughnut company next to his elbow.

He glanced down, pulled the sack open, then withdrew a French glazed cruller and bit into it as she set down two paper cups of coffee. He attempted to say, "Not bad." But, with his mouth full of pastry, his reply was barely comprehensible. He reached for one of the containers and put it to his lips. After two careful sips, he managed to swallow, then repeated with a gasp, "Not bad. After one failed attempt, I was able to come up with the appropriate password. I have just started initiating the transfer.

"There!" he said as the browser located the firm's investors' account. He clicked the button marked Transfer, and they watched as the balance of the offshore account dwindled to zero. When he toggled to website of W and H Limited's bank, the investors' account balance reflected a seven-plus million dollars increase.

"I should say so!" said Sabrina as her eyebrows arched in appreciation. "Not bad at all. That's a significantly larger amount than the ones you worked with yesterday."

Michael nodded. "Once I've transferred as much as

possible from the remaining accounts—probably by ten at the latest—I'll begin distributing the funds into our investors, starting with Breitenbach."

"Once he's appeased, the pressure should be off for a while, shouldn't it?" asked Sabrina.

"It all depends on Jordan. How's it coming with the F. B. I.?" he asked and took another bite of the doughnut.

Sabrina stiffened and her eyes widened. "Oh shit!" she said and glanced at her watch. "I'd almost forgot. Nancy and I are supposed to meet with them this morning. I think I can just make it if I leave right now. I don't suppose you can join us," she said and put down the coffee cup.

"Not unless you want Breitenbach to start a shit storm. Wait!" he said as she started to rise. "I have an idea." He opened a drawer and reached into it.

... ...

"Thank God!" Sabrina gasped as she dashed from the street onto the sidewalk, narrowly avoiding two passing cars. Brushing aside several strands of hair from her face, she told Nancy, "I was afraid I wasn't going to make it."

"You're fine, Hun," Nancy assured. "This is going to be hard enough for me to do with you here beside me. I wouldn't have gone inside alone, even if it meant missing the appointment.

"Now," she said, placing a hand on Sabrina's shoulder, "take a deep breath, and compose yourself. Did you bring everything we discussed?"

"Yes," Sabrina said and showed her the portfolio.

"Good. How are the bank transfers coming?"

"He's managed to get into almost all of the accounts and has started transferring their balances back to the firm."

"Good. Fingers crossed," said Nancy. She consulted her wristwatch, then turned and looked up. Twenty one stories high, the building before her seemed as daunting as the task they were facing. "Are you up to this?"

Sabrina swallowed hard and nodded. "I think so."

They rode the elevator to the thirteenth floor and found themselves standing in front of two glass doors etched with the insignia of the Federal Bureau of Investigation. They pushed them open and a smartly groomed woman in a white blouse and gray business suit instructed them how to pass through the security check. Once they were inside the lobby, they surrendered their driver's licenses and were directed to place their cell phones inside a locker. After receiving the locker key and visitors' badges, they crossed the gleaming marble floor to where a man, who introduced himself as Special Agent Lucas, escorted them to a conference room. Another man, attired in a black business suit and clasping a manilla folder in front of him was waiting outside.

"This is Special Agent Chan," explained Lucas. "He will be joining our discussion." He opened the door, gestured toward two empty chairs and said, "Won't you ladies please have a seat?" Once all four had arranged themselves, Lucas informed them, "I've read the notes from your appointment request, but haven't had time to explain the reason for this discussion to my associate. I'd like each of you to introduce yourselves, describe the matter that's brought you here and explain why it concerns us."

Nancy looked a Sabrina, then turned to the agents. "My name is Nancy Weeks and I am embarrassed to say that I'm here because of the financial fraud my husband, Jordan Weeks, has committed." Lucas nodded and Chan cocked his head, but neither interrupted. "I know what you're thinking. Angry wife. Marriage on the rocks. The usual reasons for a woman to take out her frustrations on her husband. But I want you both to understand, I've brought a substantial amount of evidence to back up my allegations.

"My husband," she continued, "is the CEO of the investment firm, W and H Limited. He's financially sound and has no outstanding liabilities, so I'm as puzzled as you might be why he's decided to commit such an act." She sighed, then rested her forearms on the table and leaned forward. "Jordie has stolen millions of dollars from his clients' investment accounts and transferred the money to a number of personal offshore bank accounts."

"Are you saying the funds are now outside the U.S.?" asked Lucas.

"Most of them." She hesitated, then said, "It's somewhat complicated. I'm not part of the firm, so I'm not sure about all the ins and outs. In fact, I would never have learned about any of this if it wasn't for Sabrina." Nancy inclined her head in her friend's direction. "I think it'll be best if she gives her own account of what she knows and how she learned it."

When the agents shifted their gaze, Sabrina said, "I'm Sabrina Babich and I'm one of W and H Limited's employees. I was informed about what Mister Weeks had done by Michael Sumner, W and H Limited's chief accountant."

When the Special Agents exchanged glances, Sabrina said, "I suspect that you're wondering why the source of our information isn't here to substantiate our story. I want you to understand that, while Mister Sumner isn't able to join us, he has instructed me to tell you he is willing to meet with you in person. Here is his business card," she said, and slid it across the table. When Special Agent Chan picked it up and examined it, Sabrina explained, "You will see that he's written his address and cell number on the back."

Chan flipped it over, then handed it to Lucas, who

studied both sides of the card then inserted it into the folder Chan had placed between them.

"Is he suggesting we meet him at his home, rather than at his office?"

Sabrina nodded. "At the moment, only the three of us are aware of what's happened. He's afraid that if you show up at the office, rumors will spread and our investors will realize that something bad is happening. He's located some, if not all, of the stolen funds and is in the process of recovering them. We believe it would be to their benefit, as well as the firm's, if he could complete the process before they start to panic."

Lucas and Chan nodded.

She went on to explain, "Michael was the one who uncovered the transfers. He came across them during the firm's annual audit." She went on to explain how she had disclosed the entire affair, including the one way tickets, to Warren Holmes. With that, she withdrew copies of the documents she had presented at the Tiburon café and slid them across to Chan.

The two Special Agents spent the next several minutes reviewing them, gesturing on occasion to bring an item of interest to the other one's attention. At one point, Chan asked, "And where is Mister Holmes?"

Sabrina explained his demise, adding, "Brandi, his widow, and his two deceased children, are the three other parties to whom the reservations refer."

"These don't mention their names," said Lucas, waving the documents in his hand.

"But these do," said Nancy, withdrawing stapled sheets of paper from her purse. "I found two sets of documents in Warren's desk after I'd kicked him out. This set," she said as she passed them over, "are printed copies of emails from the airlines, confirming the reservations and the names of the passengers. The second set, is a copy of what I gave to Sabrina. It contains what I had suspected to be an encoded list of Jordan's offshore bank accounts."

Sabrina picked up where Nancy left off. "I gave that set to Michael who confirmed that, in fact, it did contain coded bank names, associated account numbers, and Jordan's user names and passwords." She went on to describe Michael's efforts in detail.

"Why the rush?" asked Lucas.

Without mentioning who told her, Nancy explained, "We believe Jordie's about to leave the country and we want to make sure he doesn't block our efforts, because if he does, he will certainly change all the passwords and we will no longer have any access."

"Does he have any reason to suspect what you're doing?"

"Probably not yet. He will if he notices the accounts are being emptied. The reason we're here is that we're hoping you will arrest him before he can do any of that."

"We'll need to have some evidence of wrongdoing, that the money isn't his. Do you have any proof?"

"Oh! Of course," said Sabrina. "How stupid of me." She delved into the portfolio and produced a printed spreadsheet, as well as another document, and gave them to him. "You'll notice that the accounts in question are clearly labeled as belonging to investors."

After a brief glance, Chan handed them to Lucas. "Let's have one of our specialists see what they can do with this. I'm thinking Marcovich."

Lucas nodded. He went to the door and stepped into the hallway. Nancy and Sabrina heard him say something indistinct into a microphone they hadn't noticed him wearing earlier. A moment later, a young man appeared and accepted what Lucas gave him. The two spoke for several minutes, the young man nodding in response to what Lucas was telling him.

While the two were conversing, Chan explained, "I'm hoping we can gather enough evidence to establish a sufficiently solid case before the accounts are emptied."

Sabrina explained, "Whether it's Jordan or Michael who empty them, Michael has already archived all of the bank accounts involved while the funds were still in place in order to preserve the evidence."

Chan raised his eyebrows out of apparent appreciation for Michael's diligence.

Nancy frowned and said, "So there's still a chance that Jordie will get away scot-free."

"I hope not. It's still too early to say. If what you're telling us is true… " When Nancy started to interrupt, he held up his hand. "Please understand, it's not that I don't believe you. I appreciate your willingness to bring this matter to our attention. Not many people would. But before we can take any action, we have to be sure that an actual crime has been committed."

"Talk to Michael," Sabrina said. "As the firm's chief accountant, he can verify that Mister Weeks has no right to the money."

"Rest assured, we intend to contact him," replied Chan. He indicated that the meeting was over. Then, as the ladies rose and started to leave, he asked Nancy, "If we decide we want to speak with your husband, where can we find him?"

"I can't say," she replied. *After all, it isn't exactly a lie,* she told herself. If they interpreted her answer to mean she didn't know, when what she intended was it wouldn't be prudent to divulge the information, well then…

••• ••• ••• ••• •••

Nancy and Sabrina exited the elevator and walked toward the building's foyer.

"Were we wasting our time?" asked Sabrina. "Are they that stupid? If they pay a visit to Jordan before Michael has finished… "

"I know what you mean, Hun. It seems as if there's no sure way to take action against that son-of-a-bitch. It's like all the cards are stacked against us and in Jordie's favor."

"Are you going to end it?"

"You mean divorce him? Can you see any other way? Absolutely. I intend to cut the cord, and if it's at all possible, I intend to do it in such a way there'll be no turning back. I know myself too well. I know I can seem hard as nails, someone you'd rather not mess with. But girl, I'm a softy. A genuine marshmallow." Nancy chuckled. Then, her expression hardened. "I have no intention to let that sweet talking bastard try to ease his way back into my life after Brandi realizes what a criminal she's hooked up with. And trust me, she will. Much as I hate to admit it, that girl is no dummy. When that day comes, Jordie will realize what a good thing he's lost and try to charm his way back into my life. And there's a good chance he could, if I don't take steps to eliminate any chance of that ever happening.

"Right now, while my heart is a raw, open wound, I have to take steps to keep myself from acting stupid." A few feet from the exit, Nancy stopped and turned to face her. "As sure as he is the best con man the world has ever seen, as sure as I am the most gullible person in the world when it comes to love, I'm going to do everything I can to short circuit my inborn stupidity."

Sabrina mustered a smile and tried to counter with, "You're not stu… "

"Oh, but I am, girl. I wish I could say that I wasn't, but I am. After all these years and some of the crap he's already put me through and the way I responded, I can say with conviction that, where Jordie's concerned, I'm the dumbest sucker on earth."

27

Warren was a creature of habit. It was one of the traits that had fostered his success when he was alive and selling stocks. Every night he would program his coffeemaker so the coffee would be already brewed when he answered his alarm. He would have downed two cupfuls by the time the opening bell sounded at the New York Stock Exchange. Every morning, when he reached out to his clients, he had a good grasp on how the market was trending and what his recommendations should be.

Now, in the afterlife, he was developing another habit. For an hour or two every evening, he would return to the Tenderloin and visit the scene of his family's execution, trying to come to terms with the irrational event that had brought an end to everything. Thus it was that he chanced upon a pair of police officers conversing. He listened as one described the scene he had encountered a few weeks earlier and the events that had followed.

"You should 'a' seen 'em. Laid out on the sidewalk, right here in a river of blood," the officer gestured at several feet of concrete as he told the other one, "All of their throats slit open. It was a miracle one of them survived. My first thought was, they had to all be dead. I was radioing for help when the woman raised her hand. There was no way I could get close without damaging the crime scene, but I had to see if

I could help her." As the officer's story unfolded, and he described in detail how the woman's and the children's clothing had been torn open and the condition of their bodies. "It was bad enough that the pervs had been molesting them, but why did they have to finish them like that?"

Warren wondered, too. As his mind returned to Robert, the one who had been in charge, the one who was still enjoying himself, Warren knew he needed to address that. As he had done before, he went searching for the one whose very existence kept him in torment.

The search didn't take long. Warren found the object of his quest back again in the same part of town, limping down Mason in the same direction from which Warren and his family had come. His curious gait was pronounced, almost to the point of exaggeration, and it brought Warren up short. Robert was favoring his left leg and seemed to be talking to himself. At one point, he grabbed at the right side of his rib cage and gasped. He halted and his knees bent. He steadied himself by placing his hand against the building next to him.

Curious about this change in appearance, Warren eased himself closer. Under the glow of the street lights, he saw a gash across Robert's right cheekbone and the man's nose was misshapen, tilted off to one side with a stream of blood running down his upper lip. He saw that the sport shirt he was wearing was the same as the one he had worn in the sports bar, but not pressed and new in appearance like it had been on that previous occasion. The breast pocket had been pulled down with such force that the the fabric beside and below it was ripped open. Now that Warren began to look closer, he also saw that the knees of Robert's trousers were torn and his kneecaps were bloody.

Delighted by the man's injuries, Warren drew near and Robert shuddered, leaning away from the sudden chill. Warren spoke into his ear, saying, *It's a rough neighborhood. Bad things can happen to people in this part of town, or haven't you noticed?*

Robert's head jerked up, and his eyes opened wide. When he glanced around, looking for the one who had addressed him, he lost his balance and nearly fell. He placed both hands against the building's façade to steady himself.

Carlos and Kevin learned that the hard way. You've heard about what happened to your buddies, haven't you? I hear news travels fast in certain circles.

As Robert began edging back in the direction from which he had come, Warren said, *You look like you've had a rough go of it. What happened? Someone rob you?* He laughed, then growled, *At least you were able to walk away, unlike me and my family.*

"Leave me alone!" Robert managed between lips that were swollen and split.

Not until I'm done with you.

Robert whined, "I can't take any more."

That's good. Hopefully, that means you have some idea of what's about to happen.

Warren looked around and found that the street was almost deserted. There were some figures headed eastward across Mason a few blocks higher up, but too far away to see what was happening here. And he didn't believe that the passengers in the few cars driving downhill would notice, let alone bother to stop, when he was doing what he intended. So long as the police kept themselves to Eddy Street and not come over to Mason, he could set to work uninterrupted.

Now, said Warren. *Where should I begin?*

He was trying to come up with something original, but decided that creativity wasn't important. The only things that mattered were that he inflicted as much pain as possible and that he prolong Robert's agony. In order for those things to happen, he needed to take care not to injure anything vital. So that Robert would remain conscious, Warren also needed to avoid any injuries to the brain. He began by slamming Robert into the wall of the adjacent hotel.

"Fuck!" Robert cried on impact. He grabbed at his shoulder and started to back away. "I'm really sorry. What can I do to make you stop?"

Bringing me and my children back to life would be a good place to start.

"Do what?"

You'd need to make amends. You'd have to return things to the way they were. Your predicament is a little like smashing a tea cup, then telling it you're sorry.

"A tea cup? I don't understand."

What I'm trying to say is if you have any suggestions as to how you can return things to the way they were, I'll take pity on you.

"That's crazy! How can I… ?"

My point exactly.

Warren shoved Robert onto the sidewalk. He landed with so much force that, after his knees struck the pavement, his momentum drove him onto his face in front of a sports bar somewhat smaller than the one on Divisadero Street. Even though Robert had held his hands in front of him to absorb the impact, when he raised himself, his lips were bloody and his upper front teeth were broken. Warren didn't give him any time to recover. He grabbed him by the collar and thrust him into the ornamental base of a streetlamp a few feet farther downhill. In order to avoid giving Robert a concussion, he directed him so that his left shoulder struck. Robert screamed and Warren heard something crack. He suspected he had broken a bone.

"Oh God!" Robert cried. "I can't take any more."

Oh, but you will, said Warren, grinning at the agony he was inflicting. *Let's get you onto your feet and see what kind of condition you're in.*

Warren lifted Robert and forced him to stand, delighted that he had finally mastered his control of physical objects. A glow from the right indicated a car driving eastward on Eddy Street was approaching the intersection. Curious how he might make use of it, Warren held Robert upright and forced him to run downhill. As they passed under the cloth covered awning of a residence hotel near the intersection, Robert reached out for it in vain in an attempt to halt his forward progress. Warren would have none of it, however, and yanked Robert away from the curb, leaving the awning's support posts inches beyond his reach.

The car passed only seconds before they arrived and Warren cursed the missed opportunity. He had hoped to throw Robert against it—not into its path, where the vehicle might actually kill him—but rather against its side panel.

He glanced to the west and found that the police officers had gone elsewhere, leaving Eddy Street free for him to use. He dragged Robert into the street's center, searching for anything he could employ as a weapon.

"Please, man. Please stop!" Robert sobbed.

Wasn't that how my children begged?

Chest heaving, his knees threatening to buckle, Robert said, "Yeah. I know. I shouldn't have done it."

But you did. When they were begging for mercy, begging for their lives, you ignored them. Instead, you listened to your friends who said, "Let's do them and get out of here."

Well, now it's your turn to die.

"Then do it. Just kill me, because I can't take any more."

I'm not letting you off that easy.

Robert sobbed and whispered, "Please."

You're going to pay for what you did, and I'm going to enjoy myself and take my time.

A restaurant on the corner had a foot high, white, wrought iron picket fence topped with arrows in front of each of its windows. *What nice little weapons,* Warren said and dragged Robert to the sidewalk. The comment registered and Robert's head came up. He stared at the arrows for a second, then tried tearing himself free from Warren's grasp.

Not so fast, Warren told him, then lifted him four feet off the ground so that his torso was a full foot higher than the pickets. It also occurred to Warren that the windows might be shatterproof, so he angled Robert's body so that, if the glass failed to break, his shoulder, instead of his head, would take the brunt of the impact. Warren smiled at his choice. Since the arrowheads rose perhaps three inches above the fences' stringers, they would penetrate, but not so deep as to inflict any immediately fatal injuries. Robert would lose blood, but live for a while afterward, hopefully in a great deal of pain. *Here we go,* he said and launched Robert forward. Robert raised his arms to protect himself, but could not support his weight when Warren released him. He screamed when the arrowheads pierced his chest and abdomen, then struggled to lift himself from the metal points.

Warren backed away to get a better perspective, then grinned as he watched the man struggle to free himself. Robert fumbled as he attempted to grab the arrows' shafts, but his blood was beginning to coat them and his hands slipped each time he tried to obtain enough leverage to lift himself.

Warren was determined not to let him die before his could inflict even a few more injuries. So when he saw another vehicle coming, he lifted him again and held him above the sidewalk, remembering for a second how he had dangled in Robert's grasp. When he felt that the minivan had drawn close enough, he hurled Robert into it. Just as Warren had planned, Robert struck the van's side panel and his arms and legs splayed out in four directions. The van braked to a halt and Robert tumbled onto the asphalt, cartwheeling a few feet forward before coming to a halt with his arms and legs akimbo.

"Oh, my God!" the woman driver cried as she flung the door open and stepped onto the street. She covered her mouth with her hands and stood staring at the crumpled body. "I didn't see him," she told the youth who was just now rounding the vehicle's rear bumper.

"Me neither," he said, and came to stand beside her. He wrapped an arm around her, then stopped. "We need to call an ambulance."

"I can't stay here," she protested, already in tears. "My dad will kill me."

"We can't just let him die. Look at him," he said, already punching 9-1-1 into the keypad.

Warren heard the operator say, "Nine-one-one. What is your emergency?" As the young man began describing the situation and providing their location, Warren eased away. Blood was flowing from Robert's mouth and his movements had almost ceased. He wasn't dead yet, but he soon would be.

Another one down, Warren told himself.

28

"What was that all about?" asked Brandi.

Two men in business suits had just left the hotel room. When they had arrived half an hour ago, they informed her they needed to talk to Jordan… alone. When she started to object, they flashed badges and repeated that they needed to talk to him.

"Nothing," Jordan replied, but could not meet her gaze.

Brandi raised her voice and demanded, "Don't tell me 'nothing'! They were FBI." When he looked away, she said, "Look! I'm no dummy."

"I never said you were."

"But you're acting like it. Did it have to do with what Warren warned me about? Some kind of financial fraud?"

"No."

"Then what was it?"

Jordan remained silent, and his chest began rising and falling.

"That's it, isn't it? Warren wasn't lying, was he? You've stolen money from the investors and you need to leave the country before they arrest you."

Silence.

She stepped directly in front of him. "Goddammit Jordan! Talk to me!"

"I… "

Although she lowered her voice, it lost none of its intensity. "I can't believe it. Nancy and Sabrina were right. You're a thief and a liar and you want to make me a party to your crime."

"It isn't that simple."

"Oh, yes it is. I am amazed I didn't see through you earlier. I'm just your sex toy. Something to play with. Your marriage became a barren wasteland and you needed me to take care of your cock." She whirled around and faced the opposite direction. She, too, was breathing hard as she decided what to do next.

After several minutes of uninterrupted silence, she turned back and told him, "You realize that you've just admitted to everything I was saying, don't you?"

Jordan nodded, head averted, unable to meet her gaze.

"So all that bullshit about how you were fine with my bringing along Robbie and Rebecca… "

"That wasn't bullshit."

"BULLSHIT!" she shouted. "It was all about how you wanted to screw me… "

"It was a long time before it ever came to that," he said in a calm and even tone. "Don't you remember all of the months we spent just talking? All of the times we talked about how Warren had screwed things up? I will admit how much I enjoy making love to you."

"You mean screwing me."

"I said, 'making love.' You can't deny how much you

felt it, or you wouldn't have allowed our love making to continue."

Brandi hesitated, then admitted, "Yes. You're right. I did." Then, changing the conversation's direction and the tone of her voice, she said, "But that doesn't change the fact that you're a criminal. It doesn't change the fact that you defrauded the investors. The FBI came here for a reason and I don't want anyone to interpret my sticking around to mean that I was complicit. So good luck," she told him. She raised her voice and her expression and posture altered to reflect it. "I hope they fry your ass."

In the face of yet another betrayal, her anger gave way to despair and she broke down and cried. Despite the fact that her vision was blurred, she stormed into the bedroom, removed the first of several suitcases from the closet and tossed it onto the bed.

… … … … …

Unable to summon an apology that she would accept, Jordan watched Brandi disappear into the hallway while the bellman followed, drawing the baggage cart with him.

Suddenly alone, this part of his plan irreparably shattered, he sat in silence, unable to move. The only sounds he could hear were the hotel's air conditioning system and the blood rushing through his ears. He remained frozen for several minutes, gradually becoming aware of the growing discomfort in his damaged hands. It reminded him that, unless he stayed ahead of it, the pain would escalate to the point that it would be hours before the Percocet on his nightstand could bring it under control. Desolation gave way to necessity and Jordan forced himself to rise. One foot followed the other until he was standing in front of the bathroom sink. In need of a glass of water to rinse the medication down, he unwrapped the paper from around the tumbler that the hotel's maid service had left when they had finished their daily cleaning. With an eye on the wastebasket, he attempted to crumple the paper wrapper, but even that minimal task caused him to cry out. He dropped it. When he bent to retrieve it, but his lower back protested and he cried out once again. Determined to accomplish even that simple task, he pinched it between this thumb and forefinger, held it over the wastebasket and released it. However, the open piece of paper found its own trajectory and fluttered to a spot a foot beyond the receptacle. Jordan stared and clenched his lips, resigned to the fact there would be no second attempt and that it would remain where it was until the maid service cleaned the bathroom in the morning.

Rising again to standing, his eyes traveled from the glass to the faucet and he realized how almost impossible turning the tap would be. Wanting to give up altogether, but realizing there was no better alternative, he made his way into the bedroom and spotted the white capped, amber plastic container. If he could manage to remove the top without spilling the precious tablets across the carpet, he would place one of them under his tongue, let it dissolve and wait for the thirty to sixty minutes before the narcotic took effect.

After two botched attempts and one near fumble, Jordan's trembling fingers managed to deliver the medicine to its intended destination. The one positive aspect, he told himself, was that the drug was almost tasteless, in fact almost sweet, not bitter as he had expected the first time he chose to try this method of delivery.

As he waited for the tablet to dissolve, he realized that he could not continue living alone like this for very much longer. Having already committed Bryce's phone number to memory, he sat on the edge of the bed and reached for the telephone.

"Bryce," he said, trying to remove his desperation from the tone of his voice when the bodyguard answered. "There's been a change in plans. Can you come to my hotel room as soon as possible?"

"Of course," Whitmore replied. "Is anything wrong?"

"There's too much to go into over the phone, but yes. I need your assistance."

"Certainly. There are a couple of things I need to attend to first, but I believe I can be there in thirty minutes. Is that soon enough?"

The bodyguard's reply was better that Jordan had expected and he answered, "Yes. Anything less than an hour will be perfect."

"Fine, Mister Weeks. I'll be there as soon as I can."

Feeling more at ease than he had only a minute earlier, Jordan began to consider what he needed to do next. He would have to contact the hotel in Hamilton and find out how soon they could accommodate him, if not in the suite he had already reserved, then perhaps in something more modest until the suite became available. He would also need to check with the airline to see if he and Bryce could take something earlier. Naturally… *goddammit!*… he would have to alert them that Brandi would no longer be travelling with him. The thought left him seething for several minutes. Once he had mastered his emotions, he understood that he also needed to start transferring his money to new accounts. Since the authorities had learned about the existence of at least one in the Seychelles, possibly more, they were probably also aware he was heading for Bermuda. That would mean he would have to begin the second leg of his journey shortly after he had arrived in Hamilton.

Jordan rose and hobbled into the living area. He dropped into the impromptu computer chair and launched the browser. While he waited for the bookmarked bank account to upload, his mind returned to the federal agents' visit.

He wondered how they had found him, until he realized the task would not have been difficult. Where would any multi-millionaire go if his wife had evicted him? Such an individual would not have thrown himself onto a friend's doorstep, lest they consider him unable to take care of himself, so staying at a hotel would be a logical solution. Since there were only so many hotels in the immediate area that were able to offer five star accommodations—half a dozen at best—the same number phone calls would have led them to this one.

The stupid thing he had done was to book the room under his own name. How hard would it have been to have used an alias? He already possessed two phony drivers licenses, in case he needed to use them during the course of his getaway, as wells as corresponding credit cards. He berated himself for failing to perform the obvious when when Nancy evicted him. That alone would have short-circuited their pursuit. Now that they had found him, the chance of his being arrested increased manyfold. Of course, that would have probably caused Brandi to question his using a disguise. He knew very well that one lie always leads to another. He laughed aloud at the irony when a long forgotten quote from a college English course surfaced. Sir Walter Scott had it right when he said, "Oh, what a tangled web we weave, when first we practice to deceive!" Here he was, caught in the middle of it.

He also wondered who had alerted them. In the same instant, he realized it had to be either Nancy or Sabrina… probably Michael as well. Now, here he was, crippled and too far removed that he could not make them pay for their betrayal. Realizing that his failure to anticipate might very well be the flaw that would bring him down, he resolved to make sure he didn't repeat it.

As he returned from his reverie, he looked at the

monitor and wondered if his eyes weren't deceiving him.

That can't be right! he thought. He shook his head and rubbed his eyes.

That's impossible!

But possible it was, he realized as his eyes focused and confirmed what he had initially thought might be an illusion. He sank into the chair. The zero balance that stared back at him brought home the fact that he was in very, very deep shit. Wondering if only this bank was affected, Jordan sat up, left this website and hurried to upload another one.

Same result.

Holy crap!

So it was with the next one. And the next. And with several more after. When he came to a bank account that he had recently opened and saw that its funds were intact, he understood that Nancy must have discovered his list of user names and passwords. He forgot why he had elected to use a different set of abbreviations for this one. But when he realized that his change in strategy was probably all that had kept the hacker from robbing this one as well, he also understood that this particular change was all that had kept its balance safe and out of reach.

Having arrived at that understanding, he logged out and rushed to the second account whose username and password were similarly encrypted and was relieved to find those funds were also untouched. Realizing there was no guarantee that the new coding scheme wouldn't be uncrackable forever, he changed this account's password, then rushed back to the first, where he did the same.

Now that at least this much was safe, he transferred a portion of of money to one of the Canadian accounts. He knew that the amount he had chosen would be small enough to avoid alerting the Canadian tax authorities. He would also do the same from the second account. Despite having taken a devastating hit, the upside of where he now found himself was that he still possessed more than half of what he had taken. The downside was that the required size of the transfers mean it would take a great deal of time before he completed the task.

Afraid to remain within the United States boundaries, lest the FBI decided to arrest him, and deciding that the password changes would give him a certain amount of latitude, he telephoned the hotel to see if he could bump up his arrival until a few days from now. He was relieved when the concierge informed him that one of their executive suites had just come open, and that no one had reserved it until after Jordan's Presidential suite became available. They also explained that they could situate Bryce in a smaller room, two floors below, until his ultimate living quarters opened up.

So much for that.

The airline proved to be more difficult to work with and that complicated matters. In the end, however, changing their flight to a different airline with an overnight layover in Denver solved that problem as well.

There was a knock on the door and Jordan glanced at his watch. That would be Bryce, he decided, and rose to explain the change in plans.

29

Michael slid the baking tray of battered halibut into the oven and closed the door. He almost never found time to prepare his own meals these days, and was looking forward to a relaxing dinner of fish and chips without the din of a restaurant's patrons making it hard for him to think, let alone enjoy his meal in peace. He was reaching for the timer when the doorbell rang.

He looked at the clock and wondered, *Who the hell is that?*

As he went to answer it, he reached toward the counter for the bottle of amber ale, took a sip, then set it down.

"Can I help you?" he asked the two men in dark business suits who were standing on his doorstep.

They presented their badges and one of them replied, "Special Agents Lucas and Chan. We'd like to have a word with you. May we please come inside?"

Michael hesitated. "I'm not in any trouble, am I?"

"No, Mister… " The man consulted the business card he was holding. " …Sumner. We just have a few questions to ask. We can do this here if you'd like."

When Michael noticed the card, he said, "Please excuse me. I'd completely forgotten. My days have been kind of crazy lately." He stepped aside and gestured toward the interior. "Be my guests."

He ushered them into the living room and indicated a sofa where the men could sit. "Can I offer you something to drink? Some bottled water, maybe?"

"No, thank you," said Chan. He set his reserved expression aside, smiled and asked, "What can you tell us about the cash transfers from the investors accounts?"

Michael settled into a chair directly across from them and spent the better part of an hour recounting what had happened during the annual audit, including the reasons the firm conducted it and how they would identify anything unusual. "At first, I thought it had to be some kind of accounting error or that the funds had been moved into other holding accounts the firm maintains for various purposes. Our software, however, maintains a paper trail that most of the firm, including Jordan, is unaware of."

"And why would you do that?" Lucas asked.

"If the IRS were to conduct an audit of their own, it would provide information about any irregularities." Lucas nodded and Michael continued, "It quickly became apparent that the money had been moved to accounts in the Seychelle Islands over a great deal of time, initially in amounts nobody would have noticed. The amounts kept getting larger, however, and I suspect that Jordan was either getting nervous, or else was preparing to leave the country."

"And what makes you believe this was done by Mister Weeks?" Chan asked.

"Everyone who has access to these accounts has their own, unique login. The login identifies the user and any actions he takes."

"And who would these users be?" asked Lucas.

"Would most of the firm's executives be able to do this?"

Michael shook his head. "In order to keep these accounts as secure as possible, we limited access to our seniormost accountants—that would be myself and Noel Szymanski—a few other accountants, a few attorneys, and some of the clerical staff, who have more limited access, as well as Jordan Weeks and the late Warren Holmes."

Lucas, who had been taking notes, quickly flipped to an earlier page and confirmed, "That would have been Jordan Weeks's counterpart."

"Yes." Then, glancing at Lucas's note pad, Michael said, "I'd have thought you'd be using a tablet."

Lucas paused for a moment, frowned, and returned a questioning look. Then, as if understanding, he glanced at the paper notepad. "Ha! Yeah. Most of the other guys do. I guess you could say that I'm old school." He studied his notes, then flipped the page. He looked up and asked, "And nobody else, aside from the ones you just mentioned, would have had access?"

"Nobody else," Michael confirmed.

"Who else knows about this besides you, Mister Szymanski, Nancy Weeks, and Sabrina Babich?"

"Szymanski is on an extended leave due to health related issues, so he isn't in the loop yet. Miz Babich has contacted the SEC through their whistleblower's website and we're considering filing a Suspicious Activity Report through FinCEN."

"Considering," said Lucas, placing emphasis on the word. "Why haven't you done so already?"

Michael compressed his lips. "We're kinda new at this and our manpower's limited to Sabrina and me. Nancy's not part of the firm, so she isn't an active participant. In addition to tracking the money and trying to claw it back to our investors' accounts, we don't have as much time as we'd like to research our alternatives. We've been hoping the SEC would get back to us so we could ask them some questions about which would be a better way to proceed, but they haven't responded… at least, not yet. I'm also hoping that you can offer us other suggestions. Although, now that I think about it, I don't think that's your role."

Chan shook his head.

"I hate to say it," said Michael, "but sometimes it feels like we're flailing in the dark."

Michael ran his hands through his hair.

"Does anyone smell something burning?" asked Chan as he sniffed the air and glanced about.

BEEP! BEEP! BEEP! BEEP! BEEP!

"Holy crap!" exclaimed Michael and started to rise.

BEEP! BEEP! BEEP! BEEP! BEEP!

Chan and Lucas looked all around and Chan reached toward his jacket. The thought flashed across Michael's mind that he was reaching for his sidearm. When he stood, the words "smoke detector" slipped from his lips. As he ran to the kitchen, Michael glanced back and explained, "My dinner is burning."

BEEP! BEEP! BEEP! BEEP! BEEP!

A thick layer of black smoke filled the air at the level of his head as dark, gray streamers rose from the double oven's lower door. Bright yellow flames greeted him when he opened it. He was about to reach inside when he remembered to put on the pair of oven mitts that were sitting on the adjacent cooktop. As he reached in to remove it, he glanced over his shoulder to gauge how far it was to sink. With no regard for whether the mitts would catch fire, he picked up the baking sheet with the burning embers that were once the French fries he intended to accompany the fish. Nearly dropping it, but catching himself and increasing his grip before he could scatter the flaming potatoes across the kitchen's floor, he whirled, and in three quick steps, he maneuvered the fiery container across the kitchen and dropped it into the sink.

BEEP! BEEP! BEEP! BEEP! BEEP!

Angry that the mitt on his right hand would not allow him to turn on the water, he grabbed the mitt between his teeth. As soon as his hand was free, he turned the water faucet hard to the right. The clockwise motion released a flow of water and Michael reached for the handheld sprayer and showered the flames. Steam hissed as it rose and clouds of vapor merged with the all-encompassing smoke.

BEEP! BEEP! BEEP! BEEP! BEEP!

Michael reached for the window over the sink and slid a panel open. Whirling around, he turned the cooktop's ventilation fan to high, then opened the oven's upper door where the halibut was still cooking. To his relief, although the fish had begun to blacken, it wasn't yet burning. Forgetting that his right hand was gloveless, he reached in to remove it, then jerked it back when the tray seared his fingers.

BEEP! BEEP! BEEP! BEEP! BEEP!

The smoke detector drowned out his scream as he rushed to the basin and saw that the glove was now drenched. He fumbled to don it, then, once his hand was protected, he turned and removed the other baking tray, then doused that one in the sink as well.

BEEP! BEEP! BEEP! BEEP! BEEP!

Needing to quiet the smoke detector so that he could think clearly, Michael grabbed a step stool and carried it to the doorway where he ascended and, with a twisting motion, unscrewed the device from the wall mount and dropped it onto the floor where the air was better.

BEEP! BEEP! BEEP! BEEP! BEEP!

He turned on the exhaust fan above the cooktop, then opened the window for added ventilation. Grabbing a broom from beside the refrigerator, he cleared the air around the alarm with a series of sweeping motions until, after a minute, the beeping ceased and the apartment was once again quiet. Breathing hard, he walked to the front door and opened it allowing the wind to blow through. He removed the water logged mitt from his right hand and sucked his fingers. Only then, did he see the men from the FBI, standing in the living room.

"Are you all right?" asked Lucas.

Michael shook his head.

"Let me take a look at that," said Chan and came next to him. Appraising what Michael could see were third degree burns, he said, "I'm calling an ambulance," and reached for his cell phone.

While they were waiting for the paramedics, Lucas said, "Before I forget, there is something else I need to ask."

Michael sucked on his fingers and nodded.

"Why wouldn't Jordan have known about the 'paper trail,' as you put it?"

Michael shook his head. "Dunno," he said, adding, "Would you mind following me into the kitchen? I need to start cleaning up. As he left the living room, he explained, "He seems willfully ignorant about our security system. That's not surprising in view of how computer phobic he is." When the agents appeared curious, he explained, "He has no interest in software, except as it allows him to access the internet."

266

Michael thought about it for a minute, then said, "I guess, on one hand, that's fortunate, because it allowed him to be careless. On the other hand, if he had known about it, we probably wouldn't be in the mess we're in."

Lucas nodded and said, "Do you know what happened to his hands?"

"I haven't had a chance to talk to him since it happened, but the general consensus is that some person or persons came into the office and attacked him."

"Can you be more specific?" asked Chan. "Is there anything that suggests it might have been one of your investors?"

Michael cocked his head. "That would make sense. But, no, we don't have any idea if that was what happened. The security cameras malfunctioned. Or at least that's the best explanation why they didn't capture anyone entering or exiting the conference room where he was attacked."

The agents exchanged glances and he then went on to explain that the San Francisco Police Department had confiscated the server they were connected to, in order to have more time to evaluate whatever footage there was.

As they continued their conversation, he gave up on the cleaning, his burns prohibiting him from doing anything useful. And while the kitchen would have to remain on the figurative back burner, he knew that his first priority, after leaving the emergency room, would be to finish what he had started and complete the online transfers.

30

"Michael! What's wrong?"

Sabrina rushed to his side and sat down next to him. His head was down and he clutched it with both of his hands.

"It's too late," he gasped as he turned in his chair to look at her. "Jordan's locked us out."

She slid her chair closer and wrapped an arm around him. "It's alright. You did the best you could."

"It wasn't good enough," he objected. "Not nearly enough."

"How much did he get away with?"

"A lot."

"Do you know how much that would be?" Sabrina pressed, keeping the tone of her voice soft while avoiding any hint of accusation.

She had never seen him like this. He was always in charge, in control of both himself and his circumstances. Now, he seemed ready to fall apart at the seams at any minute. His hair was disheveled. Several buttons of his shirt were misaligned with their buttonholes, creating deep wrinkles in what was usually a pressed and freshly laundered shirt. She realized that his trousers also looked rumpled, as if he might have slept in them. It was then that she noticed his bandages.

"What happened to your hand?" When he frowned and shook his head, not appearing to comprehend, she explained, "Those bandages. How did you get them?"

He seemed disoriented and he hesitated before answering. His eyes returned to the computer display, then shifted to the dressing the PA in the emergency department had applied. He appeared to be struggling to focus, as if he had lost the conversation's thread. After another second, he managed, "Stupid mistake." He then haltingly described what had happened in his apartment.

"It must hurt like hell," she observed.

Another pause, then he nodded and said, "Sorry. I'm doped up on pain meds."

"Have you had any sleep?"

"Nope. I needed to get to work and there wasn't any time."

His head drooped and he appeared to be nodding off. He seemed to have disconnected, so she attempted to bring him back.

"Michael! Wake up!" She reached out and took his chin between her fingers, then turned it so that he was facing her. "I think I need to take you home."

"Yeah. Maybe," he admitted, before saying something apparently unrelated. "I think more than half."

"What?"

Seeming to have regained some of his awareness, Michael explained, "I think Jordan still has more than half of what he took." He took a deep breath, then sat a little straighter. "I was hoping I could have recovered more, but something, or someone, alerted him and... Damn! I was this close," he said, holding his thumb and forefinger one inch apart.

"Maybe it will be enough," she offered.

Michael shook he head. "All it will take for our little house of cards fall apart is for another investor to find that his balance has dropped to zero. Naturally, the FBI will be aware that we're not part of what happened, but the illusion of our competence will have been shattered. Can you imagine the fun the TV networks will have?" He chuckled. "Our faces will be all over the six o'clock news. That will be my fifteen minutes of fame." He yawned and added, "If I'm lucky enough that it won't stretch out to an hour… or even longer."

Sabrina stood and placed her hands under his armpits and tried to help him stand.

"Let's go," she said. "There's nothing for us to do here."

He resisted her effort for only a second. Then, nodding to acknowledge the truth in her statement, he rose and allowed her to lead him out into the vestibule that the conference room, his office, and those of several junior executives shared. Sabrina was grateful that the elevator was unoccupied, and that it didn't stop until it reached the underground parking garage. As Michael wobbled on unsteady feet, she reached inside his trousers' pocket and came up with the key to his gray 2018 Ford Taurus.

He didn't resist when she insisted on driving him home, or when she insisted on taking him to bed. The words "Oh, my God!" slipped from her lips as she walked him through the front door and then through the living room and happened to glance toward the kitchen.

Once she had undressed him and tucked him under the covers, she took time to tidy up. His apartment was colder than she wanted, so she slid the kitchen window closed and locked it.

After hanging her clothes on the closet hangers that Michael had reserved for her occasional visit, she slipped under the covers and moved next to him, spooning in an opposite arrangement from their usual one. She was resting her cheek between his shoulder blades and thinking she might want to bump up the heat a couple of degrees more when the apartment's chill intensified. Michael pressed himself against her and muttered something indistinct. It was then that Warren spoke to her.

Don't worry. I'm going to take care of Jordan.

Sabrina's eyes opened wide.

31

"Mister Weeks," said Bryce Whitmore, after opening the door at Jordan's request. The greeting had been phrased as a statement and the recognition it expressed caught Jordan off guard... until he remembered the research Bryce had conducted before accepting this assignment. He smiled at the man's diligence, then nodded.

"Please come in," he said, then stepped aside to make room for his bodyguard's unexpected physique.

Standing a good six feet four inches in height and weighing in at, by Jordan's estimate, more than two hundred fifty pounds, the bodyguard exceeded Jordan's expectations several times over. If appearances weren't deceiving, here was a man who could thwart any physical attack with ease. The look of intelligence that shone in his eyes suggested he was a man who could accomplish whatever task Jordan assigned him to.

There were four pieces of luggage on the floor where Bryce was standing. He reached for the two smaller ones and placed them just inside the doorway. The curious, oblong shape of one of them made Jordan wonder if these contained his weapons. He then lifted the two remaining suitcases, each one larger than Jordan would have cared to manage even when he was well, and stepped inside. Once he had entered, he set one down and, without having to be reminded of Jordan's handicap, he turned and bolted the door.

As Bryce carried all of his bags into the living room, Jordan was taken by the lines of his suit and how the garment moved with him, suggesting that it had been professionally tailored. He smiled at his new companion and said, "It's so nice to finally meet you." He started to reach out and shake hands, then caught himself. Instead, grimacing at the near *faux pas*, he asked, "Can I bring you something?" When Bryce raised an eyebrow and glanced at the bandages, Jordan replied, "I'm not completely helpless." Realizing how defensive that sounded, he softened his tone and asked, "May I bring you a glass of mineral water?"

Bryce smiled and returned a gentle, "No, thank you." When Jordan returned his own questioning look, Bryce explained, "We're going to be living in close quarters, so I try to maintain a degree of cordiality." He paused, then added, "Of course, if you prefer that I act more businesslike, I can do that as well."

Caught by surprise at the man's candor, Jordan chuckled. "Not at all. I just expected that since you're… well… "

"I understand," Bryce replied. "I'm your bodyguard, so you were expecting a tough guy."

Chagrinned, Jordan admitted, "Yeah. Well, sorta."

"I can be as tough as my duties require. But when it's just the two of us, I've found that a certain degree of camaraderie helps the days go by easier. You will find that I have a broad range of interests and can converse on a similarly broad range of topics. You asked for someone who could help you. I interpreted that to mean both physical assistance"— Bryce nodded toward Jordan's hands—"as well as helping to keep you comfortable with our relationship. I'm going to be at your side almost twenty-four hours, so it's important that you feel good about it."

Jordan nodded with a growing appreciation of the man's perceptiveness.

"Where will I be staying?" asked Bryce, looking around the suite.

"Please excuse me," said Jordan. He turned toward a wall that would have been to Bryce's right as he entered and pointed at a door. "While we're here, we have connecting suites.

"Take as much time as you need to refresh yourself. But I'm planning to leave first thing in the morning, so don't bother to unpack any more than necessary." As Bryce lifted one of his bags, Jordan added, "You'll find your key next to the service menu on the bureau. In another hour, I'll be sending down our orders for dinner at six. I expect you'll prefer to have your dinner served in your room."

Bryce turned to look at him. "This question is a little delicate, so please don't take offense."

Jordan frowned, uncertain what Bryce intended.

"Will you need me to cut your food into bite-sized portions?"

While this was something Brandi had done for him, Jordan hadn't considered that his bodyguard would handle this aspect of his care, as well. He compressed his lips and nodded.

"Fine," said Bryce. "I'll phone the front desk and ask them to set up a table in your living room so we can eat side-by-side."

… … … … …

Warren did not intend that Jordan go to the airport. He didn't intend for him to leave his suite. If he were to deal with his former business partner and hired bodyguard in the hallway, the lobby, or anywhere outside of the hotel, too many innocent parties could get hurt. He was a son-of-a-bitch when it came to settling scores. It was bad enough that he might have to injure Bryce—hopefully not kill him, but at least hobble him enough that he wouldn't be a factor—Warren's real target was Jordan and he intended to keep it like that. To keep things as simple as possible, he waited until both were sleeping so that he could gain the upper hand.

Jordan's bedroom was larger by far than what most people enjoy in a standard hotel room. A king sized bed was positioned against the longest wall, bookended by a pair of matching end tables. A desk-slash-dressing table stood against the wall connecting the one with the bed and the one opposite that opened onto the living room. There was a TV set and a bureau for socks, underwear, and miscellaneous elements of one's wardrobe, to the left and right of the connecting door. A table and two chairs stood off to one side of the bed in the space between it and the television, perhaps to supplement the desk, or to offer a place for playing games and writing letters. The fourth wall opened onto a walk-in closet, as well as a bathroom with shower and separate Jacuzzi bathtub.

Warren searched for something he could use to inflict injuries. Better equipped for this purpose than the conference room had been, the lamps on the end tables caught his attention, as did the chairs and the upholstered bench in front of the dressing table. In fact, the dressing table's mirror reminded him of what he had done to Kevin.

He wondered for a second if he should bother alerting Jordan to his presence. *What the hell*, he told himself, and decided it didn't matter one way or another. He raised the bench, held it above Jordan while he decided where to strike, then brought it down hard against Jordan's ribcage.

Jordan screamed, and Warren brought it down a second time.

When he cried out again, Warren grabbed him by his pajama's collar and lifted him out from under the blankets, holding him up where he could see him. It didn't matter that the room was completely dark, with no illumination other that what the alarm clock and the TV remote's LEDs provided. He could see Jordan's feet dangling. He could see Jordan's hand grabbing at his broken ribs.

Remember me? he demanded.

"Oh, God!" gasped Jordan.

Not quite, but close enough. Give me a little time, though, and I'll make sure that you meet Him.

Feet pounding against the carpet warned Warren what would happen next. The lights came on to reveal Bryce standing wide-eyed in the doorway, one hand on the light switch and the other holding a Glock.

"What the fuck!" he exclaimed. His chest heaved as he stared uncomprehending at his employer hanging above the bed.

Put the gun down, warned Warren. *It won't do you any good.*

Bryce's eyes opened wide as he glanced in all directions, the gun's barrel following his gaze. He no longer appeared the self-assured protector.

This is the last time I'm going to tell you. Put down the gun or this isn't going to end well.

The bodyguard began altering his stance. His feet shifted as he broadened the distance between them, bending at the knees to lower his center of gravity. He began moving around the bed until he was standing with Jordan dangling between him and the bathroom.

"Get me down!" Jordan demanded. "I'm hurt. My ribs are broken."

Bryce's eyes ranged over every inch of his employer's body while he tried to determine how what he was seeing was even possible. He looked up to the ceiling, perhaps, Warren mused, to see if there were any wires or guys suspending him. He bent down to look under Jordan's feet, which were pointing downward like a ballerina's. When it became obvious there was nothing underneath, the bodyguard reached out to touch him.

"God damn it, get me down," Jordan repeated.

Bryce inserted his pistol into the holster by his left shoulder.

That's nice, remarked Warren as, once again, Bryce peered in all directions, searching for the speaker. He climbed onto the bed, the mattress yielding under his feet as his weight compressed it. As he started to grip Jordan, Warren said, *I'm sorry, but I'm not in the mood to play nice*. He tore Jordan free from Bryce's grasp and hurled him across the room and into the mirror.

Glass shattered and Jordan tumbled to the floor as Bryce, knees pumping, managed to remain upright. Warren grinned at the two barefoot men, unable to navigate through the shards of glass strewn across the carpet, some of them standing upright on their edges.

"What's happening?" called Bryce.

Jordan arched his back and rose to a near sitting position. "My partner," he gasped, barely above a whisper as he moved his hand first to his ribs, and then his shoulder.

"What?" asked Bryce, cupping a hand to his ear.

Somewhat louder, Jordan answered, "It's my business partner."

The bodyguard stopped pedaling and stood staring. "You said he was dead."

"He is. He's a ghost." When the bodyguard's expression remained unchanged, Jordan said, "If you won't believe me, just look at where I am and consider how I got here." After another second, when Bryce still didn't respond, Jordan shouted, "I'm paying you to protect me! Get me the hell out of here before he kills me!"

Suddenly alert, Bryce studied Jordan's situation, then moved near the end of the bed where the pillows were. He leaned forward and grabbed the blankets. Then, as he tore them free, he moved back to the bed's center. Holding the bedding with both hands, he shook it so that it was hanging freely. His eyes travelled from where Jordan was sitting to the bed and back again, assessing the distance, then tossed the covers so that they spread and arced through the air with one edge draped over Jordan's legs, the rest falling across the glassy daggers.

Without losing any more time, he stepped down and tread carefully across the carpet, avoiding places where what was hidden beneath the blankets created ridges. Glass crunched as he stepped, but did not deter him. When he was standing beside Jordan, he reached down and said, "If I'm going to get you out of here, I need to lift you. I promise it's going to hurt, but there is no other way."

Jordan nodded and reached up to assist him. Studying where he placed his feet, Bryce moved close where he could gain better leverage.

"Ready?" he asked.

Jordan nodded.

Bryce inhaled deeply, then said, "Here we go."

Using both hands, he pulled Jordan to a sitting position, then leaned forward and, in one swift move, pulled Jordan up and draped him over his shoulder. With Jordan's torso on top of his back, Bryce rose to standing. Securing Jordan's legs with one arm while extending the other for balance, Bryce turned and started running toward the door.

Smooth move, Ex-Lax, but not smooth enough, said Warren as he slammed the door before Bryce could get there. Bryce reached for the doorknob with his free hand, but Warren threw him back, forcing him to fall and let Jordan go.

Kinda tough, isn't it, to be in a situation where your guns and hand-to-hand combat training can't help. I'll tell you what. You have two choices: Leave Jordan alone with me and I'll let you stay healthy. Or try to fight me and I'll make sure you lose and lose badly.

Bryce rose to his feet and opened the door, then turned around and bent down to lift his employer again.

Certain people would find your commitment admirable. Me? I find it a pain in the ass.

Before Bryce could get a solid grip, Warren lifted him into the air. *Look what you've gone and made me do. I promise you one thing. This isn't going to go well for you.* With that, Warren hurled the bodyguard into the wall beside the door. He struck hard, then dropped to the floor and Jordan's eyes and mouth came open. His body sagged when his bodyguard was slow to recover. He looked at the door to the living room and extended a hand to reach the doorknob.

Your client is running out on you, Warren told Bryce.

Bryce shook his head to clear it, then kicked out his legs in order to counterbalance his attempt to rise. Placing a hand on either side of him, he pushed his torso to vertical, drew his feet back under him, then knelt for a second before standing. Warren responded by hurling him into the wall by the dressing table. A pounding on the wall and muffled shouting told Warren he had gained the attention of the adjacent suite's occupant. Jordan responded by crying, "Help! Somebody help me! Help!"

Warren needed to shut him up. If that party decided to phone the front desk and the hotel's staff responded, it would cut into the time he needed to execute his plan. He decided to escalate.

He picked up a chair and swung it horizontally, striking Jordan in the side of the head. He studied him for a second, hoping he hadn't damaged his brain. When Jordan started to move, Warren became optimistic, because he would eventually need to make use of his cognitive abilities.

Bryce moaned. When Warren turned to evaluate him, he saw that the man had risen onto all fours and was starting to look around. While Warren didn't want to kill him, he needed to keep him incapacitated for the next several minutes. He raised the chair above him and brought it down hard against his head. Bryce collapsed under it, his arms and legs splayed in four directions.

Now, good buddy, he said to Jordan. *I have plans for you. Let's hope you don't disappoint me.* He opened the door and dragged Jordan to the table where his computer stood. *I need you to show me how to log on to the two bank accounts for which you changed the passwords*, said Warren as he lifted him and dropped him onto the chair in front of it.

"I don't know what you're talking about."

Seriously? I can cause a great deal more pain if you decide not to cooperate.

"Do you think I'm that stupid? Do you really think I'm going to leave myself without… "

Without any money? That's your greatest motivating factor, isn't it? Well, let me clue you in. You're not going anywhere. Bermuda is out of the question and so is Canada.

Jordan looked around, as if doing that would help.

You don't really give a shit about Michael and Sabrina. You don't even care about your clients. But if you don't start helping me right now, I'm going to start hurting the one person you do care about …good buddy.

Jordan folded his arms in front of him, but Warren grabbed his left arm and managed to extend it despite Jordan's struggles to protect it.

You've probably noticed that I am now able to exert a great deal of control over things in the physical world. Allow me to demonstrate how much control I do possess.

Although Warren was pinning Jordan's hand beside the computer's keyboard, eight or so feet across the room to Jordan's left, a vase containing a bouquet of flowers rose from a table and hovered. Jordan's jaw dropped.

Nice trick, wouldn't you say? asked Warren as the vase began moving toward him.

How much pain do you think it's going to cause if I drop it onto your hand... the surgery being as recent as it is?

As Jordan opened his mouth to respond, Warren asked, *How much damage do you think it's going to cause if I bring it down with the same force I used to throw you against the wall?*

Jordan gasped and his eyes opened wide.

You should know by now that I deliver on all my promises, so I promise you this: I intend to dwarf anything I did to you in the conference room.

When the vase had travelled half of the distance between where it had started and where Jordan was sitting, Warren said, *So let's see. You've trashed your marriage. You've lost Brandi. Michael and Sabrina have recovered a large part of what you've stollen. The FBI is on to you. I've disabled your bodyguard. You're now at my mercy and you're holding out for… what? As I see it, you're in a no-win situation.*

The vase was now beside where Jordan was sitting. It started to rise until it hovered in place a couple of feet above Jordan's hand. Perspiring profusely, Jordan said, "I can't type very fast."

Warren laughed. *I'm not in so much of a hurry that you won't be able to do what I'm asking, so long as you start typing NOW!*

Jordan moved one of his hands to the the trackpad and navigated to the first bank's website. Once he had entered the user name, he moved the cursor to the password field and paused.

"Do you want me to write it down?" he asked.

Just type, said Warren.

Jordan did as he was told. Once the page revealed the account information, Warren instructed, *Now the next one.*

Jordan complied. With the second bank's user name and password firmly etched in Warren's memory, Warren commanded, *Now, let's move on to the rest of them.*

"The rest of… "

Don't play coy, said Warren.

"I've done what you asked me to do," pleaded Jordan, turning his head to where he possibly assumed Warren would be.

Don't play stupid. You know what I want. When Jordan remained frozen in front of the monitor, Warren asked, *Do you really think those hands can take any more abuse? I'm fully prepared to leave you permanently crippled.*

Lips clenched in anger, Jordan moved from the second bank's website and entered the URL of yet another bank.

Good boy, said Warren. *And when you've shown me what I need to know about this one, keep going to the rest of them. If, at any point in time, I suspect you're holding back on me, I won't give you any more warning. Those hands of yours will be two flaps of crushed bone and mangled flesh. No surgeon—I don't care how gifted he might be—is going to be able to form them into anything even remotely human.*

For the next five minutes, Jordan, trembling and in tears, navigated from one site to the next, while Warren's now perfect memory recorded every keystroke until, at one point, Jordan stopped.

"That's it. That's the last one," he said and leaned back into the chair, his remaining strength having abandoned him.

You know, said Warren, *you've got quite a memory. So many usernames and passwords and you remembered every one of them. I'm seriously impressed.*

"What are you going to do with them?"

Now that's a stupid question. Why, hand all of that information to your top accountant and your Marin County salesperson. Do you seriously believe I might have any other use for it? Maybe set myself up like you were planning to do for you? Give me a break. A knock at the suite's front door reminded Warren that he still had work to do. *And now I'm going to give you everything you deserve. You remember the phrase 'just deserts,' don't you?*

Jordan's eyes came open. Suddenly finding new strength, he moved the chair away from the computer and started to rise. He was turning around to face where the knocks, and now the voices, were coming from when a large upholstered chair that had been standing by the suite's entrance flew at him.

Knocked back on top of the one where he had been sitting, Jordan reached back to arrest his fall and screamed when one of his hands came between his falling body and the chair that was under it.

Thought you could screw my wife and I wouldn't know? hissed Warren. *Nobody fucks with me and gets away with it.*

Jordan yanked aside his hand to avoid falling onto it. With it now out of the way of his descending two hundred pounds, Jordan tumbled onto an armrest, pinning the other hand. In response to his cry of agony, the knocks on the front door grew louder and Warren knew that he didn't have more than a few seconds before someone came up with a door key.

Stupid Warren's dead, so I can do whatever I want. Is that what you thought? Come on. Admit it.

Jordan nodded in a series of short, abrupt jerks. "I'm sorry," he cried and started sobbing.

Why is it whenever one of you sons of bitches thinks he's going to die, he develops a conscience? Do you think that apologizing is going to make me forgive you? Do you think that it's going to make me decide, "Well, hey! He's not such a bad guy after all. What he did doesn't matter, now that he's said those two magic words."

WELL, FUCK YOU, SON OF A BITCH!

Shoving Jordan onto the carpet, Warren raised the chair again and brought in down repeatedly, making sure that one of its four wooden legs or its pointed corners landed on Jordan's skull each time the chair descended. After half a dozen blows, Jordan stopped moving. Half a dozen more and Jordan stopped breathing.

"Mister Weeks?"

Warren turned at the words coming from the bedroom doorway. Bryce had entered. Warren had no grudge against this innocent bystander, but he was in no position to prevent what was about to happen next. The sound of voices and the front door opening told Warren that the bodyguard was going to have a lot of explaining to do.

32

Warren left the hotel and went out into the city, exhilarated by what he had done and by all he had accomplished. The trio of thugs were dead. So was Jordan. Warren was about to give Michael and Sabrina all of the information they needed to keep W&H Limited functioning and its investors unaware of the damage Jordan had done. Brandi's affair was over. Even though Warren was slow to admit it, he was still in love with her and he was glad she wouldn't screw up her life by running off with his ex-partner. Her inheritance of Warren's interest in his soon-to-be-resurrected firm would maintain her lifestyle for as long as she wished. Nancy was also assured of a certain and stable future, now that Warren had eliminated her need to file for a divorce and the investors would not be going after her assets.

With little else demanding his attention, Warren turned to the problem of whether he could return to his children or if he was doomed to remain in exile. In view of all the positive events that had resulted from his actions, he could not believe that what he had done to the street thugs and his partner would truly warrant the penalty Bertrand had predicted. Needing to pursue his earlier discussion further, he set off in search of him.

Because he was still learning the ropes of the afterlife, including how he could sense the presence of others like him, he still had no way to determine where he might be. He headed to Washington Square, hoping Bertrand would be notice him and meet him there.

It was just past the evening rush hour and the typical array of evening shoppers, lovers, and sightseers were sauntering up and down Columbus Avenue or around the park in front of Saints Peter and Paul Church, in search of whatever might meet their needs at eateries offering Italian dining *al fresco*, shops selling pastries, focaccia or espresso, even at a shop that creates custom made hats. But after Warren had lingered for almost an hour, he was unable to detect any sign of his friend and decided to see if scanning the city would reveal anything useful.

He rose above the treetops until he was level with the church's roseate window, high enough that he could see the distant outline of Golden Gate Park. The cross atop Mount Davidson was standing gray against the setting sun, its rays casting Coit Tower with pastel shades of rose, tangerine, and violet. Street lamps and office buildings, homes and businesses were starting to glow as the city's drab promenades began to transform into a glowing webwork of lights.

Off to the west, a spark brighter than Venus appeared against the deepening darkness above the Pacific. Warren watched in fascination as the spark grew in luminosity until it became obvious that its apparent increase marked an object's high velocity approach. He was wondering what this strange phenomenon might be when, abruptly, it transformed into a ghostly specter in front of him.

Get away from my church! The spirit shouted.

But I wasn't...

GET WAY FROM MY CHURCH!

Why was the spirit coming after him, Warren

wondered? He never had anything to do with the Roman Catholic Church... or had he?

All at once he saw himself wearing the black cassock and white surplice of an altar boy. He was in the sacristy of Saint Mark's Church, in a city whose name he could not recall, at a time before his family had moved to California. Father... *Damn it! What was the priest's name?...* McFarlane was pouring a glass of sacristy wine and encouraging him to take a sip, and then a swallow. Warren remembered how, even though he found the alcohol relaxing, he knew what Father McFarlane was doing was wrong. "No, Father," he protested as the gray haired priest delved a hand underneath his garments, touched the front of Warren's pants, and made him feel something previously unknown, but far more pleasurable than anything he had ever experienced. He could still hear McFarlane saying, "You're a good boy, Warren. The Lord will reward you for making an old priest happy."

Fragments of long repressed memories began rising to the surface, like bubbles in a pond. Warren remembered how the priest had asked his parents if their son could work in the rectory to answer the phone and receive sick calls, to take down information from new parishioners in order to free up McFarlane and the other priests to go about their duties.

From time to time Father McFarlane would appear unexpectedly and it would be just the two of them inside the priests' residence. The old priest would make some attempts at small talk, asking Warren if he had remembered to collect the money parishioners had deposited into a slot when they paid for votive candles, or about the family of Hungarian immigrants who had come in hopes of joining Saint Mark's Church and whether they had had any difficulty completing the necessary forms. Eventually, however, Father McFarlane's interest in these subjects dwindled as he turned his mind to other matters, largely focused on his and Warren's erections and how Warren could help him take care to them with a little manipulation so he return his thoughts to more holy matters.

You are defiling God's house with your presence, the spirit cried, interrupting Warren's reverie. All at once, Warren's mind returned to his conversation with Bertrand about Saints Peter and Paul Church and the ghost named Ricca. In that instant, Warren believed he understood the reason for Ricca's outrage. It wasn't merely because of Warren's presence. It wasn't merely because, as Tolliver had explained it, there was some connection between him and the Holy See. Rather, it was because of the acts he and Father McFarlane had committed inside the rectory, inside the sacristy, in front of the altar and the very sacrament it contained: Christ's body.

Dear Jesus! he cried at the understanding. The moment the words slipped from Warren's lips, Ricca hurled himself toward him and Warren dodged the attack.

I'm sorry, he heard himself say an instant before Ricca came at him again. *I was too young. I didn't understand.*

Apparently, the apology did not matter. Ricca launched a series of attacks and Warren barely avoided each of them. Knowing he could not remain on the defensive forever, Warren wondered how he could change things. He heard Bertrand telling him, *Imagine the kind of creature you need to be to turn the struggle to your advantage.*

How? he asked.

Envision yourself as a beast of great power. I can't describe it any better than that. But if you don't figure it out in a hurry, you're doomed.

Understanding that all of his previous successes had been the result of focusing his thoughts and using his imagination, Warren remembered the creature Bertrand had been during that previous struggle and tried to envision himself as something similar.

When Ricca came at him again, Warren, preoccupied with his transformation, was slow to react. He felt something collide with him and watched as something that looked like vapors flew away from him. Although Warren possessed no physical components, he felt somehow lessened.

You can't let him do that again, shouted Bertrand.

Caught between needing to avoid being struck and the need to go on the offensive, Warren began moving away from Washington Square, hoping that by distancing himself from Saints Peter and Paul's, Ricca might not continue. The spirit, however, was not so easily appeased and kept launching new ones.

As Warren began imagining his body covered in scales, his exterior began transforming. When he imagined himself growing larger than his attacker, Ricca began to seem smaller in comparison. He imagined himself with dagger-like fangs and claws and was immediately taken by how his limbs and mouth felt different.

His view of San Francisco whirled as another strike sent Warren tumbling and, once again, he felt himself lose more of his substance. While he could not define exactly how the loss affected him. He certainly felt weaker.

As his tumbling ceased and his vision of the world began to stabilize, Warren worried what might happen if these attacks were to continue. He couldn't die, but if he lost more of his substance, would he just cease to be?

Warren saw the great beast that was Bertrand Tolliver flash by. He collided into Ricca and the beasts began fighting. Uncertain how long this distraction would occupy Ricca and whether Bertrand would prevail, Warren returned to his transformation.

He sprouted a tail and a pair of batlike wings, the kind he associated with dragons. *All the better to maneuver with*, he told himself. Next, he imagined a series of stegosaurian ridges along his spine for protection from attacks from above, and six spikes at the end of his tail. Last of all, Warren focused on his desire to become more substantial. As Warren's mass increased, he found himself sinking, so he flapped his wings and became giddy when he found himself flying.

His exhilaration became short-lived, however, when he heard someone cry out in pain and realized that it sounded like Bertrand. Turning toward the battle, Warren saw that Ricca had sunk his teeth into Bertrand's neck. Fearing what might happen to his friend if this were to continue, Warren launched himself at Ricca. Just before he collided, he spread his wings and arrived at a nominal speed. He spun around and spiked Ricca's body with his tail. Ricca released his grip and Bertrand backed away, shaking his head, appearing dazed and uncertain.

Ricca also looked shaken as he shook himself free from Warren's spikes. He stared at his new attacker as wisps of vapor flowed from the wounds Warren inflicted, then backed away and stared at his two opponents. And while a similar substance also flowed from the wounds in Bertrand's neck, he turned to face Ricca as well.

Ricca watched Warren advancing, then looked in the opposite direction to see Bertrand on the offensive, too. Finding himself outnumbered, he started backing away, then turned and flew back in the direction from which he had come.

Are you alright? Warren asked after Ricca had vanished.

As he returned to his normal form, Bertrand nodded and sighed, *I believe I'll survive.*

What is this stuff? asked Warren as he, too, lost the shape of the beast he had created and gestured toward the dissipating vapors that were flowing from both of them.

It's what we're made of, the stuff that allows us to manifest ourselves to the living.

Is that what happened to me when Ricca struck me?

Bertrand nodded.

After giving the matter some thought, Warren replied, *You told me that, after the first blow, I shouldn't have allowed him to continue.*

That's right. If you kept losing your… essence, I guess you could call it… at some point you would disappear.

So it's a little like losing blood, Warren offered.

It is, but it's more profound. Some time ago, another one of us allowed herself to lose some of her substance when Magnus attacked her. During subsequent attacks, she grew progressively weaker until, at one point, she lost her ability to communicate. After a while, she was barely visible. I was with her, trying to see if there was anything I could do for her, when she vanished before my eyes. I haven't seen her since.

Warren stared at Bertrand, unable to express himself for several seconds. He finally managed, *That frightens me.*

And so it should, replied Bertrand. Taking a good look at Warren, he frowned and said, *You've been up to something, haven't you?*

Warren wanted to deny it, but suspected that another darkening of his aura would make it clear he was lying. *Bertrand,* he began in a tentative tone. *I've only been trying to address the damage that others had done to me and my friends. Why should this be something terrible?*

Without specific knowledge of what you've done,

Bertrand answered, *I can only conclude it has to do with the way that you handled it.*

Warren related the things he had done and to whom, as well as the reasons behind his actions. At one point, Bertrand interrupted. *Look*, he said with an exasperated sigh, *I don't make the rules.*

But...

You're preaching to the choir, Warren. Given half a chance, what do you think I would have done to the bullies who put me here? But as much as I sympathize, I can't begin to emphasize strongly enough that you're digging yourself into a pretty deep hole. I feel for you, my friend. But I also have to tell you that, from this point forward, you're going to have to fend for yourself.

I'm not your enemy, Warren objected. *I would never do anything to hurt you.*

You probably wouldn't have dealt with these people the same way when you were alive. When Warren didn't contradict him, Bertrand said, *Your silence speaks for itself, so I have to believe that, while you might not intend it now, if I do something that offends you—Lord knows, I'm probably offending you as I speak—I need to keep away from you or the two of us are apt to have the same kind of confrontation as the one I had with Ricca.*

Good-bye, Warren, Bertrand said as he turned away. *And good luck. You're going to need it if you run into Magnus.*

As for Warren, he set off to perform the only redeeming act at his disposal.

33

"You need to get something into you," Sabrina insisted. When Michael refused and turned his head, she set the slice of toast next to his scrambled eggs. "Maybe try a little fruit salad," she suggested. When he shook his head and clenched his lips, she sighed and sat back in her chair. "This isn't going help," she said, picking up her now cold cup of coffee and putting it to her lips.

After a minute, he broke the silence. "I never thought it would come to this. I… " He hesitated, then turned to look at her. "If I only had another few minutes."

She placed her hand on his and said, "But you didn't." She set down the cup and held his hand between hers. "It isn't your fault. You did everything you possibly could." When he opened his mouth to object, she touched her finger to his lips and smiled. "I'm amazed you were even able to crack his code. Do you realize what an accomplishment that was? Not many people could have managed to get into even one of his accounts, let alone… How many?"

"Twelve."

"Yes," she said. "You got into twelve of his bank accounts and transferred what was there back to the firm. You should be proud of yourself."

"But I didn't get everything."

"No. You didn't. But that's nothing to be ashamed of."

He sat in silence a minute, then took a deep breath, and nodded, then reached for his fork.

··· ··· ··· ··· ···

They were finishing up the dishes and putting them away. Sabrina had suggested they go for a walk. "I think it will help clear our heads and give us a healthier perspective." She was placing their glasses into the cupboard when she found herself shivering.

"Michael, did you open the window?"

Sliding the silverware drawer shut, he said, "No. I didn't." He turned and looked around the kitchen. "Warren!" he called, and Sabrina looked around as well. "Warren! We know you're here. Please say something."

Sorry, Warren replied. *Something's happened that's made it harder for me to manifest. I apologize.*

"Not a problem," said Sabrina. She replaced the dish towel and furrowed her brows. "What's up?"

I have some good news for you. I overheard your conversation...

"Goddamn it, Warren!" Sabrina shouted. "That was private."

I understand. And like I said, I apologize. I wanted to let you know I was here, but I couldn't. Like I said, something happened.

Sabrina pulled out one of the chairs at the table and seated herself. "Is it something serious?"

Kinda. But it's hard to explain and it doesn't affect you anyway, so I'd rather not go into it.

"Alright," she said. "So tell us, what brings you here?"

Like I said, I've brought you good news. Pull up a chair, Michael. When Michael was slow to respond, Warren said, *Please sit, because what I'm about to tell you is going to drop you onto your ass if you don't.*

Once Michael was seated, Warren asked, *What would be the best news anyone could give you? What would be the one thing you'd most want to hear from me or anyone?*

Michael thought for a minute, then offered in a skeptical tone, "You've brought me all of Jordan's passwords."

Bright boy!

"Wait! What?" When Warren didn't contradict him, Michael said, "Are you serious?"

Can you think of anything better?

"Seriously?" asked Sabrina.

When have you known me to be anything but? When the pair remained silent, waiting for something more, Warren said, *Meet me at your office.*

··· ··· ··· ··· ···

Michael flicked on the light switch and peered inside. Sabrina leaned over his shoulder. Unable to sense Warren's presence, Michael went to his desk and turned on the computer. When the login screen appeared sat down and entered his password. The task bar had just appeared when Warren told him, *Launch the browser and let's get down to business.* Surprised by the abrupt intrusion, but curious as to what the moment held in store, Michael hesitated an instant, then interlaced his fingers and cracked his knuckles and did as Warren instructed.

Warren provided the first in a series of URLs he wanted Michael to visit. When the bank's logon page appeared, Warren told him how to enter the case sensitive user name and password.

When the accounts page appeared, Sabrina exclaimed, "Michael, look at those account balances."

"Holy shit," whispered Michael as he studied the numbers. "This is so much larger than any of the other accounts."

And I promise, this is only the beginning.

"How did you convince Jordan to give you this?" gasped Sabrina.

Let's just say I have a very persuasive personality.

"I'll say!"

They spent almost an hour emptying the various offshore accounts, each of them with far larger balance than Michael had expected.

"I don't understand," he said. "I'm the firm's chief accountant. Why wasn't I aware of how much money was involved?"

I suspect it's because the theft started about the time W & H Limited brought you onto its team. You spent the better part of your first two years getting familiar with our business and accounting practices and putting new ones in place. During that time, you would have hardly had room on your plate for anything else. You did uncover the fraud, however, once you had finally settled in and things were running the way you wanted.

Michael nodded.

Those months were more than enough time for Jordan to dummy up accounting reports. Stop for a moment to consider how long it takes for the I.R.S. and its teams of specialists to unravel what many corporations have concealed over similar periods. Then remember you're just one man—one gifted man I will grant you—but still just one.

Once Warren had assured them that they had secured everything Jordan had stolen, Michael spent the next several hours making transfers to each individual investor.

"I can't say it's completely accurate," said Michael once the project concluded. He leaned back in his chair, laced his hands behind his head and sighed. "But it's pretty damn close."

I think it's close enough to assure the investors that what they see is what they should be expecting.

"Thank you, Warren," Sabrina told him.

You're welcome. He paused for a second, then added, *Before I go, I just want to say, take good care yourselves. You're two wonderful people and have a nice future ahead of you, whether together or on your own.*

Sabrina moved behind Michael and wrapped her arms around his shoulders. She kissed him on the cheek and Michael turned and pressed his lips against hers.

Don't botch things up like I did with Brandi, although I suspect you won't.

"What's wrong?" she asked. "Why do you sound so sad?"

Like I told you before, something has happened that I still need to deal with.

"Is there anything we can do to help?" Michael asked.

I wish you could. But, no, I'm afraid not. His tone hardened. *This afterlife stuff is a bitch.*

34

Warren travelled to Sutro Heights Park where he could sit high above the old Cliff House, atop the stone wall that rimmed the park's western boundary and gaze over the ocean and down the Great Highway. He smiled when he noticed a wedding procession leave the beach where the ceremony had been held, the celebrants dressed in costumes that portrayed what people might have worn a couple of centuries earlier across the Atlantic. Bridesmaids were holding the bride's train above the drifting sand and a pair of riders were mounted on horses whose colorful livery was marked with heraldic crests. The bridegroom, walking beside his wife of just a few minutes, was decked out in the costume of a noble. The priest, who was appropriately balding, was outfitted similar to Robin Hood's legendary Friar Tuck. Others were dressed as courtiers, jugglers, monks, and nuns, making the procession the kind of whimsical distraction Warren needed if he were to forget his woes.

Starting to feel more at ease, Warren moved to the park's center where a nearly vanished concrete foundation marked the outline of an eighteenth century bath house. Two college age kids were lying face to face on the grass the outline encircled. They were prostate on their bellies, his hand delving into her blouse, her lips pressed hard against his, too caught up with desire and a budding romance to notice the people meandering along the walkways that encompassed them. The sight of this couple returned Warren to a romance he once had, all those years ago when he was as young as these two. He and his girlfriend had been similarly enamored and caught up with the heady excitement that hormones bring. Warren paused when he recalled that she had broken off with his former schoolmate and grew troubled when he remembered her calling him… was it Jordan? That couldn't be right, he decided and cast the thought aside, concluding it was too great a coincidence.

A blow from his right slammed Warren hard to his left. Dazed and shaken, he looked up and saw the rump and tail of a large beast moving away from him. Had he not experienced a similar attack a short time ago, he might have taken his time to recover. As it was, Warren knew that, in almost no time at all, the beast would return and strike again.

Scrambling to remember how he had transformed himself in that previous encounter, Warren began creating the scales, claws, fangs, and spikes that he needed. His limbs and body grew and he began to sprout wings as the great beast wheeled in the air to confront him. Hoping he had done everything necessary to defend himself, uncertain to what extent, if any, the laws of physics might apply, Warren started circling the distant enemy out of fear that lack of momentum would make it difficult to set his stationary self into motion.

This is nuts! This is absolutely insane, he told himself. *Is this what Bertrand has to do to survive? Is this what I have to do?*

His eyes widened as the creature came at him again and he avoided its attack by scant inches. He had enough presence of mind to lash out with his tail as it passed, and saw its spikes dig gouges along the enemy's flank. The victory was short-lived, however, because the creature was outfitting its tail with similar weapons. Warren was breathing hard after just two attacks and that worried him. After losing some of what

Bertrand called his "essence," he felt noticeably weaker. He lacked the almost limitless energy he possessed right up until his encounter with Ricca, as if some essential part of him was missing. He doubted he could continue much longer and he looked around for somewhere to hide.

To Warren's amazement, the people strolling through the park seemed unaware of this deadly battle. A mother holding the hand of her unsteady toddler, who was obviously learning to walk, walked through the tail of Warren's attacker. Warren cringed when the spikes passed through them, half expecting the two would either be bludgeoned, or else be fatally impaled, but the pair moved along without incurring any harm, completely unaware. He smiled with relief when the child pointed at a flittering butterfly and the mother smiled in delight at his discovery, oblivious to anything else. It was only when movement at the edge of his vision alerted Warren that the creature was on the move again that he began to assess his readiness for combat. His strength was fading rapidly and if that thing suspected how weak he was, it would certainly escalate its attacks and finish him off in a matter of seconds. He decided he needed to convince it otherwise and that a show of force was his best option to do so.

When the beast had drawn to within one dozen yards, Warren opened his mouth to expose rows of needlelike teeth and impressive canines. Rising onto his hind legs, he raised both forelegs to display his nearly foot-long claws. As Warren had hoped, the creature slowed to assess what it was facing.

Warren had another flash of inspiration. Before the thing had time to decide what action it should take, he visualized himself standing near a pond in Golden Gate Park. Thought became deed and instantly Warren found himself hiding beneath a grove of trees at the water's edge.

Unlike Sutro Heights, this portion of Golden Gate Park was deserted. The predominant sound was of branches shifting in the breeze, although the distant sound of motor vehicles was also in the air. He heard a woman's laugh in the distance but, aside from that, Warren believed he was alone. Uncertain whether that creature could follow him, he stared through the branches, trying to see through the glare of the midday sun.

He remained like that for close to half an hour, but eventually he decided it might be safe to leave his concealment and move into the open. He was abandoning the shape that had given him protection when someone spoke and the sound made him jump.

Hello Warren.

Bertrand?

Bertrand replied, *What you've been doing has caused me a great deal of concern.*

How did you find me and what are you talking about? When Bertrand hesitated, Warren asked, *For that matter, why should anything I've done be any of your concern? I've been giving the matter some thought and what you've told me doesn't make any sense.*

Such as… ?

That thing about my behaving myself and how it would affect whether you could trust me. How the hell does how I treat my enemies have any bearing on how I treat my friends? …assuming you are my friend.

I'd like to be your friend, Bertrand began. *It's just that…*

Before Bertrand could finish, Warren cut him off. *Don't give me that crap! When I was alive, I started seeing a pattern in how certain people communicated. For example, when someone one I knew said, "People are going to tell you I'm a thief. Don't believe them," and then I eventually learned that person really was a thief. Or when a girl I knew in college said, "People are going to tell you I sleep around. Don't believe them," and then I learned she was screwing all of my friends. Then you come along and tell me that you are going to harm me if you find I've been addressing past grievances, but you really are my friend. So I have to question your sincerity. You see, while these situations aren't exact parallels, they do have one factor in common: if someone tells me to ignore something that sounds awfully suspicious, I should go with my gut and question their intentions.*

You tell me I should trust you, but you don't trust me. Something doesn't exactly fit and I'm wondering why. And to top that off, after I almost lost a battle to some creature I don't know… Ricca or Magnus— assuming there really is a Magnus… and then you show up out of nowhere, I have to ask myself what the hell you're doing here. You haven't answered me, and I have to ask myself why.

I need your help, said Bertrand.

Really? In what way?

I'm not sure where to begin. Bertrand sighed. *I'm wondering if we can perform a sort of… transfusion, I'd guess you would call it.*

Transfusion?

I'm wondering if you can donate some of your… Bertrand hesitated. *…essence.*

Seriously?

I know that what I'm asking sounds like a great imposition, but…

Warren cut him off. *A great imposition? You're asking me to give you some of the stuff that keeps me… well, not exactly alive, but in existence.*

Y- yes.

Tell me why you followed me. For that matter, tell me how you followed me, then maybe I'll consider it.

Bertrand remained silent, then turned his head and gazed into the distance, avoiding Warren's eyes. After a few seconds, Warren noticed streamers of... *could it be essence?* Warren wondered... flowing from gouges along Bertrand's side. Warren grabbed Bertrand by the collar and shook him.

Where did you get them?

In a voice that sounded innocent, Bertrand asked, *Where did I get what?*

THESE! Warren shouted, pointing at the grooves running along Bertrand's side.

I...

It was you who attacked me; you imitating Ricca's attack. I need an honest explanation because—and I promise you this—if you don't tell me something that sounds completely credible, I will do everything in my power to destroy you. Here. Now. On this very spot. The fears you expressed about what I might do will be nothing—NOTHING, DO YOU HEAR? Warren's voice dropped almost to a whisper as he concluded—*compared with what I am actually going to do.*

Bertrand seemed to grow smaller as Warren berated him. Cowering, he whimpered, *I'm sorry*, and wrapped an arm around his head as if to protect it from Warren's accusations.

Warren leaned close and growled, *Just tell me why.*

I want to go back, Bertrand began, then hesitated.

Go back? Go back where?

I want to go back to the Light, and I'm terrified that I'm going to be stuck here.

Warren came upright and asked, *Why should you be terrified? You said there's a chance that…*

I know what I said, but I don't know that for certain. When I asked Magnus about it, he told me that, if I performed a sacrifice, he could help. With that, Bertrand broke down and started sobbing.

So you were going to sacrifice me?

Bertrand gave several confirming jerks of his head.

You're disgusting, said Warren. After pausing a moment to think, he asked, *Why would you ask Magnus about it?*

Magnus is different from spirits like you and me. He's darker, more… powerful.

And you thought he might help you?

I don't know what I thought. I've been here so long I was starting to get desperate. I guess you're not going to help me after all.

By giving you a transfusion? Warren sneered. *Not likely.*

But you're not going to hurt me, are you?

After pausing to consider it, Warren told him, *No, regardless of what my inclinations tell me. Go on. Get out of here.* As Bertrand was starting to leave, Warren said, *Wait! If I wanted to get in touch with Magnus, how would I contact him?*

Bertrand replied, *Just concentrate on your desire and he will appear.*

As simple as that, said Warren.

Bertrand nodded and confirmed, *As simple as that.*

After he had gone, Warren wondered if it had been wise letting Bertrand leave like that. He did so because he was growing tired of all the killing, but wondered if, by allowing Bertrand to live, he wasn't setting himself up for another attack down the road. Since that issue was moot, he would just have to see how matters with that one unfolded. Magnus, however, was the one great unknown he needed to learn about if he were to survive.

35

Who, exactly, is he, Warren wondered, *and why would he want Bertrand to perform... a sacrifice?* The concept disturbed him and gave him a hint at what Bertrand intended when he described Magnus as dark and powerful. Knowing how this afterlife presented unexpected problems at almost every turn, Warren realized that he might need some kind of protection if he decided to speak with him. Understanding that the meeting and its concomitant danger was inevitable, he was mulling over how he could deal with it when his eyes drifted eastward and fell on Mount Davidson and the one hundred foot concrete cross at its summit. In hopes that this structure would be more than symbolic and could actually offer some sort of protection should Magnus prove to be as evil as Warren feared, with no better solution in mind, Warren headed toward it.

Mount Davidson is the highest point in San Francisco and is located near the city's geographic center. It commands sweeping vistas of the surrounding area and, conversely, is visible from most parts of the city. Warren wanted to be somewhere Magnus could easily find him and he could think of no better place. But now, as he was poised to reach out to a possibly maleficent spirit, he had to ask himself if he really wanted to do this? Was it even necessary?

It occurred to Warren that what he wanted wasn't part

of the equation. He didn't *want* to commune with someone evil. He didn't *want* to endanger himself. And while he *wanted* to return to his children, more than anything else Warren *needed* to learn if he might also be required to perform a sacrifice in order to return to the Light, because, if that were the case, he knew it was not a condition that he could accept. In the back of his mind, Warren suspected that Magnus had been toying with Bertrand, if, in fact, Bertrand had been honest when he offered his explanation about the attack. Ultimately, Warren *needed* to learn the answer if he were to move forward on, so to speak, solid ground. Consequently, as was the case with all of his other accomplishments, Warren began focusing his thoughts on the problem at hand.

He had been concentrating for almost an hour without any results and was about to abandon the effort as fruitless when a voice asked, *Who are you to bother me and what do you seek?*

Understanding that the way he responded would affect his and Magnus's relationship, Warren decided that any initial mention of the alleged sacrifice might make him sound fearful or deferential, either of which would put Magnus in charge. In addition, Magnus might perceive those allegations as threatening. If he were, in fact, someone to fear, Warren did not wish to anger him. But if Magnus was not the monster that Bertrand had painted, if it turned out that Bertrand had manufactured everything about him and Magnus was just another spirit caught up in circumstances beyond his control, such a beginning could destroy a potential alliance before it ever began. Hoping that this reply would sound sufficiently neutral, Warren answered, *Someone has told me certain things about you and I want to determine if they are true.*

When Magnus replied, *And so you came to the source,* Warren relaxed, believing he had set the right tone.

Yes, he said.

In a voice whose inflection suggested deep curiosity, Magnus asked, *What did they say?*

Warren spent the next several minutes providing a background to what he was about to deliver, including his first encounter with Bertrand, Bertrand's account of his murder in the Castro, his explanation of why it might not be possible to return to the Light, an account of Warren's own demise and his desire to reunite with his family, as well as an account of Bertrand's attack against him. He completed his tale with Bertrand's insistence that the attack only occurred because Magnus required him to offer up Warren as a sacrifice.

A brief silence followed and Warren struggled to keep his mind from proceeding down the dark avenues the pause suggested. Finally, Magnus said, *I know him. He is not to be trusted.* Then, after another pause, Magnus asked, *Have you let him into your mind?*

I don't understand.

Have you let him read your thoughts?

No. Why would I do that?

That's good. It's probably not something that would occur to you. But if he ever suggests it, don't do it. It will give him a way to find you wherever you are.

Thank you, Warren said. Feeling more alone and isolated than ever before, and needing some additional information about his situation, Warren asked, *Do you know if what he told me about the Light is true?*

In what regard?

My chance of returning, Warren explained. *Is there any chance I can ever see my children again?*

Magnus sighed and said, *I'm afraid that part is true. If there was any way to return, I and most of the rest of us would have gone back a long time ago. You should start to resign yourself to the fact you're here for all eternity. You should also learn how to protect yourself from spirits like Bertrand and Ricca.*

Warren found the concept disturbing, so he asked Magnus if transforming himself into a monster was what he meant.

That's one technique, answered Magnus. *There are other methods as well, depending on the circumstance.* Before Warren could ask him to be more specific, Magnus said, *Should you continue to survive, you may learn about each of them when the situations present themselves. I wish I had time to go into all of the details, but there are some pressing matters I need to attend to. So, if you will excuse me, I must leave you to work out your problems on your own.*

Warren was relieved that Magnus had not posed the threat Bertrand had promised. And because Magnus hadn't threatened him, he had to accept that at least some of what Magnus had said might be true. There were certainly enough ghosts haunting San Francisco to make Warren wonder why they had not returned to the Tunnel. Bertrand had already proven himself dangerous on at least one occasion, and so was not the friend he had pretended to be. These two factors alone lent themselves to Magnus's credibility... although liars sometimes tell the truth and the things that basically honest people say cannot always be relied on. Without something compelling to establish whether either of these spirits could be trusted, Warren had to accept that he might be utterly alone and without friends.

Where did this leave him, Warren wondered? He had already exacted revenge on Jordan and the gang of street thugs. He had short circuited Brandy's love affair, but had no desire to cause her any further harm. It was yet to be seen if the firm would restructure or be sold to a larger entity, now that he had given Michael access to Jordan's offshore bank accounts, thereby returning it to a solid financial footing. In any case, he had taken care of the investors. Michael and Sabrina would be able to carry on as a couple for as long as they cared, and Nancy was free to do whatever she pleased.

As for himself, karma appeared to be weighted toward the negative, so he could never return to the Light, no happy-ever-after ending for him. In the event he was mistaken, he would continue to do what he could to protect his friends. He would also try to keep himself safe from malevolent spirits until the sun burned out, the world died off, and he was left to an eternity of darkness.

ABOUT THE AUTHOR

Raymond Bolton lives near Portland, Oregon with his wife, Toni, and their cats, Max and Arthur. He has written award-winning poetry and has published six novels.

His crossover epic fantasy/sci-fi quartet, The Ydron Saga, which consists of *Awakening* and it prequel trilogy, *Thought Gazer*, *Foretellers* and *Triad*, are published by WordFire Press, publisher of many bestselling and award-winning authors including Frank Herbert, Kevin J. Anderson, Jody Lynn Nye, Alan Dean Foster, Brian Herbert, Tracy Hickman, and David Farland, as well as the Dune and Star Wars series.

His work has been endorsed by the late Mike Resnick, who says, "In *AWAKENING*, Raymond Bolton presents us with an intricate and interesting problem, characters you care for, aliens who <u>are</u> alien, and a carefully-thought-out future." International award-winning author of more than 100 books,

Paul Kane, describes his work as, "Thoroughly imaginative, with an eloquent writing style and characters that live and breathe on the page." D. J. Butler, author of *Witchy Eye*, calls his fifth novel, *Folder*, a self-published Young Adult science fiction novel, "A wild young-adult alternate-worlds adventure that will leave you guessing right up to the end! Fans of Philip Pullman's *His Dark Materials* will love this!"

Wraith received a pre-publication endorsement from Michael R. Collings, who was named Grand Master at the 2016 World Horror Convention:

"Raymond Bolton's *Wraith* presents an intriguing view of the intersections between the living and the dead. Beginning with a triple murder, this dark paranormal novel explores the consequences of betrayal, greed, infidelity, and vengeance on both sides of mortality…and in each instance, provides unexpected twists that propel readers onward, page after page. Bolton deftly shifts perspectives between the world of the Wraith and those he pursues with a fury that transcends death itself."

Another endorsement for *Wraith* came from Paul Kane:

"Bolton gets into the meat of relationships, and makes you care about his characters—which is all too rare, yet essential, in horror. Combined with a cracking story, it makes for quite the read!"

To purchase Raymond Bolton's other titles, go to his website,

http://www.raymondbolton.com

then go to the Books link at the top of the Home page. You'll find a purchase link when you click on each title.

www.ingramcontent.com/pod-product-compliance
Lightning Source LLC
Chambersburg PA
CBHW072052190726
48294CB00005B/1475